SPLASH

A Sable World Novella

Baine Kelly

Winterloch Publishing

This is a work of fiction. Names, characters, places, and incidents are products of the author's imagination or are used fictitiously and are not to be construed as real. Any resemblance to actual events, locales, organization, or persons, living or dead, is entirely coincidental.

Winterloch Publishing
P.O. BOX 35368
Richmond, VA 23235

Copyright © 2013 Baine Kelly
Excerpt From "Blood Loss" copyright © 2013 Baine Kelly
ISBN: 098936920X
ISBN-13: 978-09893692-0-6
www.winterlochpublishing.com

DEDICATION

For my amazing husband

BAINE KELLY

.

CONTENTS

BAINE KELLY

ACKNOWLEDGMENTS

I will try to keep this short but there are so many people I would like to thank. First to my family and friends that have supported me through this journey of becoming an author. I couldn't have done this without your guidance and support. Thank you to Barry, Lisa, Jim, C.J., Laurie, Tim, Mikayla, Randal, Sharon and my parents.

Next I would like to thank my fellow authors who have spent week in and week out helping me develop The Sable World into a great series. Thank you Tina Glasneck and Lori Justice.

Thank you to Michelle for catching all the editing mistakes.

Thank you to Brian Pickral for the beautiful picture of the orange moon.

Thank you Tammy Shackleford my media queen.

Now for a special thank you to my husband and son for their continued daily support and encouragement for me to follow my dreams. I couldn't ask for anything better. I love you both.

BAINE KELLY

SPLASH

BAINE KELLY

PROLOGUE

1859

Nathaniel was running late, as usual. He hated his responsibilities of a farmer's son. He didn't mind helping when it wasn't a burden to his own wants. *He was selfish back then.* He had a prior engagement the night of the attack. Danielle Tucker, daughter of the towns tailor, had agreed to sit near the water's edge with him. It was a step he wanted and one she had finally allowed after months of courting.

Before he left to meet Danielle, father told him to walk Sariah home from a delivery. Sariah Ann Bartlett, the daughter of the butcher and younger than he. Her father, Joseph, was a couple of towns over delivering meat to

3

local shops, leaving Sariah to make the deliveries near their home. He should have gone to walk her straight away, but no, instead he went to the water's edge first, and was disappointed when he found himself alone. Danielle was nowhere to be seen.

Irritation of the night ruined Nathaniel stomped toward the Peterson house, where Sariah was making her delivery. The solitude of the night was unnerving, something was off.

Nathaniel quickened his pace to a steady jog. Everything about the night seemed different, the smell, the soundless atmosphere, until a ruffling utterance drifted from the town's edging forest. Startled, Nathaniel sprinted leaving his jogging pace behind.

With his long strides, he took three steps at a time onto the Peterson's porch and began knocking on the door. A long, slow creak broke the evening silence as Mr. Peterson pulled open the door.

"Good evening Nate. What brings you out so late?"

"I am here to walk Sariah home, sir. I was running late. Is she still here, by chance?"

"No, afraid not. She left a bit ago. I did offer to escort her myself, but she refused. Didn't think much of it with it being quiet. Only troubles cross the Foster boys."

"Thank you, sir. I am sure I can catch her on her way back." Nate turned toward the steps as a high scream pierced the air.

He and Mr. Peterson raced across the field toward the forests edge, where they now only heard a faint moan. Quiet laughter faded slowly away as they entered the forests opening. They slowly walked, listening for the moan and looking for whom it belonged. The need to run away dominated Nathaniel, yet he forced himself to stay. His heart pounded with fear erupting all around him. He slowly followed Mr. Peterson into the mist of night. Laughter no longer heard they followed the sound of the faint, diminishing moan.

They approached a large oak tree and saw a shape silhouetted by the rays of moon light through the trees. Taking a few minutes to focus their eyes Mr. Peterson whispered, "Nate, stay here," as he continued onward towards the large oak.

Nathaniel stopped, and stood motionless while his eyes searched the trees for who else might be out here. But nothing. He couldn't see anyone. He couldn't hear anyone else. His attention snapped back to Mr. Peterson's fearful voice.

"Oh no! It's okay. It's okay now, honey. You're safe. Be still. Be still. Please honey, be still." Mr. Peterson's voice crackled low with each comforting word.

"What is it sir?" Nathaniel asked as he approached the tree. Then he stopped, sucking in air between his teeth as his stomach began to twist in protest.

Sariah.

It was Sariah Bartlett.

She lay on the ground, clothes torn, shoes missing and body battered. Blood covered her entire torso; her uncovered legs sprawled to the side. Her moans became more of a gurgle as blood pored over her swollen lips. She kept trying to lift her head, but weakness planted her where she lay. One of her swollen eyes barely opened, the other was swollen closed and darkened.

Proof of her horrific attack.

"Nate. Nate, son." Mr. Peterson yelled, "Go. Go now and get help. Fast, Nate. Go fast!"

Nathaniel shook with fear as he turned to head back to the Peterson's house when a gust of wind swished past him, and spun him around. He fell head first into the decaying foliage. He took deep breaths, steadied himself and stood just to be thrown back down again by an invisible force.

Staying where he was Nathaniel had forced open his tear-filled eyes and looked toward Sariah. Her limp body lay beneath the large oak showing no sign of life. Mr.

Peterson was nowhere in sight and two unknown figures towered above her.

ONE

Sariah sat on the edge of the large canopy bed, shaking. She had been confined to the Manor for so long the thought of leaving terrified her. What if she lost control? She wouldn't be able to live with herself if it happened again. She turned and zipped her suitcase closed and reached for her purse. She wasn't sure what to expect.

Would she finally be free? Could Nate really make this happen? She hoped so but why was he doing this for her? She hadn't seen him in decades. She remembered him from their small village. She had liked him back then. Before the attack. Before their deaths. Now she wasn't sure what to think of him. He'd left her over one hundred years ago and she hadn't heard a word from him since. He used her. They had a lot in common back then which brought them closer together. But in the end she was only a passing thought. Yesterday she was informed to pack because she had to travel to Virginia to participate in a trial for a new drug. He invented this drug that was supposed to curb the cravings. She would have to see him.

"Ms. Bartlett, are you ready?" Sariah glanced toward the door where Liam Hirst stood wearing his usual security attire of a black shirt, black cargo pants, and black military boots. She normally teased him about his broody attire, but not today. She was too nervous. His uniform didn't hide the well sculpted body that lay beneath the clothes. She knew firsthand how fit he was.

Liam was an older vampire, physically built, and well trained in combat. She remembered being afraid of him at first when she saw him in a battle to help save her life. He was quick and efficient when he killed, and had been her personal trainer for decades. He was now her personal bodyguard for her long trip to Virginia.

"I think I have everything." Sariah stood up and reached for her suitcase. Before she could grab it Liam held it in his hands. Sariah arched a brow.

"It would hurt my manly honor if you would not let me carry your belongings." Nothing would hurt his manly honor. He liked to take charge of all situations and enjoyed everyone following him. She had learned that during their training sessions. She still couldn't beat him, but she came close once. It was a low blow but if you had to fight for your life you used what you could. Her kick had stunned him as he dropped. Too bad he recovered quickly. Sariah smiled and strutted right past him through the door, he would have to *follow* her to the car. *Ha!*

Sariah was overwhelmed with a mix of excitement and fear. She had never ventured from the confines of the Manor because she was afraid Josiah would find her. Or worse she would hurt someone again. Over the decades she had learned how to recognize her urges and try to hold back, but there were times when it was more difficult than others. Anger or fear would ignite the monster quickly.

Liam pulled out of the Manor and headed toward the airport. She had never been on a plane before and her excitement spiked overshadowing her fears. She was finally leaving the Manor. Part of her was saddened by the fact but a larger part was relieved. She wouldn't have to endure anymore of the silver room. She looked back at the Manor one more time as they drove further away from it. On the outside it looked like a normal average sized house. You wouldn't know this house had over fifteen bedrooms and bathrooms below the actual structure of the old home.

Inside, the Manor was more like a small prison complete with an underground medical facility. The underground facility also supplied silver lined rooms that were used as confinement cells for vampires who were caught doing bad things.

Like killing.

Sariah shuddered. Thank goodness she was no longer in one of those cells. She had moved to a top floor suite roughly thirty years ago when she had learned to control most of her emotions. She had worked hard every day to keep her controlled status and avoid being put back in the cell. No one outside of the vampire world knew what really went on there at the Manor. Most thought it was an old rich guy who owned it. They were right, Garrick was old.

Sariah had never seen such a pretty sunny day. She was restricted from outside access. She stared out the window up to the clear blue sky and smiled. So much had changed from the eighteen hundreds. The houses, cars—the people. She watched a young mother walk with her child. The boy smiled as he swung his backpack around. Sariah grinned. She had always wanted a family. When she was raised a woman's purpose was to have babies. It's not that way anymore. Liam had gotten her a telly of her very own when she moved into her new suite. Watching shows gave her glimpses of today's world.

Liam accelerated through the yellow light.

"We have company." Liam glanced into the rearview mirror again.

Sariah turned in her seat to see that a black sedan followed them. She had wondered if it would be safe for her to leave the Manor. It had to be Josiah and his men. Liam had assured her that he wouldn't let anything happen to her. The night she died was horrific. Not a peaceful fulfilling life that came to an end, but a brutal attack that left her a monster.

One capable of murder.

Josiah was responsible for the slaughter of multiple villages. She had never believed in the stories told to scare the children from wondering off. She had found out the hard way they were true. She had died by the hand of one of those evil bastards.

She had lain curled on her side sprawled across the dirt floor of a drafty old condemned cabin. Nathaniel lay unconscious next to her, his face swollen and bloody. Someone had beaten him. She cringed when she heard men laughing and carrying on with another girl from the town. Danielle Tucker, the tailor's daughter, had finally stopped struggling. Her whimpers grew less and less as the men took their turns. Sariah closed her eyes sending up a prayer. Please don't let me be next...

Liam interrupted her thoughts. "Here, take this" Sariah reached out and took the slick black 9mm pistol he handed her with shaky hands. She wasn't sure if the shiver that racked her body was from the thought of that night or the thought of using the weapon against someone. She'd been trained to use it by Liam but had only used it in a training room. If only she had known how to defend herself back then. Maybe she could have stopped them from taking turns with Danielle.

With her.

Sariah briefly closed her eyes and wished her prayer had

come true that night. But didn't it come partially true? She thought of Nathaniel.

"Are you sure? You think it's that bad?" Sariah tried to hide her rising discomfort but her voice still cracked. Of course it was needed. She should have never left the Manor. She was safe there. Safe from him. Which him was more dangerous to her?

"I'm betting on it. Be ready to use it Sariah. Just like we practiced. I don't know how many are in the sedan so our best wager is to get away quickly. If we have to we'll run for it. I am going to try and get us as close to the underground as possible."

Sariah peered in the side mirror. Hadn't she suffered enough? All she wanted was to be free. Free from the hunger. Free from herself. Free from Josiah. She shuddered. Josiah was his own category of evil. Anger flushed her cheeks quickly followed by regret, fear, and sadness. Josiah was the worst of the men who slaughtered her town. She was lucky to have escaped him the first time.

She looked at Liam comforted that he was by her side. She didn't want anything to happen to him. Too many innocents had already died. Liam had been with her for almost a century. He was her fierce protector, determined teacher, and calming hand that was always there for her. She felt safe with him by her side. At one time she had wished for more but Liam had always turned down her advancements. She hadn't understood why for many years, until she noticed he never accepted advances from any woman… *It's Always the cute ones.*

Sariah glanced back out the rear window. The sedan was closing in fast. She could make out at least three figures in the car. She braced herself right before the sedan rammed into the back of their car. Her purse flew to her feet and landed on the floor board. Liam cursed and spun the car around and quickly turned down a side street. Sariah pushed her bag over some and braced her feet firmly against the floorboard to steady herself as she pulled the slide back on the pistol to chamber a round. She didn't like using weapons but had grown accustomed to it over the years. Sometimes you had to do what was needed to survive. Why were weapons easier than feeding? She needed blood to survive but still couldn't bring herself to violate a person that way. Her anger spiked.

Sariah was suddenly thrown forward as the sedan sideswiped them. She leaned back, bracing herself again. "I see at least three in the sedan Liam"

"Fuck!" Liam tossed her his phone. "Ring Garrick now."

Sariah struggled to tap the screen that showed Garrick's face with all the bumping and swerving.

"Put it on speaker." Liam swerved again, barely missing a pedestrian who walked across the street. The car lifted up over the intersection crashing down hard. Sariah winced, the screech of medal hitting pavement pierced her sensitive hearing. Liam accelerated again.

"Halo mate."

"We are under attack. Black sedan. At least three people in it. We're heading for the Underground."

"Bloody hell!" Garrick shouted through the phone. "I'm on it. Keep your phone on. I'll be in touch. And Liam."

"Yea."

"You bloody better keep her safe and get here!" Garrick disconnected the call.

TWO

The murmurs of the gathered guest lowered as Jonathan stepped up to the microphone. "He did it! Our future holds a new light. No more feeding on humans, no more worrying about bagged blood. Now we can have a little red capsule in your favorite flavors. It has been a long and trying journey to achieve this but here we are. Every blood type in a small capsule that dissolves in liquid, making a bloody treat for our survival. This is a huge break through that can help many a vampire." Nathaniel stood and listed to his assistant Jonathan go on and on about the capsules. Little did Jon know that his reason for developing Splash had crystal clear blue eyes that reminded him of a mid-summers morn just as the sun raised. He spent decades obtaining multiple medical degrees so he could find a way to help her.

He completed the first trial a week ago with promising out comes. He should be just as thrilled as everyone here but he was on edge waiting for Sariah. She would be the true test of accomplishment. Not just for the development of Splash but for the healing of his heart. His pulse raised, his heart swelled with every thought of her. Her delicate frame and sweet smile. Her eyes used to light up at the littlest things. He used to think it was trivial until he could no longer share the little things with her. Could she forgive him? Maybe he should have tried to contact her decades ago.

"Please raise your glasses. Here is to Nathaniel Collins, the brains behind Splash, an easier way to ensure our futures!"

Now it was his turn to say something. Something inspiring. A pair of crystal blue eyes looking up from beneath him invaded his thoughts. Now that was inspiring. Nathaniel's pulse spiked with the anticipation of seeing her after all these years. *Sariah*. She was on her way here now, and this capsule could help her get her life back. He lifted his glass with everyone else and took a long swig of AB positive. His favorite.

Nathaniel set his glass down and stepped onto the stage. "Thank you all for coming. As my colleague Jonathan expressed, this has been a long and trying journey. One with many ups and downs. But all worth it in the end. We now have a new way to feed that is easier and more convenient for all. No more coolers full of bagged blood, no more searching for humans to feed on. Instead you can drop one small capsule into liquid and make your favorite blood type on the spot. This can help us blend in with the ever changing world around us."

This can help Sariah.

Nathaniel cleared his throat and continued. "The world

is full of pills that help multiple health concerns. Even powders that mix with drinks. It's about time our world caught up. I see a lot of good with this invention, so please help yourself to the bar and try your favorite drink. And remember if you add your capsule to an alcoholic beverage, well let's just say be prepared to enjoy a buzz!" The crowd cheered.

Thank god it was almost over. Nathaniel went to the bar and ordered bourbon with a splash of AB positive. He glanced around the room watching everyone celebrate. He'd celebrate once Sariah arrived. The bartender handed him his bourbon and Nathaniel took a long cooling drink just as his phone rang. He checked to see the caller's name. *Garrick.*

"Hello." He listened to Garrick explain what was happening with Sariah and Liam.

"What do you mean they are under attack?" Nathaniel yelled. Every head in the room turned toward him, not a sound made. Nathaniel stormed out of the ballroom quickly. "Garrick. You can't let anything happen to her. She's been through enough, dammit!" Nathaniel's eyes darkened making his sight clearer, stronger. His gums burned urging his fangs to slide down.

"I know Nate. I'm on it. Liam left his phone on and I am tracking it. Ivan is on his way there now. She will be fine. Remember I know what I am doing, mate."

Nathaniel took a deep breath. Garrick was the leader of the Trackers. In the vampire world there were laws to follow. If you broke one a Tracker would find you and the punishment was always harsh to ensure you never faltered again. If you did you were met with Garrick's silver knife. "Garrick I want to help. I can leave now."

"No! You are staying at the lab. I have just as much riding on this as you do. Now stay put! I'll get her to you."

"No. It's been too long and I left her once. There's no way in hell I'm going to sit back and do nothing this—."

"Don't say it Nate. She will need you there to help her.

Stay put. I'll let you know when I have an update."

Nathaniel couldn't argue, Garrick hung up.

Shit.

Liam raced through more than half the city, finally losing the black sedan. He pulled into a parking structure and drove to the top level and parked the small two door Mercedes between two large SUV's. "The car should be hidden pretty well here, at least for a bit. Grab only what you need Sariah. We are going to foot it to the Underground and head for the airport."

Sariah grabbed her purse and hid the pistol inside. "This is all I need. Let's get out of here before they catch up." She watched Liam twist the gear selector and pull it out.

Liam smiled as he placed the selector in his jacket. "Best part about working for Garrick. The toys! The car is lined in silver, and the gear selector pulls out as a silver stake." *Wow.* Just when Sariah thought she knew everything about the Trackers.

"Let's move."

They stayed close to the walls of the parking structure and moved quickly to the ground floor. Liam snagged a couple of hats to help hide their appearance as they made their way pass street vendors. About fifteen minutes later they were safely on the tube headed toward Paddington Station. From there they would finish the trip to Heathrow Airport where a private jet was awaiting them.

Sariah sat back in the far end of the train car while Liam sat toward the front. The seats were limited with the amount of passengers getting on and off. The smell of sweat was strong enough to curl her stomach. It almost masked the sweet scent of blood pumping through so many people. A woman sat with her infant right behind Liam. He shifted to the side to answer his phone. It was probably Garrick. *The Tracker.* She had hated him for the longest time. Why couldn't he have let her die that night?

It took decades to forgive him and realize he was trying his best to help. Garrick had been the one who comforted her when Nathaniel left. Was she that bad that Nate couldn't stand her anymore? They had become quite close over the first few years of their turning. Then they slept together. It was the best night of her life. So passionate, they were so in love back then. He left her the next day.

The sliding door to the train opened and a very tall man, encased in solid black, walked into the train car. He glanced around slowly as he walked down the aisle. Passengers unconsciously shied away from him as he passed. They must sense the posing threat of danger. There were too many people on the train and she hoped they wouldn't end up injured. Not here. Sariah curled herself into the corner of her seat and lowered her hat hoping her face wouldn't be as noticeable. Her heart raced, could it be one of Josiah's men? He smiled as he approached taking a seat across from her. *Shit!*

She looked at Liam whom still talked on the bloody phone. Sariah shifted closer to the wall and placed her hand into her purse clutching the pistol with a sweaty palm. Her heart pounded louder with the fear of capture, her gums stretched as adrenalin coursed through her body, her fangs slowly slid down filling her mouth. Her vision sharpened. She slanted her darkened eyes toward the mystery man prepared to move quickly. A baby cried toward the front of the car. Sariah glanced up, distracted by the needy cry of the infant. Before she could react the man jumped across the aisle and grabbed her. He moved quickly, pinning her against the wall of the moving train car. A pistol pressed into her side.

The man hauled her out of her seat and dragged her toward the sliding door. She noticed Liam reach for the silver stake as they passed and Sariah shook her head. *Please not here.* Too many innocents. The man rushed forward as the train slowed. Just as the door slid open at the next stop another man blocked their exit off the train. Ivan. *Oh, thank goodness.*

"Vho's your friend Sariah?" Sariah smiled. Ivan was one of the best Trackers from Russia and wanted Josiah and his men dead even more than she did. This mystery man had no idea what was going to happen to him.

"Some asshole that can't keep his hands to himself!" Ivan chuckled.

"Vell don't let me stop you." Ivan moved to the side leaving just enough space for them to step onto the platform.

The man glanced around sharply before dragging her through the doors before they slid closed. His fingers dug painfully into her arm as he pressed the gun harder into her side "Stay back or I will shoot her."

"No, stay calm. No one's gettin' hurt today."

"Except you, you bloody wanker," Liam murmured quietly from behind them. Sheeh! She hadn't even heard him approached. Everything happened so fast. Sariah was thrown to the ground as Liam and Ivan engaged the man. She sat up on her knees and looked frantically for her purse. She had lost hold of it when Liam grabbed her and tossed her like a rag doll to the ground at the same time Ivan lunged for the man. It didn't take long for them to unarm him, and pull him off to the side of the platform, away from human eyes.

Thank goodness this wasn't a busy stop and only a handful of people exited the train and rushed off to their intended destinations. Luckily they were all in a hurry and rushed off. Sariah grabbed her purse that had slid to the edge of the tracks and withdrew her pistol. She followed the men around the corner and took aim.

"Who sent ye mate?" Liam asked. When the man didn't answer Ivan stabbed him completely through his arm with a silver stake.

"No vories, I von't kill you with the stake. But you be vishing me had." Ivan was one of the scariest vampires she had ever met aside from Garrick. She knew very little about the Russian vampire. His family was killed when he was turned and now he worked for Garrick as a Tracker. One thing she knew for certain was if Ivan was coming for you you're better off staking yourself than letting him catch you.

Liam asked again. Sariah winced as Ivan stabbed the man a second time. This time in the stomach. He fell to his knees. Blood dripped down the man's shirt and pooled around his knees. Sariah's nostrils flared. She had to turn around away from all the blood. People were starting to arrive for the next train. They would start to notice what was happening soon. They needed to be hurry.

The man laughed. More blood dripped down his chin. Ivan had hit him hard when they first got off the train. "You think I'm alone?" His wicked smile widened.

"Who cares? Ivan." Ivan smiled before he rammed the stake straight through the man's heart. The unknown vampire turned to dust and crumbled to the ground within seconds. Liam narrowed his eyes. "Let's go. Nice timing by the way."

Ivan laughed. "Come. I've got car parked."

"He said he wasn't alone. Shouldn't we be looking for the others?" Sariah asked.

"Nyet. He had two buddies. I introduced myself." Ivan winked.

Liam chuckled and slapped Ivan on the back. "I'm sure they didn't enjoy the introduction, mate."

THREE

Nathaniel paced his office. Garrick pissed him off. He needed to get to Sariah. Everything inside him screamed to go to her. He tried, only to be stopped by Doran. Now Doran and his brothers were stationed outside his office. *Fucking babysitters!* Nathaniel's phone rang. He stomped across the floor and plopped down at his desk. "What."

"She's on the plane. She'll be arriving tomorrow morn. Have Sorin take you to meet her. But Nate."

"Yeah."

"Be careful. Josiah's men are after her. Ivan confirmed it with one of the guys he killed in London." Nathaniel could hear the anger with each word Garrick spoke.

"Got it. You want me to keep her here?"

"Yeah. I will see you sometime tomorrow."

Nathaniel hung up the phone, relieved. She was safe and she would be here soon. Was she just as beautiful as he remembered? Would she still love him? He put those thoughts aside, for now. He needed to prepare.

Nathaniel walked into the private studio apartment connected to his office. There was a small kitchen living room combo to the left, a king size bed to the right with a door leading to a private bathroom. This should work. She would stay here with him so he could protect her and observe her through the testing of Splash. Hopefully the medication would fulfill her hunger and help her lead a full, fearless life. He remembered how her eyes looked after she killed the family in that small town after months of starving herself. It wasn't her fault.

Full of regret.

Sorrow.

He never wanted to see that again. He moved into the kitchen. He'd have to stock the fridge with blood bags just in case. Fill the kitchen with beverages too. What does she like? He walked back into the bedroom area and smiled. One bed. Huh, should he tell her the couch folded out?

"Doran!"

Doran opened the office door before venturing back to the small studio apartment. "Yeah."

"I need some supplies Mr. babysitter." Doran's eyes narrowed. "I need a stocked kitchen. Beverages, blood. AB positive and B negative." He hoped that was still her favorite. "And I need this place softened up some. It's too manly. Sariah needs to be comfortable when she arrives. Her favorite color is purple. Go and fetch some new linens, pillows, and blankets. The works. And have someone come in to clean up a bit. This place is a mess."

Doran stared at him, speechless. His jaw set he turned back toward the doorway. "I'm not a fucking babysitter and I's sure as hell not an interior decorator." Doran walked out.

Nathaniel followed Doran out into the security office. This used to be a normal looking reception area but not anymore. The room was now blocked off from the hallway with silver lined doors, security monitors housed one long wall and a guard's station with computers, phones and weapons housed the other wall. His damn windows were even blocked with silver lined plates.

Not a babysitter my arse!

He felt slightly ashamed with his frustration. Sariah had lived this way for decades because of him and he couldn't stand it for a few lousy months. Garrick forced the security changes on him. "Some may not be as excited about your medicine Nate. We need to protect you and your product." Garrick had argued.

"My work is safe and I don't need any changes. It will all be fine. The lab has fine security."

"Do you want Sariah to come or not?" Garrick asked softly.

"Yes, of course I do."

"Well then you better bloody take the extra security. Do it for her."

That had been then end of their conversation. He would take extra precautions for Sariah.

"Can you believe him?" Doran shouted to his brothers. "He wants me to be his fucking gopher!" Doran stomped to the small corner of the office that held a small kitchenette, thanks to Garrick, and poured himself a drink. Doran had two brothers Sorin and Nolan. All three were his personal guards now. The Trevena brothers were triplets and almost impossible to tell apart unless you knew their unique personalities. *Death, stupid, and intelligent.*

Sorin sat at a table cleaning a large black rifle. He was the most dangerous of the triplets with his black shirt and black leather pants. He was missing his long leather duster that he normally wore. His jet black hair and dark brown eyes did nothing to make him look sane. Nathaniel mentally shook. *Death.*

Nolan sat behind the desk, his fingers clicking away quickly over the keys of his laptop. He was the brains with a less intimidating appearance of jeans and a button down shirt. He looked harmless unlike Sorin but Nathaniel knew Nolan could be just as dangerous. *Intelligent.*

That left stupid. Nathaniel looked at Doran. Doran always got himself into some type of trouble. Regardless he was just as lethal as his brothers when pushed.

There was a reason these three were the best guards known in the vampire world and Garrick recently assigned them to be his personal detail. Some unknown individual supposedly made a threat about Splash and wanted it all destroyed so Garrick stepped in and Bartlett Laboratories had stepped up security.

"He can't leave the facility Doran. So if he needs something move your ass and go get it!" Nolan said while not missing a beat on his computer.

"No way! Why do I have to go out and do this shit? You go! I'll watch the monitors."

Sorin's dark laugh was low, threatening. Nathaniel took a step back. "You think you could take on Josiah? What if he showed up? You're better off shopping like a little bitch."

"Sorin—let it go." Nolan stopped typing and eyed his brother.

"Fine, but watch yourself Doran. You screw up again nothin' Nolan can say will save your stupid ass." Guess Nathaniel wasn't the only one who was through with *stupid.* Sorin stood and walked to the weapons cabinet, stored the rifle he had cleaned, then walked out of the security office.

"I don't care what the hell is going on between you three but someone better get what I need. Tonight!" Nathaniel walked back into his office slamming the door behind him. *What the hell?*

Finally the plane touched down. It had been a long flight. At first Sariah couldn't sleep. She kept looking for someone to jump out at her and kill her. Or worse take her again. But nothing happened. Ivan had told them about one of the men he so called "introduced" himself to at the Underground. He had been hired by Josiah. His mission was to capture her and bring her to him. Chills erupted up her neck working their way slowly over her scalp. She'd rather die. Apparently Josiah wasn't happy that she got away from him over a century ago. That's one big problem with the vampire world. Grudges could literally last forever! *Ugh.* She couldn't keep thinking about him.

She focused her thoughts on freedom. What would it be like to go somewhere? Anywhere? A movie, dinner. Maybe even a real date. *Dancing!* She spent so much time at the Manor she hadn't realized how much the world had changed.

Sariah folded the blanket and stored it in the side cabinet next to her seat. Liam was right, Garrick's toys were cool. She was shocked when she first boarded the plane. A private suite, large bathroom, and plush leather chairs with everything you needed at your fingertips. She refused the suite wanting to stay close to everyone.

She was tired of isolation.

Ivan stretched his long legs, his arms touching the ceiling. "Finally."

"Do you need anything before we reach the hanger?" Liam asked as he removed the headphones from his ears. He had spent the entire flight sprawled out on one of the leather seats, his headphones blaring.

"I'm fine, thanks. I am nervous Liam. What's it like here?" Sariah asked, softly twisting her hands together in her lap.

Liam tilted his head in thought. "It's nice here. It's been awhile but I remember the trees. The fall is beautiful. Maybe you will be here long enough to see it."

Sariah shook her head. "Don't think so. Not to be mean but I want this pill and then I am headed back to England as soon as possible."

"What about Nate? Wouldn't you want to hang around a bit?"

Sariah huffed. "What makes you say that? He was the one who ran away. He was the one who couldn't handle things when things got tough. Why in the world would I want anything from him? The only reason I agreed to see him was because *he* invented this damn pill." *How dare he ask about Nathaniel!* She was here for one reason and one reason only and then she was on her way back to England. Sariah closed her eyes taking a deep breath to cool her temper. Liam chuckled. "What?" Sariah snapped.

"You just seem a little—passionate about him is all."

Sariah fumed. "Passionate? You think this is passion Liam? Try anger!" She stood, grabbed her purse and stumbled toward the front of the cabin before the plane came to a stop.

Maybe she should have used the suite.

Sariah rushed off the plane the moment the door opened. Down the steps and into the warm air. She couldn't still like Nate, could she? Not after what happened. To be honest she was embarrassed to see him. What if all he remembered was an uncontrollable blood driven monster?

"What the bloody hell are ye doing?" Sariah turned to find Liam standing right behind her, scowling.

"Getting off the plane. You know one foot in front of the other, down the stairs and then straight to the waiting car over there"

"Stop being a smart arse. You know what I mean. You still need to wait for me. Josiah and his men could already be here preparing to snag you."

Liam could be a real pain in the arse sometimes. There was no way Josiah could be here already. "I'm fine and tired of being treated like a baby." She walked toward the car just as Garrick stepped around from the back of the car.

"Sariah." He greeted.

"Nice plane Garrick. Thanks again for everything."

"He gets a thank you? Vho had to kill thri people to get here safe?" Ivan muttered as he walked past them headed toward the car.

"Put the bags in the boot mate. I have to head out, but I will be back later. I just wanted to see that you all arrived okay."

Liam held out his hand. Sariah put her bag into his hand with more force than was necessary. He smiled. She wanted to scream.

"Here you go." Garrick held the back passenger door open for her.

"Thanks." She started to get into the car only to pause. *What?*

Nathaniel sat next to the door across from her. She'd have to ride with him? She thought she would have more time before seeing him.

"Get in. You two are going to have to work things out." Garrick nudged her forward. She got in seated as far from him as the car would allow.

Liam and Ivan got into the front with Liam driving. Sariah kept her mouth closed and her eyes forward. Her heart raced, did he always look this good? She wiped her sweaty palms on her jeans to calm her nerves. She felt a demanding urge to touch him.

"Are you hungry?" Nathaniel asked softly.

Of course he would go there! She looked at him, eyes narrowed. "Sorry to disappoint but no I'm not. The plane was fully stocked." She looked away. His eyes were the same shade of green that she remembered. She had always loved his deep dark red curls and how his green eyes seemed to glow with excitement. She clutched her hands together in her lap. Everything inside her screamed to look at him, touch him. *No, he had left her!*

The rest of the drive was awkward. No one said anything. She wiped her sweaty palms on her jeans again. It was hot in here. Was there air conditioning? She was smoldering. She pushed the button on the door to roll the window down. Nothing happened. Was it broken? She tried it again.

"The windows are locked. For safety." Nathaniel spoke softly.

Just great!

"There's a car following us." Ivan stiffened and turned around to peer out the back window. "Don't worry. They're my bodyguards." Nathaniel said and then murmured something about babysitters.

About thirty minutes later Nathaniel instructed Liam to turn down a narrow alleyway. At the end of the street an old painted door slowly open. They pulled the car through the hidden door and into a small dark garage. The door closed leaving the garage barely lit. Thank goodness they all had great night vision.

Sariah hesitated when Nathaniel got out of the car. She needed a minute. Did she really want to do this? Liam opened her door. "Come. This is a back way into the facility. Only a handful of people know about it." Just as she stepped out of the confines of the car the garage door "that no one knew about" opened again spilling in a flood of sunlight before quickly closing again. Liam shoved her back inside the car.

FOUR

As the other vehicle came to a stop, Nathaniel yelled "Hey! It's alright. My bodyguards park back here too."

Nathaniel winced when Sariah stepped back out of the car. Her face was flushed, her hair tossed from the force of Liam's push. She looked beautiful. He wanted to make her flushed for a whole different reason. Damn. From the moment he saw her get off that plane she was beautiful. His view had been limited from the back seat of the car but once the door opened and he had a clear view of her. Double damn. Gorgeous.

Her blonde hair fell it waves to the top of her buttocks. Her shirt showed her slight curve, her pants emphasized her rounded hips. The car ride was agonizing. He tried to be gentlemanly in his offer of sustenance. She obviously took it as a low blow from their past. Truth, he hadn't even thought about it. His mind was swarming with other ideas like how would she liked to be kissed? Gentle, demanding, both. How would she look naked lying beneath him? It had been so long. Nathaniel shifted his jaw and turned away. He had to get himself under control. His gums burned with the need to extend. His eyes darkened sharpening his vision. Crist!

"Calm down you guys. He's in England not here. I'm perfectly safe from him. You're all being paranoid." Nathaniel watched as Sariah strutted toward the door in front of the vehicles. "Can we go now?"

It took a minute for his brain to realize she was waiting for him. "Umm. Yeah." Nathaniel walked to the door and punched in his twenty digit electronic code. Next he had to have his finger print scanned. Soon they may even add a retina scanner. Nathaniel thought it was all too much and sometimes you just have to live without fear of something happening every second. All the Trackers lived their lives ready for danger to jump out of every dark corner. Or every garage door that opened. "Humph". The door dinged and slid to the side.

"Hurry. The door is on a timer and won't stay open long." Nathaniel waited for everyone to grab their belongings then followed them into the building.

Once inside Nathaniel punched in his code again to ensure the door was securely locked.

"This way." Sorin walked ahead of everyone.

"He's not much of a talker." Nolan chuckled. "Are you ready to see the facility?" Nathaniel asked.

"Sure." Did she hesitate? She had her head down.

She still wasn't going to look at him. Maybe she would soften up a bit once she saw the name of the facility. He had named it after her, Bartlett Laboratories. Maybe the room she would be staying in would win her over. He just hoped Doran came through with the changes.

Nathaniel led them down a long stale white hallway to where the laboratories were located. He had to go through the security measures of codes and fingerprints again to open the doors to his private lab.

"Top secret huh. Cool." Ivan stepped over to a table full of equipment and picked up one of the pill bottles that sat on the table. They were arranged per blood type. "Hov this vork?"

"Well first you have to spin down the donors' blood to separate the plasma. Then the plasma is freeze dried. I add a couple of things to help stabilize the proteins needed and then package it in a little red capsule. It takes about thirty seconds for it to dissolve in liquid." Sariah sat down at one of the tables. She was listening. Her face lit up when he went into the many details about the freeze drying process. He took a step toward her.

"First we added the capsule to water and then one night I thought about putting it in alcohol. Honestly I didn't think it would work." Sariah tucked a few stray strands of her long golden hair behind her ear and leaned over to peer into one of his microscopes. His groin tightened. He needed to focus. He took another step toward her. She was the reason for everything he had done. Would she understand? Nathaniel cleared his throat and glanced back to Liam. What was he saying? Oh. "I didn't think it would work but sure enough, after mixing the capsules in whisky I was feeling quite a buzz."

"Drunk? That is cool. I vant to try this!" Ivan's excitement made Sariah laugh. It was the best music he had ever heard. His anger spiked, Ivan shouldn't have her affections. Dammit, he wanted them. "Of course you would go straight for the booze Ivan." Sariah smiled.

"Da, it good. I can't remember the last time I drink." Sariah laughed again. Nathaniel had an intense urge to punch Ivan in the face.

"So how long does the blood in the capsules last?" Ah, finally she spoke to him. Nathaniel took another step. She looked up, a brilliant flush colored her cheeks. She looked away. Damn.

"One capsule should last the same length of one bag of blood."

"Even if it's dropped in a small amount of liquid?" She was challenging him.

"In a small amount of liquid it is more potent than in a larger amount of liquid. Either way you receive the same dose."

"This would stop me from having blood transfusions?"

Nathaniel hesitated. "Maybe."

"What about needing bagged blood?" Liam questioned.

Crap. No one understood that stabilizing proteins was difficult. In long term use the need for fresh blood would still be imperative.

"It will sustain your hunger for a great length of time, but unfortunately you may still need a transfusion or fresh bag of blood periodically." Sariah frowned. "You see, everyone's body is different and some may need bagged blood more often than others. We won't know how long your system can take the capsule until we start a personal trial with you."

"How long would this so called personal trial last?"

He wished Forever.

"Not sure. Until your body craves more proteins then what the capsules supply."

"I thought this was a done deal. This pill works, yeah and all that bullshit." Liam stepped in front of Sariah blocking his view of her. He was protecting her. Was there more to their relationship or was Liam just protective because he was paid to be?

"It works, but for long term many vampires find their body craves a higher amount of proteins. So, every now and then they have a bag. It's no big deal. The convenience of this is amazing."

"She will decide how long she stays. If you know the effects already then she should be fine in England." Liam turned toward Sariah. "You okay. Whatever you'd like to do."

Sariah shifted in her seat. Tears filled her eyes. Nathaniel knew she had had a hard time excepting bagged blood. She couldn't stand the sight of the blood, it reminded her too much of that brutal night. The little boy's tear stricken face still haunted him too. Who knew what it did to her.

"It's okay Liam. If I need to go through another trial to have freedom then I will. At least this time it seems promising. Nate, you have a week. Now where will I be staying for this trial?" She ran her delicate hand across her eye. Nathaniel's heart cracked. He wouldn't ask what happened to frighten her from a simple trial. He already had a good idea.

And it was because of him.

Sariah followed Nathaniel back down the long windowless hallway. No signs or paintings. Just bare walls. Memories of her first years at the Manor came rushing back. No windows, no doors, only blank walls. She was strapped to a gurney with silver cuffs burning her wrists and ankles. She rubbed her wrist, a reflex when she was nervous. Liam placed his hand on her shoulder.

"I'm here Sariah." He knew what happened. He had helped her for many years. He understood. She swallowed, her throat was dry. Her gums tingled. Fear was one way to ignite the demon hidden deep inside her soul. Liam gave her shoulder a reassuring squeeze.

They walked to a single door at the end of the hall and Nathaniel had to do his code and finger thing again. Why so much security here? They stepped into a small security room. There were two identical looking men sitting around a table. She turned back towards the door when another man, identical to the two, entered behind them. She lifted a questioning brow.

"Triplets. If you need anything talk to Nolan. He's the smart one." Nathaniel smirked.

One of the men at the table grumbled. "More of a nerd."

"Stop it all of you. Show some respect."

Nathaniel introduced everyone. After shaking hands Ivan joined the "dangerous" brother Sorin and they immediately went to the weapons cabinet and talked about the best and quickest way to kill efficiently. Liam joined the "smart" brother Nolan behind a security monitor to observe how their security system worked.

"So from here you can see everything in the facility?" Liam asked.

Nolan smiled. "Everything except the bathrooms. I knew you were here before the garage door opened."

"Sweet." Liam took a seat next to Nolan.

The other brother stood across from Sariah staring at her with a creepy smile. Weird. She glanced around realizing this place was just like the Manor. A prison with cells. Not one with bars, a much nicer one but still a cell just the same. Guards always watched your every move twenty four hours per day. This place was just missing a few silver lined gurneys.

Sariah turned toward Nathaniel. "Does a wall fold down into a bed or is there another place for me to stay?"

Nathaniel walked to a door at the back of the security office. "My office is through here and connected to a small studio apartment." Thank goodness. She needed to get away from this cell.

Sariah followed Nathaniel into his office. Creepy brother was right behind her chuckling. Was she missing something? Nathaniel's office smelled of him. A soothing spice. He must spend a lot of time in here. He had a large dark wooden desk in one corner with overflowing bookshelves against the two walls surrounding his desk.

Creepy brother plopped down onto the long burgundy leather sofa which sat across from one of the bookshelves.

"Is there a reason you're following us Doran?" Nathaniel's tone was stern, frustrated.

"Just doin' my job." Doran leaned back and planted his feet on top of the coffee table and smiled.

Sariah walked over to look at one of the unorganized bookshelves. Medical text books were stacked in every direction. He must have worked really hard to obtain a medical degree. She hadn't had that opportunity while she was locked away in a cell. "You've been busy. How many degrees do you have?"

"Nine. I had to learn many things to ensure the invention of Splash."

"Hmm." Sariah walked toward the other bookshelf. More text book.

"Through here is the studio." Sariah turned to find Nathaniel standing near the back wall. Another hidden door. "Okay." Sariah walked toward him. Doran stood to follow. Nathaniel growled.

Sariah stepped into the studio apartment and froze. Everything was purple. Everything!

"Is this your place Nate." She looked at him when he didn't answer. His jaw was tense, his eyes narrowed. His lips parted and fangs ripped through his gums filling his mouth.

"What the fuck Doran?" Nathaniel rasped through his long fangs. She took a step back. Whoa!

"Shouldn't make me your little bitch, asshole." Doran laughed and walked out of the apartment.

Sariah was shocked. What was going on? If this was Nathaniel's place then why was he so upset? Was Doran supposed to get rid of all the purple? Maybe Nathaniel was embarrassed. Or? That had to be it! He was gay. That made sense. Maybe that was why he left her so long ago— she wasn't his type. Sariah thought about Nathaniel's reaction with Doran. Could it be a lover's quarrel? She knew Liam was gay but he didn't really care for all the frilly stuff. Sariah looked at Nathaniel. Crap. Maybe she had blamed him for something that wasn't his fault.

She shouldn't be angry with him if this was his reason. Suddenly she felt guilty.

"Are you gay?"

"NO!" Nathaniel screeched between his elongated fangs. Okay then. No longer feeling guilty and moving right back to angry.

Did he have a girlfriend who was apparently obsessed with the color purple? That would make sense. She couldn't expect him to have waited for her. Did she want him to have waited for her? Her encounters were few because of being locked in the Manor. She was limited to staff or delivery personal if she wanted anything more. And she did, just not with any of them. She had only wanted one. "Do you have a girlfriend Nate?"

Nathaniel stalked toward her. His eyes darkened to an almost black. Only a slim rim on the outer edge of his pupil remained slightly tinted with green. His chest moved rapidly as his breathing increased. He stopped right in front of her. His heavy breath drifted over her face. She forgot how tall he was compared to her. She leaned her head back to look at him. Her own breath caught. He was magnificent in his vampire form. Her breathing quickened as her face heated. He was so close. Would he kiss her? Did she want him to kiss her? She didn't want to admit it but deep down she still loved him. She squeezed her hands into fists at her sides to stop from reaching out to touch him.

No, dammit, he left!

His eyes closed and after a deep calming breath his mouth slowly closed as his fangs retracted. When his eyes opened again they looked normal. He stepped even closer. She stepped back.

"I know it's been awhile Ria, but did I seem gay to you?" He used an old nickname that her father had given her in her youth. No, that night he was anything but gay. Gentle, yet demanding. He had taken his time with her helping her through each moment of her first time. Did he remember that night as clearly as she did? Then why did he leave? She wished she had the courage to ask. Maybe then she would understand. Maybe, she didn't want to know the real reason. Her.

She swallowed taking another step back. Time to change the subject. She glanced around the small studio apartment. The entire room was draped in different shades of purple. She peered around him to the kitchenette. The fridge was covered in purple magnets. The table cloth covering a small two person table was a bright purple lace.

"You can't blame me for asking, I mean your decorating skills are—questionable." The curtains were even a sheer soft purple, and the couch. The couch was a dark purple covered in different shades of purple accented pillows. And then there was the bed with at least six different shades of purple and lace. It was the most ridiculous thing she had every scene. Sariah bit back the urge to laugh.

FIVE

Nathaniel glanced around his apartment that he had called home for way too long. With his research it was easier to stay here most of the time. He rarely ventured to his home outside the city. What had Doran been thinking? No wonder Doran's brothers always wanted to kill him. His anger spiked. He was going to kill him. No, death would be too easy for the bloody bastard. He would wrap him in silver and stake his sorry arse outside in the garden and hope birds shit on his stupid head.

Sariah was holding back a smile. Did she like it? Maybe he could turn this around in his favor. If not Doran wouldn't see tomorrow.

"I remembered you liked purple and wanted you to feel comfortable while you were here." His voice low.

"Hey, it's okay Nate. I do like purple, not normally this much purple, but thank you for your effort in making me feel comfortable." He smiled. She appreciated his efforts. He'd settle with just staking Doran in the garden then, no silver needed.

"It's a small place but has everything you need. The kitchen is stocked with bagged blood and beverages. We need to start with the capsule right away so when you feel the urge to feed let me know."

Sariah winced, "I hate the sight of blood Nate."

"Still?"

"Yeah. It—It makes me think of that night. I'm not sure if I can use the bagged blood or not. And I'm worried that I won't be able to drink the beverages once the pill is added. Won't it look like blood?"

Nathaniel listened to the hesitation in her voice. He remembered both nights too. The night they were taken and turned by Josiah and his men. The torture they both had endured was horrific. He remembered praying for death to come and relieve the pain. And that was before Sariah lost control years later attacking a small town. It was all tragic. He had to help her find a way to tolerate blood not given through a transfusion.

"What if we disguise the blood? Put it into a closed cup."

"I tried that once. The orderly laughed about it and split opened a bag of blood in front of me. I haven't tried it since." Bastard.

"Would you be willing to try it again?"

Sariah glanced down to the floor. "I guess." She was rubbing her wrist again.

"Is your wrist okay?"

She looked up sharply. "Of course. Why would you ask?"

"I noticed you rubbing it while we walked down the

hallway and thought maybe you injured it when Liam pushed you back into the car." Why was she so defensive over her wrist?

"Oh."

"Are you feeling hungry?"

"Not now. Do you have a bathroom? I could really use a few minutes."

"Sure. Right through the door next to the bed. Take your time. Oh, I almost forgot. Garrick had clothes sent over for you. They're sitting in a bag on the counter in the bathroom. He said you lost your bag in England."

"Thank you Nate."

Nathaniel watched her walk into the bathroom and gently closed the door behind her. What had happened to her? She seemed—sadder than he remembered. Was the Manor that bad of a place? What was with this orderly? He would talk to Garrick immediately over that situation. Garrick had assured him that the Manor was the best place for her. Once she was doing better Garrick wouldn't allow him to contact her anymore. They didn't want anything or anyone interfering with her progress by bringing up past circumstance. He had called many times and received information on her progress for years even though he couldn't talk to her. Once she began to control her thirst and moved out of solitary Nathaniel thought it best to let her move on. Even if he never could.

Sariah gently closed the bathroom door behind her and let out a small laugh. Purple everything. She turned on the light and gasped. The bathroom was almost worse than the rest of the convenient yet small studio apartment. The shower curtain and rugs were a matching shade of lavender. The toilet was draped in a dark royal purple. *Ha!* The curtain surrounding the window matched the royal standing of the purple on the toilet. There were purple towels stacked on a shelf behind the toilet and even a purple toothbrush with her name on it. Sariah couldn't help but wonder if Doran had something to do with this. Either way she was flattered that Nathaniel had gone to so much trouble trying to make her feel comfortable. She did like the purple, although after spending a week here she might think about finding a new favorite color.

She looked in the bag and found a weeks' worth of clothes and undergarments. She decided she needed a shower and stripped out of her dirty clothes. Her shirt had a small splatter of blood that she hadn't noticed. Sariah cringed. She tossed her clothes in the trash bin next to the sink.

She turned the water on and gave it a couple of minutes to warm up before she stepped into the large three person shower stall. The shower had three shower heads beating down from different sides. It was heaven. She turned slowly in a circle enjoying the constant throbbing of warm water cascading over her body. The Manor didn't have a shower like this. The Manor was old and had plumping installed much later. She remembered when a running bath was the most exciting thing to happen. She would have to have a shower like this when she lived on her own. Should she dare hope? Would she be able to have her own place? She took her time washing her body and then her hair. She chuckled. There was a brand new purple razor on a shelf in the corner of the stall. She smiled, maybe she'd love purple even more now.

Sariah had just finished her shower when her stomach started to cramp. Her gums burned with an overwhelming need to feed. Why all of a sudden? Her eyes darkened. She glanced in the mirror. She hated her transformed self. It reminded her that no matter how much good she did she would always be this. Uncontrollable. A killer. She wished she could manage to survive like the other vampires did. Like Nathaniel. He made it look so easy. He had even achieved medical degrees in order to help their world.

Her throat began to burn with the intensity of her hunger. She needed blood now! Guess she would be trying

Splash sooner than later. She doubled over and crashed to the floor bringing the shelving unit behind the toilet down on top of her. She had tried to grab a towel but the cramps were intense. She lay there on her side panting. Her fangs ripped violently through her gums.

The door crashed open and Doran, the stupid brother with the creepy smile, walked in.

"Holy hell!" He reached above her and lifted the shelving unit with one hand placing it back in its spot. "Are you alright Sariah?"

"Need to feed." She moaned.

"You got it. Hold on." Sariah wanted to protest when Doran leaned over and picked her up but all that came out was a shallow groan. He carried her into the living area of the studio apartment and eased her down on the small sofa.

"Stay here." He walked away. Sariah leaned her head back against the soft fabric of the sofa. Her hands still clutched her stomach. She could get through this. She thought of how great things had been at the Manor this past year. She was able to have many freedoms she lacked before. She was even allowed to have a dance instructor come to her so she could have lessons. Everything faded away as she thought about spinning around as he pulling her close. She loved the feel of a man holding her. Making her feel special.

Like she belonged.

She had even made Liam learn a few of the dances so she could practice. She smiled. Liam had grumbled the whole time. But he enjoyed every minute of it.

Her throat started to cool down and the cramps began to lessen. She was calming down.

"Here." Doran handed her a glass. "I don't know what you like so I made you a girlie drink." Sariah took the glass and sat up. She sniffed it, sweet. Hmm. It didn't look especially bloody either. "What is it?"

"Take a drink first. My ex-girlfriend liked this a lot."

Ex-girlfriend?

Sariah tried to take a sip but her fangs hadn't retracted all the way. She took a deep breath and thought of dancing. He was holding her hand as she twirled around. She laughed and then he pulled her close. Almost. Her fangs were sliding back in. The man she was dancing with lifted her chin and kissed her. Nate! Her fangs shot right back out.

"Whoa!" Doran took a step back. "I just wanted to help. No need to get all freaky on me chick."

Sariah closed her eyes again. Nathaniel kept invading her thoughts. Her chest swelled from his kindness. She still loved him. She hadn't realized it until today when she looked into his green eyes. Her fangs slowly slid back into place. She opened her eyes to find Doran hovering near the door his head low. She did it. Why would thinking of Nate calm her so quickly?

Sariah lifted the drink to her mouth and took a slow sweet sip. *Wow! It was good.* She quickly gulped down the rest. "That was great Doran. Thank you."

Doran looked away. "No problem. It was pineapple juice mixed with coconut rum and a Splash of A positive."

"Well it was good. Do you mind if I have another?" She grabbed a soft velvety purple blanket off the back of the sofa and covered her naked body. Doran kept looking at the floor avoiding her, his cheeks flushed. She hadn't thought much about her nudity making him uncomfortable. At the Manor she rarely had privacy. Nudity was a normal thing and didn't really bother her. If only Nate had been the one to rescue her and carry her off. But he hadn't.

"Where is Nate?"

"He was called down to his lab. His assist Jennifer needed something. I don't get all that mumbo jumbo but he said somethin' about protein and left. He did tell me to listen for you just in case you needed somethin'. Can we leave the fact that you're naked between us? I really don't

42

want Nate to lay into me over carrying his naked woman around. He already screamed at me over the purple shi— stuff."

Purple, what? She was still stunned over what she just heard. His woman? Did Nathaniel still have feelings for her? Should she say something to him? Ask him? Or just make a move to sate the building urge that kept rising through her?

"Umm. You said something about purple?"

Doran blushed. "I was pis—upset over having to go shopping for him so when he said your favorite color was purple—well you can see for yourself."

Sariah laughed. Doran's wide smile spread across his face. He was handsome when he smiled. He had a little dimple in his left cheek. She wondered if his brothers had the same dimple.

Doran's smile faded. He backed away pressing his back against the counter. She concentrated on the movement outside of the apartment. Nathaniel was back. She could hear him talking.

Nathaniel walked into the apartment, a confused look on his face. Sariah pulled the blanket higher which then uncovered part of her leg. She quickly tucked her leg back under the blanket. Why did she feel nervous about Nathaniel seeing her naked. He had seen her naked once a long time ago. He turned with a scowl toward Doran.

"What in bloody hell is going on?"

Doran stuttered. "Umm. She fell and I helped her. That's all."

"What do you mean she fell and why is she naked?" Nathaniel's voice raised.

Before Doran had a chance to answer Sariah stood, wrapped the blanket around her body and headed toward the bathroom. "She is right here! If you want answers maybe you should ask me. Nicely."

The bathroom door slammed, hard.

SIX

Nathaniel stared at the closed bathroom door. She was angry. It took everything in him to stay planted where he was and not go straight into the bathroom and yell at her for being naked in front of another man. Instead...

Nathaniel turned toward Doran. Doran threw his hands in the air. "Hey man, she needed help, I helped. That's it. Don't be gettin' mad at me."

"Why didn't you call me?" Nathaniel tried his hardest to keep his emotions calm.

But when he saw Sariah barely covered on the couch and Doran standing across from her he was furious. He wanted to pull her to her feet and scream at her. He wanted to pull her close and kiss her breathless. When he was finished she would never even think about being naked with another man. Images of that night came flooding back.

Sariah and Danielle, another young girl from the town, lying on the dirt floor of the old drafty cabin. Josiah dragged him in by his hair and threw him down hard enough to slam his face into the ground and break his nose. Blood poured from his nostrils into his mouth. He tried to fight back but he wasn't strong enough. Each time he tried to get up his legs gave out and he dropped back down onto the dirt. Sometime had passed while he was unconscious on that cold floor but when he woke up.

Bile rose in his throat.

Nathaniel opened his eyes and watched as Danielle was dragged to the back of the cabin. Her high pitched screams were deafening as the men tortured her. Movement next to him caught his eye. Sariah. She was on the ground turned away from him naked and crying. What had they done to her? He winced when he tried to scoot close to her. His body hurt everywhere and his face was on fire from his broken nose.

"Sariah." He whispered. She didn't move. He needed to get them out of here and quickly. Now would be their chance with the men busy with Danielle. His heart sank. How could he leave Danielle behind? He had to at least try to get away. He would find help and come back for her. He held his breath through the pain as he lifted himself up onto his elbows. Sariah cringed and moved away the moment his hand touched her.

"It's okay. We have to go Sariah, now. Come." Nathaniel stood and lifted her up in to his straining arms even though his entire body protested. He struggled to the door and was amazed he was able to wedge his foot into the corner of the door and opened it. He stepped outside into the cool night air. He paused taking in the scent of victory. He stumbled as he hurried across the abandoned field.

He took coverage in the forest and sat Sariah down next to a tree. He pulled off his mud covered shirt and covered her bare body. He felt so weak, tired. He had only sat down and closed his eyes for a minute before he heard Josiah's dark laugh.

He was never going to let anything happen to her again. He turned to Doran.

"Next time if she needs something you come and get me immediately! You are not to touch her again! Do you understand?"

Doran shook his head and murmured whatever as he left the room.

Nathaniel went to the kitchenette and poured a drink adding a Splash of AB positive. He was angry. No, he was jealous. Doran had helped her instead of him. Doran had seen her beautifully sculpted body. He had to make amends and help her somehow. He wanted to be the one to see her incredible body. He adjusted himself from another growing problem and sat on the couch to wait for her. They were going to talk. When they were finished talking he hoped they could spend the rest of the evening rolling around on the purple bed. He would show her just how much he missed her.

Nathaniel smiled.

Sariah couldn't believe the nerve of Nathaniel. What right did he have to be angry? She was the one sprawled out onto the bathroom floor losing control. She pulled her pants on then grabbed a plain white shirt. At least her clothes weren't all purple. Sheesh. She left the bathroom and found Nathaniel staring at her while he sat on the couch.

"What happened?"

"Oh, now you want to talk. Maybe you should have tried that before you came in here thinking you own me!"

"That's not what I think." Nathaniel shouted.

"Really? Why were you so angry? You know what? Never mind. I am going to let Liam know the little red pill worked so we can leave."

"It worked?"

"Yes it worked. I almost lost control while taking a shower. I fell and the shelving unit came down on top of me. Doran helped." That was all. Why was he so mad?

"That's why you were naked?"

Sariah huffed. "No, I threw myself at him for his heroic actions in saving me! Of course that's why."

"What type of drink did he make you?"

"Some coconut thing with A positive blood. It was good too. I even had a second one and now I feel great. So if you'll excuse me I am going to talk to Liam. I want to go out. I am tired of being confined to one place and Liam promised me dancing.

Sariah walked toward the door then halted when Nathaniel spoke.

"I'm sorry Ria. When I saw you there, naked it brought back memories I thought I had gotten past. I kept thinking of Josiah and what he did. Can we please talk? I think it can help us both move on."

Sariah hesitated. Tears threatened to fall. Did she really want to talk about it? She needed to know why he left. "I will talk with you only if you tell me why you left." She waited for his answer before turning around.

"Okay. And I will tell you only if you go dancing with me instead of Liam."

"Okay." Sariah sat down next to him. There thighs touched with the small size of his sofa. He shifted and his leg slightly rubbed against hers. She shivered with need.

"I have regretted that night every day. I shouldn't have left you Sariah. But I needed to be able to help you. After you attacked that town, I knew I had to do something because I didn't protect you the night you were attacked by Josiah."

Sariah started to get up. Nathaniel reached out and touched her arm. She could see the pain in his eyes. The regret. Was there love in his gaze?

"Please Sariah. Let me finish." Nathaniel lightly tugged her hand and she sat back down next to him. He kept her hand firmly grasped in his.

"You shouldn't be ashamed of what happened. You

had been through a lot and trying to deal with it. I struggled too. After the night we were attacked and turned all I felt was guilt. Guilt for not protecting you. Guilt for leaving Danielle behind."

"You hid it better than me. Nate I am sorry for what happened. All those people. I don't even remember killing them. I only remembered the burning hunger growling deep inside me. I felt starved."

"I know. You weren't feeding after you were turned. That's why you lost control. That's why I have spent decades researching. You're not a monster Sariah. You just have to accept yourself and learn that it's okay to feed." Tears ran down her cheeks.

Nathaniel wrapped his arms around her and held her close. "Shh. I left to find a way to help you. You're the reason Splash exists Sariah. I made it for you."

Sariah was speechless. He made it for her. He still loved her. She could feel it in his touch, hear it in his voice. She sniffed and wiped away the tears that were showering her cheeks. "I thought it was because of me. That you didn't want me anymore after we were together."

Nathaniel lifted her chin and peered down at her. "Never. Making love to you was the best night of my life Sariah. I loved you so much. I still love you. The moment I saw you get off that plane I wanted to wrap you into my arms and never let go. When you said you were going to leave back to England my heart stopped. I can't lose you again." Dare she believe him?

Sariah tried to blink away her tears, but they spilled over in a steady stream.

He loved her.

SEVEN

After all the time she had been alone she finally felt like she belonged. Nathaniel's hands brushed away the tears sliding down her cheeks. When she glanced up and caught his intense look she knew he had been hurting just as much. The center of his eyes darkened like all vampires leaving a small green edge. He scooped her up and held her tightly in his lap. Before she realized what she was doing she looped her arms around his neck and kissed him. He reacted quickly and took charge. His mouth moved firmly over hers—demanding. She squeezed him closer still—her tension already building. She wanted to be with him more than anything. Right here, right now.

49

Was it too soon? Take your time her mind scolded, yet everything in her body screamed to be with him now.

She wiggled and felt the proof of his need growing underneath her bottom. She pulled him even closer and opened to him. He accepted by thrusting his tongue inside her mouth with a desperation that warmed her heart.

He needed her.

She had never thought about what that night did to him. She only understood her own anger. She returned his kiss with desperation of her own.

Sariah trailed her hands over his muscular body. All vampires had perfect bodies, except her. She had starved herself refusing to feed for so long she now had a malnourished frame. He cupped the back of her neck and pull her flush with his body. One hand rested on her lower back holding her firmly in place. She couldn't wait any longer. She reached for his waist band needing to satisfy her own tension that was spiraling out of control.

He chuckled. "Oh sweetness. I am trying to go slow but if you keep that up I am going to throw you down right here."

Sariah smiled and wiggled her bottom again. Nathaniel groaned.

She shifted and wrapped her legs around him then rubbed her center against him. Her body soared as she rubbed herself against the thickness she urgently needed. It had been too long since she had been with anyone. And the few she had been with never compared to that one night with Nathaniel.

His kiss became fevered. She wanted more. Chills spread over her heated body as his hands slowly moved up and down her spine. With an uncontrollable need she frantically pulled at his shirt. She wanted him naked now! He broke their kiss to allow his shirt to be pulled over his head then quickly crushed his mouth to hers again.

Sariah spread her hands and rubbed them across Nathaniel's bare chest. She loved the feel of his strong body. He groaned when her fingers drifted through the sprinkle of reddish hair and toward the waist band of his jeans again.

He stopped her exploration. "No hurry love. By the way, you have too many clothes on. A shirt for a shirt." He gave her a devastating smile and then pulled up the hem of her shirt and tossed it to the floor. He gripped her sides and slowly ran his hands up her back. His thumbs softly grazed her breasts. Sariah shivered with anticipation. She could hear his heart beating frantically in time with her own. She felt her bra loosen as he unsnapped the clasp. She was relieved to find there were many bra and panty sets in the bag of clothes that were left for her. Thank goodness. *Maybe she should buy a purple set?*

He slowly pulled the straps down her arms and added it to the floor.

"Beautiful." He bent his head low and took one pink nipple into his mouth while his other hand squeezed and teased her other nipple bringing it to a hardened pebble. Sariah arched her back pressing Nathaniel closer. He switched sides and suckled her other nipple. She moaned. Moisture pooled from her core. She pulled his head up and shoved him down and kissed him uncontrollably.

They had been very young the first and only time they making love. There was a nervousness to it that lacked this time. This time it was a quick, needful coming together.

He tightened his hands around her waist as he rose. Never breaking their kiss, she tightened her legs around his waist as he carried her to the bed. He tossed her down.

She bounced with a laugh. "In a hurry now are you?"

Nathaniel smiled. "Never. I want to see you. I can smell your excitement." The edge of his eyes started to glow brighter.

Sariah blushed. He was bolder than she remember. His nostrils flared. She squeezed her legs closed. He stood above her in only a pair of jeans— His body powerful. He used to work on his father's farm— hard physical labor.

She would sit on the hill near his house and watched him. She wanted to see every part of him first.

She sat up. "You first."

Nathaniel was stunned. His sweet Ria wanted him to disrobe first. He remembered how shy she was their first time. Well, it had been decades. Who else had she been this forward with? Jealously snuck up on him again. He didn't want her to ever be with another man.

He chucked off his shoes and zipped down his pants with vampire speed. He paused with a finger sliding over the elastic to his boxers and watched her eyes grow brighter with each slow tug down. His erection sprang out as he dropped his boxers and stepped out of them. He took a step toward her. She was beautiful laying there topless—a perfect handful with pale pink nipples. They were still hard and reddened from his play. He wanted more of that play.

He untied one shoe and the other slowly taking them off. Her socks followed.

She lifted her hips so he could pull down her jeans and underwear. *Stunning.* Her blonde curls were already glistening and ready for him. He lifted her leg and lightly kissed his way up to her knee. She moaned the closer he came to her center. She pouted when he stopped and grabbed her other leg.

Nathaniel groaned. He struggled to keep a slow steady pace when all he wanted to do was ravish her.

"I can't take anymore Nate. Please." Sariah panted.

His control snapped and Nathaniel covered her with his body and kissed her soft lips impatiently. She parted her legs ready for him and he entered her with one full forceful thrust.

It was heaven. He had forgotten how good she felt. No other woman felt like home—like he belonged. He started a leisurely pace wanting to know her every movement, her every sound. He gently kissed her savoring the feel of her tightness wrapped around him. He wanted to go oh so slow but was quickly losing the battle. Her nails ripped into his back and his thrust became fevered. He was so close but wanted to put her pleasure before his own. He moved his mouth to her neck and licked the pulse beating just beneath the skin. He sank his fangs into her delicate throat and listen to her scream as her orgasm rushed through her. His pace faltered as his own release exploded. He pulled her into his arms as he dropped down next her.

EIGHT

Peering into the microscope, Jonathan exclaimed, "It's stabilizing well with her." Nathaniel looked into the microscope. Sariah's blood work was stable. "How come it's working for her but not others?" His assistant Jonathan was just as stunned that after a week of Sariah taking Splash her body hadn't faltered once. He knew better than anyone just how good she was feeling. At first he felt ashamed for making love to her their first day together. He should have had more discipline but the moment he realized she wanted him just as bad all thought vanished.

Since that night everything was on hold. He spent time in the lab only to make sure Sariah was handling Splash, the rest of his time was spent in bed—with her. He smiled, that morning she begged him to stay for a little longer. They both knew that if he did a little longer would have turned into hours later. He had to check her blood so he forced her to give him a sample and promised to be back soon. She had uncovered her luscious naked body and stretched, arching her back making her breast bounce in the air. *Vixen!*

"What do you think Nate? Why?" Jonathan asked again.

"It's probably because her body needs fewer proteins."

"Its' amazing either way. I'm going to lunch, are you going to be here later or do you have important work back at your office again?"

Nathaniel knew everyone had known what he was off doing and he didn't give a damn.

"I'll be busy. Enjoy your day Jon. I will see you tomorrow." Nathaniel grabbed the printed results of Sariah's blood work and headed back towards his office.

He found Sariah asleep and still naked in his bed. His heart swelled with the love he had denied himself for so long. She was here and finally his. What if she wanted to go back to England? He would just have to make sure she never wanted to leave.

He quietly slipped out of his clothes and climbed into the bed next to her. Her eyes snapped open then softened when she met his gaze.

"Hi."

"Hi back."

She pushed him over and climbed on top of him.

Sariah stood, letting the shower sprays massage her back. She loved this shower with the multiple shower heads and large seated bench. She enjoyed being here and felt panicked with the thought of leaving. She didn't think she could ever leave here, or him. She loved waking to see Nathaniel next to her every morning. She felt at peace every time they made love.

She dried off after her shower and dressed in a long blue spaghetti strapped gown with a beautiful small silver pin that clasped the material between her breasts. Nathaniel had bought it for her while they had shopped on line because they still weren't allowed to leave the building. He was frustrated about all the security and wanted to have some time alone with her. Even in the apartment together they weren't truly alone. Both of their multiple bodyguards took shifts right outside their apartment door in the security office.

Tonight they were sneaking out to go dancing—just them, free for a night. They had a plan to escape their shadows and her stomach fluttered. Could they pull it off?

She stepped out into the small living area and waited for Nathaniel to return. He had opted to use the shower in his private laboratory while she used the one here. She knew why he left, if he had stayed to shower here they would both still be in the steamy room. Sariah bit her lip thinking about how gorgeous he was. The first day they made love it was frantic and needy. Since then they both had slowed down and made love gently taking time to explore every part of each other. He had found many ways to bring her to the screaming edge just to try and find another way to do it again. *She could never leave him.*

Nathaniel couldn't bring himself to take a full breath. His heart thudded as he tried to breath. She was beautiful. No, more that beautiful. Words could not explain how she looked. He had to make her see why she should not leave. It was a struggle to leave their bed to get ready for tonight, but he knew that if he stayed they would never leave. He had picked a suite with a blue button down shirt to match her pale blue dress. He had never really gone dancing before and didn't want to embarrass her and he couldn't ask for help without letting someone know their plan. So he had watched a couple of "How to dance" videos before showering.

"You look amazing Ria."

"You're not so bad yourself."

"We better go before that dress finds its way to the floor. Are you ready?" Nathaniel opened the door.

He held Sariah's hand and walked her to the dining hall located at the back of Bartlett Laboratories. She had been speechless when he explained the name of the facility. When Garrick offered to purchase the property he had jumped on it requesting he was the one who named it. Garrick agreed and Nathaniel had been leading the research teams ever since.

He led her to the table near a glass wall located at the back of the facilities dining hall. The table was draped in red linens with wine glasses set for two. A vase with one long steam purple rose sat in the center, and music played in the back ground over the intercom system. He wanted tonight to be perfect. Their bodyguards for tonight were Doran and Ivan. He kind of felt bad about ditching Doran. His brothers were going to give him all kinds of shit over this. Nathaniel smiled, deserves him right after seeing Sariah naked.

"Here." Nathaniel pulled a chair out for Sariah to take a seat.

"This is lovely Nate." Sariah reached for the purple rose and smiled. "Thank you."

"I figured after this week purple was our thing." Nathaniel chuckled and took his seat across form Sariah. He poured red wine in each of their glasses and then added Splash.

"How was my blood work today?" Sariah took a sip of her wine.

"Perfect. I guess your body needs less proteins. It's amazing really. Everything has looked fine for your whole trial."

"I'm glad. I thought it would be harder to drink with everything being tinted red because of the pills but it's not. I've enjoyed it and have felt better than I have in a long time."

"I can tell." Nathaniel's eyes sparked with need. She smiled as her eyes began to darken as well. He took a long swallow of his wine.

"So why do you think my body is so different." Nathaniel gulped. He didn't want to tell her but knew he had to. Here goes.

"Honestly I think it's because of your lack of feeding for so long after the turn. Your body didn't get everything it needed to form fully as a vampire."

"Really."

"Now for the problem. I've noticed changes in you Sariah. I think the more you feed with Splash the more your body will heal. Soon you may have to drink fresh blood."

"You think I will be stronger and have more of a vampire body."

"You are beautiful just the way you are Sariah, but yes. I think over time your body will look healthier."

"Why didn't the blood transfusions do this?"

"My best guess is that the transfusions didn't last as long. Your body needed more but was restricted to scheduled feedings. With Splash you get more blood at multiple times during the day. The transfusions only kept you alive Sariah, but Splash will let you live."

NINE

ariah couldn't believe it. Splash was working. What would happen if she had to have fresh blood? Could she do it? She would do it for Nathaniel. He had done so much for her expecting nothing in return. He worked his whole life to find a way to help her and he never stopped loving her. She could do this for him. He was right, she felt stronger. Better. She felt alive and her fears of hurting others disappeared. She hadn't lost control due to her hunger once. And the times she did lose control it was for other reasons entirely, like seeing Nathaniel naked. She had zero control of her urges in those moments and loved it.

"Let's dance."

Sariah took Nathaniel's hand and followed him to the back of the room. He had the table placed back here on purpose and told everyone that he wanted to dance with her near the windows where the moon light could spill in. Security finally agreed. Little did their security detail know they would be dancing toward an exit and then running for it. He was a little clumsy with his footing and blushed. Did he know how to dance?

"Have you ever danced before Nate?" He looked so bashful.

"I watched a lesson on my computer."

She laughed. He would even go to this length for her— embarrassing himself and admitting to research dancing on his computer.

"Dancing is something you have to experience to learn. Here, let me show you. We'll start with a simple slow dance. Put your hands around my waist." Sariah then slipped her hand around his neck and interlocked her fingers together. "Now just move your feet slowly back and forth."

He caught on quickly and before she realized it he took charge moving gracefully around the dining hall. He leaned down to whisper in her ear. "Are you ready?" Sariah shook her head not wanting to give anything away of their plan.

They zoomed toward the back exit. Nathaniel had changed the security code for this door to make it more difficult for their bodyguard's to get through. She heard the deep voice yelling from behind as they exited. They made it the car he had parked in a private secluded lot next to the office area of Bartlett Laboratories. He had told her he kept it there for emergencies. If they had to evacuate the building for some reason he always had a quick way out.

Sariah laughed as they pulled out of the parking lot. She felt free. She couldn't believe their luck at pulling this off and loved that she could spend an evening with Nathaniel all alone.

"Will we get passed the gate?"

"Nope. That's why I am taking a secret route. There is a back way to and from Bartlett Laboratories that few know about. Garrick constructed it for emergency transports. We don't want humans seeing everything that comes through the doors."

"Brilliant. So where are we going?"

"You said you wanted a date. I've already danced with you so our next stop is the movies."

Sariah squealed with excitement. The movies!

He pulled down a back alley and around the corner to park. "Let's go." When Sariah hesitated he added. "We have to walk from here. Doran will look for my car. It should be pretty well hidden here and once we are inside the theatre it will be harder for them to find us."

They walked hand in hand towards the theatre. The evening was cool and the stars bright in the sky. She loved it here. The buildings were older but kept in good condition. All of a sudden he spun her around and pressed her up against one of those buildings.

"I love you." He kissed her. Sariah kissed him back with all the love in her heart. He was the most amazing man she knew and was happy they had found each other again. His hand slid up the long slit on her dress and she arched her back wanting more of him. He left her lips to move down her cheek then over to suckle on her ear lobe. He moved to graze his fangs over the side of her neck. *Yes!*

"Well looky what we have here."

Nathaniel pulled away quickly placing his body in front of Sariah's. He had never seen the man before but his instincts told him the man was dangerous.

"Sorry, man. We will be going now." Nathaniel grabbed for Sariah's hand but only met air. He spun around to find her held tightly by another man. "What the fu—."

Nathaniel collapsed. A silver dagger protruding from his chest.

TEN

Nathaniel groaned. He was on fire. The flames were spreading, torching him from the inside out. He tried to move to find more pain ripping through his arms and legs. What the hell?

"Nate. Don't try to move. They have you strapped securely with silver." It took him a minute to realize it was Sariah's voice he heard.

Sariah!

Someone had her! He struggled to get up tearing his skin open from where the silver cuffs held him down. *Shit!* He looked at Sariah and couldn't hold back his growl. She was strapped to another medical gurney next to him with silver cuffs around her wrists and ankles. Her eyes were swollen form crying.

"Are you okay sweetness?" He tried to keep his voice from crackling but failed. His heart was slowly withering away from the sight of her battered body. She was bleeding from wounds on her beautiful face. Blood was tangled in her blond curls. Her pale blue gown was ripped in half leaving her breast exposed. He tugged harder with his wrists biting back the pain it caused. He had to get free. He had to get to her. Everything from that night came flooding back. Nathaniel screamed in agony.

No! Not again! His fangs exploded violently through his gums. The taste of his own blood coated his tongue. His eyes shifted, darkening to an almost solid black leaving very little green to show his humanity. He refused to be helpless to do anything again.

He would kill everyone!

"Nate. I'm okay. Please, Nate. Look at me." Sariah sobbed again. "They beat me up because I tried to get to you. Then they strapped me here. I hate these damn gurneys."

Nathaniel closed his eyes and thought of the last week of his life spent with Sariah. His fangs slowly retracted and the darkness of his eyes lessened. He looked at Sariah again. "You've been strapped to a gurney like this before?"

"Yes. I was strapped to one in a silver lined room for decades." Tears streamed down her face. "I thought I had gotten away from them. It looks like this is Josiah's plan."

Nathaniel could hear her fear and it tore him apart. "We can get through this Ria. Stay focused and we can do this together. Can you move your arms at all?"

Sariah lifted her arms up slightly. "I have some room but not much."

"That's a start. Can you wiggle yourself some to get what's left of your gown to fall?" He watched as she began to move. She never cried out once even though he knew for a fact those damn cuffs were tearing into her skin. "Great. Now try to reach the silver pin. It's real silver and you might be able to pick the lock on the cuff with it and use it as a weapon."

She started shifting back and forth to reach the pin just as a door opened. Sariah stilled not giving away her intent. Nathaniel saw a man walk through the door.

"Looky who's awake." He stepped closer to Sariah and ran his hand down the side of one of her breast. Nathaniel struggled to get loose with a vicious growl. The man laughed. "Someone's angry. If you really wanted to protect her you would have never left with her alone. Now I will enjoy my time with her while we fly back to England."

"Wouldn't Josiah be angry with you if he received me damaged?" Sariah spoke softly.

"What he doesn't know won't hurt him." The man ran his dirty hand down Sariah's torso stopping to cup her between the legs.

"No!" Sariah screamed and fought against the man with all her might. The door opened again, this time a small woman with short spikey brown hair came strolling into the room with them. She wore a pair of black leather pants and a tight red top showing off her petite figure. She looked familiar but he couldn't quite place her.

"Frederick back off." Nathaniel stared at the woman. Did he know her?

"Why. It's a long trip and I just wanted to have some fun before we go."

"And Josiah will neuter you the moment he smells her on you. Now get out! I need a minute with our new friends."

"You're not to be left alone with them. His rule."

The small woman confidently walked over to Frederick and grabbed him by the front of his shirt and tossed him across the room. He slammed into the far wall with a thud.

"Who do you think he trust more? Now get your ass out and don't come back until I tell you too." Frederick picked himself up from the floor and scrambled out the door.

"Thank you." Sariah whispered.

The woman laughed. "Don't thank me just yet. He would have just raped you. I am going to enjoy watching you see Nate die, and then kill you myself." She finally turned toward him.

Oh my god. *Danielle*! She was still alive. He had thought she died. When Josiah grabbed her that night he thought she was Josiah's human shield. He had no idea she was still with him—and it was all his fault.

"Danielle."

Sariah gasped when she heard Nathaniel whisper the name. Could it be?

"So you remember me, do you?"

"Yes. I looked for you. I thought you had died."

She laughed. "No not really dead. I have been waiting for a chance to kill you and your little whore. Now I have it." Danielle looked at Sariah. "Don't worry, after you watch him die you will be begging me to kill you." She walked over to a table and retrieved a silver knife. "Let's see how much pain you can endure shall we?"

Sariah screamed when Danielle plunged the knife into Nathaniel's stomach. How could Danielle do this? Why was she doing this? "Danielle, please stop. Why are you doing this?" Sariah sobbed as Nathaniel lay there unable to move. His eyes stayed locked onto her own. Loving her until the end.

Her anger began to spike. She forced her fangs to heel. She needed to stay focused in order to save them both. She had to do it for Nathaniel.

"Why? Why you ask? You little bitch messed everything up for me! Josiah punished me for years because you got away. And you're the only reason I was stuck with him in the first place. Nate saved you instead of me. Josiah wants to keep you instead of me. So you ask why? Because you are worth nothing to me and will die today at my hand." She plunged the knife into Nathaniel's stomach again.

"Please Danielle. We didn't do anything to you. Please let us go?" Sariah almost had the silver pin in her hand. She needed to keep Danielle talking so she could have more time to free herself and save Nathaniel. "We tried to save you. We both went back looking for you for days. If we had known you lived we would have found you."

"It no longer matters. Nate had always chosen you. I wanted him back then but he was always helping you with deliveries. Did he tell you the night you were attacked he was supposed to be with me. Only Josiah found me first. He could have saved me."

"No, he couldn't have." Almost there. Just a little more. "No human could stand against Josiah."

Danielle stabbed Nathaniel again. This time in his leg. "Listen to me, he can help you now like he's helping me."

"Help how?"

"He's helped me learn to feed sufficiently after decades of not feeding because of what happened that night."

"I don't have a problem feeding. And I won't regret killing a town. You are weak, a coward. This should break you though." She stabbed Nathaniel again.

Sariah couldn't hear Nathaniel's soft cry any longer. Was he dead? Is this really how she would lose him? Finally she got to the pin. She began to work on the cuff. The first one clicked opened softly and Sariah covered up the sound my kicking her leg against the gurney.

Danielle smiled. "Now you get a little fight in you, huh?" She stabbed him again while Sariah freed her other arm. Now how to free her feet without being notice?

A loud noise sounded outside of the door, someone screamed. Ivan came crashing through the door with Frederick flying in midair. Fredrick was thrown into Danielle knocking them both into the wall.

Liam followed at a slower pace into the room with another man. Sorin. She had never been happier to see death himself as she was in that moment.

Sariah freed her ankles and ran to Nathaniel. Before

she reached him Danielle grabbed her by her hair and slammed her head into the side of the gurney. Sariah fell to the floor.

Letting her control dissolve Sariah's fangs sprang forward and her pupils blackened, darker than a starless sky at night. With a pained cry Sariah grabbed Danielle's arm and twisted it around. Danielle screamed and Sariah finished by kicking Danielle into another wall. All Sariah saw was blinding rage. She would no longer let her demon control her. She would no longer stand by and let someone else get hurt because of her.

She attacked Danielle with a fury she had never known. Not uncontrolled but strategically to fight for those she loved. She pulled out the silver knife that Danielle had left in Nathaniel's chest and ran for her again. Danielle screamed and took off for the door but Sariah was faster and was a good aim. She threw the knife. It hit its mark dead on and Danielle crumbled to the floor. Only a pile of dust remained.

Sariah ran to Nathaniel. Ivan had Frederick contained in silver cuffs. Sorin and Ivan said something about getting the other guy and took Frederick with them as they left the room.

"How did you know?" Sariah asked when Liam approached her.

"Tracking device in your shoes. We'll talk later. Let's get him in the car and take him back to the lab. Sorin and Ivan will deal with our new prisoners. Garrick wants them in custody." Liam gave her a stern look then walked out the door. *Shit!* He was mad.

Liam drove them back to Bartlett Laboratories. Sariah sat in the back seat with Nathaniel across her lap. She couldn't lose him. Not after everything he had done for her. Nathaniel's staff ran out and took Nathaniel to the infirmary immediately. Liam stopped her from following.

"We need to talk."

"Now?"

"Yes. Let's go." With no choice she followed Liam to the studio apartment.

"He's safe. There isn't anything more you can do for him right now. Go shower and get yourself cleaned up. I will be here on the couch waiting."

After Sariah was cleaned up she sat down next to Liam with a Splash of AB positive added to a glass of wine.

"I'm sorry."

"You know we would have taken you out. Why did you guys have to go and put yourselves at risk? I am so pissed at you right now!"

"We wanted to be alone. Truly alone Liam."

"Do you love him?"

"Yes, I do. And I am going to stay here."

"I figured. You know I have to go back."

"I do."

Doran walked into the apartment. "He's awake and pissed as hell. He wants to see her."

Doran hadn't even looked at her. He must have gotten into a lot of trouble.

Sariah could hear Nathaniel's scream before she reached the infirmary door. She rushed to his side and stoked his face.

"I'm here. It's okay." His eyes were unfocused and looking around frantically. Finally he saw her.

"Sariah! Thank god!" He grabbed her and pulled her down on top of him.

"Careful. You need time to heal."

"All I need to heal is you. Oh, god I thought I had lost you, again." Nathaniel squeezed her tight.

"I'm here Nate, and I'm not leaving."

"You mean you plan to stay. Here with me?"

"Yes. Here with you."

Nathaniel stood up taking Sariah with him. She clutched his neck to keep from falling. "Let's go." He walked out of the infirmary with Sariah nestled in his arm.

"Where are we going"

"To our place to celebrate."

"Oh, no! Put me down now. You need time to recover."

"Trust me I am fine. Jonathan gave me a new drug I have been working on. This one rapidly excels the production of blood cells into the body. I'm good to go. I want to be with you now and forever Sariah."

EPILOGUE

Three Months Later...

Laying wrapped in the purple silk sheets, Nathaniel gazed upon Sariah. "Again?"

"Yes, again."

Nathaniel chuckled and rolled with Sariah in his arms until she was pinned underneath him. "I, Nathaniel Collins take you Sariah Bartlett to be my wife in sickness and in health, for richer, for poorer until death do us part."

"Thank you! I love hearing you repeat your vows. I love you Nate!"

"I love you too Sariah."

"Now we better go back to our guests. They are probably wondering where we snuck off to." Sariah sighed.

"Why did you have to invite all these people?"

"I told you. They are all my family. The whole Crest of Garrick's line is here for this. It's not often we have a reason to celebrate something good so when we can we go way out."

"Garrick seems sad."

"Well that's because he hasn't found his true love yet. Not everyone can be lucky like me." Nathaniel bent his head and kissed Sariah deeply. She kissed him back with all the love she had ever felt. She was finally free. She finally belonged...

Coming Fall of 2013

Winterloch Publishing, LLC.

Baine Kelly

The unforgettable smell of fuel scorched her nose moments before the flames sparked, the night glowed brightly as fire engulfed the street. Smoke suffocated her with each breath, heat surrounded everything in its deadly path. Flames of hell heaved toward the heavens.
Screams pierced the night.

Cries of help never to be heard.

Never to be answered.

Baine Kelly

Blood Loss

Baine Kelly

Baine Kelly

Natalie heard the tires squeal as the vehicle skidded sideways moments before the loud boom of impact. Sparks rained down showering the street, wires ripped forcefully from their holdings. The telephone pole crashed down violently trapping those inside. Their never ending cries for help rang through the night as she watched from beyond unable to reach them. Natalie shielded her face as the flames grew brighter, sweat beaded her brow.

The explosion shook the ground throwing her backwards, slamming her to the asphalt. Her ears rang from the deafening blast and still she glanced up searching for every detail, not wanting to remember them but needing to know them. Pushing herself from the ground she noticed a slight movement. He was here again.

A large figure, shoulders broad, tall and encased in black. He stood motionless in the midnight air, watching. His unnatural eyes glimmered in the shadow of the flames. Natalie tried to focus only on him. She needed to know why he was there. Did he cause it? Why wasn't he helping them? She glanced to the pavement near his feet and knew what she would see next. A small tennis shoe, discolored, spotted crimson. Their bodies trapped in the car, unable to escape. The lone figure turned and walked away, doing nothing. She refocused on him trying to gain the slightest detail of who he was. Why was he leaving? Either way it didn't matter, she was too late to do anything but watch. Trapped by time, unable to save them.

A soothing English accent broke through the vision and the images flashing before her slowly faded away.

"Are you alright love?"

Natalie took a deep breath and wiped her sweaty palms on her jeans. Seated in a soft cozy chair she tried to clear her hazy mind from what she'd seen. The smell of freshly brewed coffee reached her and she remembered. She was in a bookstore and had just finished a cup of coffee while reading a book when the vision took its hold. Slowly

Natalie opened her eyes to find an unknown crisp blue set staring back at her. The unknown man was kneeling in front of her, concern strained his masculine features.

"Fine, thank you." Natalie answered hoarsely, her throat still burned from the smoke, the stench of fire still lingered. It always took some time for the impact of the visions to damper. Usually the visions only occurred when she slept, but lately she kept seeing the same one over and over again no matter what she was doing.

"You sure 'bout that? You looked ghastly pale there. Thought you might fall right over."

"Long day. Thank you." Natalie replied as she stood, swaying slightly. The stranger caught her arm steading her. She stepped away from his grasp and looked for the book she had brought with her. With shaky hands Natalie bent down and picked up the book that had fallen to the floor and quickly placed it into her bag. Natalie grabbed her empty coffee cup off the table and hefted her bag over her shoulder.

"Can I do anything for ye love?" The stranger asked.

"No thank you. Like I said, long day. I need to be going." Natalie walked passed him and headed toward the exit tossing the empty Styrofoam cup into the trashcan by the door.

Taking in a deep breath of fresh air Natalie stopped outside the bookstore and glanced up at the stars shining brightly above, wishing she could see her family just one more time. Two years had passed, each night she relived every moment of that fatal day caught in the throes of the reoccurring vision. Tears began to blur the bright lights of hope together as she sent up a silent prayer to her boys.

One day mommy will hold you again.

Wiping away the tears dripping down her face, Natalie rummaged through her bag for her keys and headed for her car. The visions were uncontrollable at times and were getting worse. Something was wrong, she could feel it. She needed to find out who the figure was and why he was there and hoped finding out would help ease the guilt churning her stomach each and every day.

The guilt of not understanding what was happening, of not stopping it.

The guilt of not saving them.

* * * * *

He watched as she tossed her long blonde hair lightly to the side, slowly sipping her drink as she tried her hardest to flirt with the man sitting next to her at the bar. Crossing her legs, her short black dress slid up showing a glimpse of her thigh. Still she had no luck. He wondered why? She wasn't bad looking. Prostitute, maybe? He found himself curious enough and focused his heightened senses and listened to the late night chatter in the club and discovered there wasn't a guy in the bar willing to go home with her. Their blatant insults amused him: *slut, bitch, been there done that, and so on.* Not interested was better for him. He searched for women like her, those who were liked by few and despised by many. He knew the type.

She was perfect.

People like her made the easiest prey in his experience. He observed her smile, strained, faked. Her laughter halfhearted. Taking a healthy swig of whisky he watched her turn that smile toward another man seated at the bar... Another failed attempt of flirting.

Patrick knew better, but couldn't help himself. The moment he saw the blonde-haired woman he was assaulted with need. Craved her body, craved her blood. He sat in a darkened corner of the club to wait. She clutched a ridiculously large purple handbag to her shoulder, one she probably bought instead of necessities like food and shit. Her very short black dress showed off long slender legs. Long legs he liked. She was tall with the help of heels and would be close to his height which could make things fun. Okay looking tits although small, generous ass.

He was cautious when he chose a woman, had to make sure no one would miss her. She was the one. He wasn't supposed to indulge, but fuck the others. He wanted her and by damned, he was walking out of here *after* her. Because he couldn't very well be seen walking out of here *with* her. He ordered another drink and waited, impatient as uncontrollable need grasped any sanity he had left. He wanted this, craved it more than the others. He would wait it out and hope he could have her before the others showed up. No sharing tonight. He wanted to be the only one to touch her, taste her. The only one to watch her fear filled face as she exhaled her last breath. Patrick lowered his gaze hiding the dark changes that blackened the world to him and swallowed down his excitement of what was to come. Patrick smiled as his body responded to the image of her naked body on display.

Dying by his hands.

"Halle-fucking-luiah!" Patrick whispered, getting to his feet he made his way across the bar slowly following her through the crowd and out the door. The moment Patrick stepped outside his senses were overwhelmed with the stench of fried food, strong perfumes, the river and urine. Closing his eyes and breathing deeply he focused on one scent. Hers. Cheap perfume mixed with rum and pineapple juice floated toward him on the evening breeze. She was to his left.

Tilting his head lightly he listened to the steady rhythm of her heels clicking on the cobblestone walkway. She was walking toward an alley.

Keep making it easier for me sweetheart.

He lingered for a moment not wanting his prey to know he was near. Not yet anyway, the chase made it more exciting, more pleasurable. Slipping his hands into his pockets, Patrick lowered his head, his gaze swiftly taking in his surroundings as he walked leisurely down the side of the buildings. His nostrils flared, his smile broadened. The hunt had begun.

* * * * *

"Oh, come on, you have to go with us! I need a girls' night out and it's about time you get out too Nat." Natalie listened to Loren whine about needing a night out while starting a pot of coffee. "I promise we won't make you dance. It's a new club and we are all going, please Nat."

No dancing, Natalie thought, whew that made it better! The visions always drained her emotionally and physically so all she really wanted to do was curl up in bed for the rest of the night. But when she got home from the bookstore Loren had been impatiently waiting for her in the driveway. "I really don't feel like going Loren. It always starts fun and ends with 'the' conversation," she grumbled, remembering the last time they talked her into going out.

'The' conversation being it's been two years, it's okay to move on and have a little fun while you still can, and her favorite, please, please get yourself laid!! Maybe that will put a smile on your face! No, she didn't want to go there. Not again. Not tonight.

"Nat. Nat. Natalie, will you go with us tonight?" Loren repeated anxiously.

"Huh? Tonight? It's already, like 9:00 p.m." Natalie huffed.

"You weren't listening to me again, were you?"

"No, not entirely. Sorry Loren, I'm just not that sure about a dance club. Besides I didn't get a whole lot of sleep last night and I'm exhausted."

The vision in the bookstore was nothing compared to

the one she had last night. After waking from the intense vision she couldn't settle down enough to go back to sleep. So she'd done what anyone would have done, cleaned out the cabinets, fridge and closets all before heading to work. "I'll buy you a drink." Loren said, her smile sweet, eyes eager, then continued, "Come with us tonight. I got our names on a list at a new club that opened up about a month ago. It's supposed to be the newest hot spot, called 'Second Sun'. Please, come with us. It will be so much fun with just the four of us."

Knowing Loren wouldn't give up until they were headed to this club for the night Natalie reluctantly gave in. "Fine, I will go. Stop pestering me!" Shaking her head with a light laugh, Natalie reached for a mug and poured a cup of coffee. She was going to need it.

"Great! I will call Jane and Jess to let them know you're in." Loren dashed from the kitchen toward the living room for the phone.

Without her friends, she would still be sleeping her days away in the darkness, silently wishing it would take her too. Their support had helped her start working, eating, and seeing daylight again. Natalie knew her friends saw her as a single women yearning to be found again. Natalie saw a thirty-four year old woman, now widowed, no longer a mother. It hadn't been easy, but she had learned to put on a strong face and carry through. Saving the breakdowns for when she was alone.

"Okay, I will be back to pick you up around 10 p.m. You better be dressed and ready or I will drag your ass down there in your underwear if I have to!" Loren mumbled as she ran out the front door.

"Great. I couldn't be more excited!" Natalie mumbled, sarcasm dripping from each word as the door slammed closed.

Natalie looked around at her empty house. Maybe one night out wouldn't be so bad. It sure beat sitting around here all alone, with darkness bearing itself nearer.

Newfound determination invaded. She headed for the shower. Tonight she'd take her time. She washed her hair and then slowly cleaned her body, still using the same perfumed body wash that Bob had liked. The scent reminded her of him. Better times.

She thought about the first time she used the lavender and vanilla scent. Her boys told her she smelled better than all the other moms. She pushed back the tears threatening to spill and picked up her razor and began to shave. When finished, she tipped her head back and enjoyed the comforting caresses' of warm water as the droplets trickled down her back. Steam rose, the scent of lavender surrounded her, engulfed her in serenity for the last few minutes before she reluctantly turned the shower off.

Wrapped in the softness of a sage towel, she wiped the mirror clean from the steam and peered at her reflection. Sadness still lied beneath her eyes. She may *think* going out was a good idea, but she still didn't *feel* it was but wanted to be with her friends because of everything they had done for her.

Knowing her friends would be pissed at her lack of clubbing clothes and not caring, she grabbed a pair of jeans and a tank top from her closet. After drying her long dark hair, she pulled it into a ponytail and donned her shoes. There, she was ready as ready could be. No way was she getting all dolled up to go to some stupid club.

She wished with all her might that some type of hope would cross her path.

Wished that someone out there could completely understand her as she was now.

Not as she was before. She walked out of her bedroom right as the doorbell rang and fists started pounding on the door. Natalie sighed while walking to the door listening to three grown women scream like teenagers.

* * * * *

Garrick glanced down to the lower rooftop a moment before he leapt with effortless ease, landing silently. He hadn't yet started his approach full force, instead he kept pace enough to watch, to see who was about in the dark night the whole time thinking *what the fuck*. He should have noticed him sooner. The way he walked with his head tilted down showing no interest in his surroundings, yet somehow still knowing everything that was going on around him.

But no, instead the light scent of lavender wafted up to his senses paralyzing him in a single moment, distracting him. Garrick couldn't resist looking for the owner of the tantalizing scent that had drawn him over the edge. Over the edge was exactly it too. He had almost fallen from the rooftop searching for her and almost missed the asshole he was chasing down now.

"Bloody hell," Garrick murmured from the shadows, recognizing the bloke who stalked the young blonde woman down a back alley. She hadn't notice her stalker yet, her pace was steady. Her skirt swayed with each strong stride, her heels clicking on the pavement as if nothing could touch her. Garrick knew her type a little to well. The way she carried herself, strong, overly sure of herself and doomed to all ends. Easy prey for sure. If she were willing then Garrick would concede and return to the pub but if this blonde wasn't willing the fun would begin. A moment passed and she clutched her large purple bag closer to her. Holding it tight as her pace sped up, almost matching her now speeding pulse. She must have realized she was no longer alone.

Her fear sifted in the light breeze tearing through Garrick's senses forcing his pupils to blacken. His sight shifted, his vision darkened as he fought against every instinct to attack and sate his own need. Garrick swallowed down the urge that rose beneath his chest. The urge of the monster he had become, unwillingly. The urge that wanted to show his dominance over the other male and take the fear filled prey for his own. As difficult as it was one thing often won; self-control. Something that took him decades to master yet remained flawed.

Garrick watched while fighting down the need to intervene and take her for himself. The stalker walked along the shadows of the alley quickly approaching his prey. Before the women could scream she was thrown up against the wall, pinned. Her arms fell slack; her purple handbag fell to the ground as her stalker pressed against her. His head tilted down as his fangs punctured her neck.

Garrick's nostrils flared, taking in the sweet scent of blood. With one quick, silent move, Garrick found himself standing, unnoticed, behind the stalker as the woman's heartbeat slowed. Garrick struggled, his body demanded he feed. He took a silent step back. How long had it been since he indulged in fresh blood. Tapped blood straight from the soft curve of a woman's neck.

"You've been a bad boy Patrick." Garrick whispered, taking a step forward.

The stalker spun around and found himself staring into black orbs of death. Patrick's eyes blazed, brow creased, unshed tears glistening from within. He searched the alley for a way to escape. His voice shaky Patrick asked, "Not doing nothing' you haven't done before Garrick. Did you want a taste?" Patrick tilted his head towards the blonde women who now laid slumped on the ground in offering.

Garrick glanced down at the dying women. Temptation burned his throat as he watched blood flow from her neck staining her blonde hair. He pushed back the roar building inside him and looked straight into the eyes of the man he once knew. *What happened to him?* "That may be, but you have indulged too many times old Chap. And stupid enough to be in my pub while you're hunting. Not good for business ye know."

"Yeah. Well. I was on my way through." Nervousness drifted from each word Patrick said. "In fact I was leaving tomorrow. I mean….umm…tonight. Yes…I was planning on going tonight to meet up with Octavia." Running his hand down his face he continued, "You'll never see me again Garrick. Promise."

Ahh, so that's what happened. Octavia. With one last look at the dying woman, Garrick ran his hand through his hair and said, "You be right about that mate." Before realizing it, with a movement as natural as breathing, Garrick's arm lashed out right below Patrick's rib cage. Patrick's eyes widened as the blade slid into his skin and pushed up into his heart.

ABOUT THE AUTHOR

 Baine Kelly was born and raised in the Chicagoland area but currently resides on the east coast with her husband, teenage son and assorted four legged babies. Her greatest enjoyments in life are family, reading, writing, training her dogs and camping in the mountains.

Baine has always been drawn to the myths of the supernatural, vampires, werewolves and all creatures of the night. She is working on a series called "The Sable World" that brings fantasy to life. Baine hopes you will follow her through the daring journey of her "Sable World" and enjoy the ride.

Baine would like to encourage each of you to reach for your dreams because you only live once and can accomplish anything you set your mind to. So Baine says, "Go for it!"

Baine knows your time is valuable to you, so she appreciates you taking a moment to check out her site. She loves to hear from readers. Your encouragement is what keeps her creativity flowing, bringing forth more stories for your enjoyment. Please take a minute and send her a message, she is looking forward to hearing from you.

To learn more about Baine Kelly, Check out her web site – http://www.bainekelly.com or follow her on Facebook and twitter (@bainekelly).

Made in the USA
Charleston, SC
21 November 2014

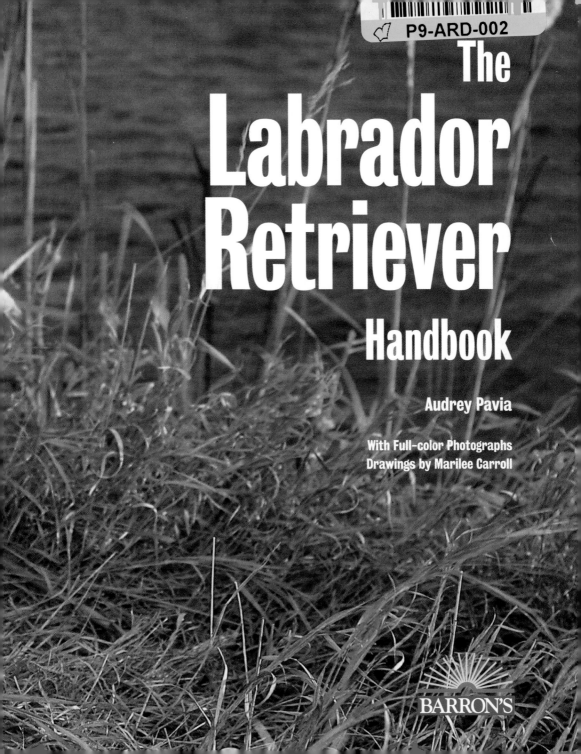

The
Labrador
Retriever
Handbook

Audrey Pavia

With Full-color Photographs
Drawings by Marilee Carroll

BARRON'S

Acknowledgements

The author would like to thank Bob O'Sullivan; Grace Freedson; Christopher Wincek and the Labrador Retriever Club, Inc; Liz Palika; Randy Mastronicola; Betsy Sikora Siino; and Ruth, Baxter, and Hanna Strother.

All inquiries should be addressed to:
Barron's Educational Series, Inc.
250 Wireless Boulevard
Hauppauge, New York 11788
http://www.barronseduc.com

International Book Standard No. 0-7641-1530-8

Library of Congress Catalog Card No: 00-031186

Library of Congress Cataloging-in-Publication Data

Pavia, Audrey.
     The labrador retriever handbook / Audrey Pavia.
    p. cm.
    ISBN 0-7641-1530-8
    1. Labrador retriever. I. Title.

SF429.L3 P38 2000
636.752'7—dc21   00-031186

Printed in Hong Kong

9 8 7 6 5 4 3 2

About the Author

Audrey Pavia is an award-winning freelance writer specializing in animal subjects. She has authored 11 books, including Barron's *Careers With Dogs*. In her 16-year publishing career, she has written hundreds of magazine articles for *Dog Fancy*, *Popular Dogs*, *Dogs USA*, *Puppies USA*, *The Puppy Guide* and a number of other animal publications. Former senior editor of the *American Kennel Club Gazette* and former managing editor of *Dog Fancy*, Audrey holds a bachelor's degree in journalism and is a member of the Dog Writers Association of America.

A Word About Pronouns

Many Lab lovers (including this one), feel that the neuter pronoun "it" is not appropriate when applied to our four-legged friends. However, for purely editorial purposes, to avoid the clumsiness of "he or she" throughout the book, we have decided to use a gender-neutral "it" when speaking in general terms. This should not in any way be interpreted to diminish the importance of Labradors, and for that matter, all pets, in our lives.

Photo Credits

Norvia Behling: p. vi, viii, 5, 11, 12, 17, 19, 27, 31, 32, 35, 39, 41, 48, 53, 56, 63, 66, 72, 75, 77, 83, 84, 90, 94, 96, 100, 107, 108, 111, 113, 116, 118, 120, 121, 122, 123, 127, 130, 155, 157, 158, 159, 160, 161, 162, 163, 164; Kent and Donna Dannen: 9, 15, 23, 44, 50, 59, 70, 79, 98, 102, 136, 139, 143, 146, 149, 153; Tara Darling: 67, 114, 131, 134, 141, 151.

Cover Credits

Front Cover: Norvia Behling and Kent and Donna Dannen; Back Cover: Norvia Behling; Inside Front and Back Covers: Kent and Donna Dannen

Contents

Preface

In my years as an editor, writer and dog lover, I have never seen a breed of dog more deserving of its popularity than the Labrador Retriever. Friendly, gentle and fun-loving, the Lab comes as close to being the perfect dog as any canine possibly can.

I've known many Labs throughout the years, and each one has been a very special dog in its own right as well a great ambassador for its breed. Take Lydia, for example, a young black female who belongs to some friends of mine in Austin, Texas. Lydia is the ultimate family dog. She is best buddy to the family's 10-year-old daughter and babysitter to their 2-year-old son. Gentle and quiet with both children, it's hard to believe she's the same dog when it's time for a raucous game of fetch with the kids' athletic father.

And then there's Hanna and Baxter, two black Labs who live with a couple I know. Hanna is a dignified old matron, enjoying her twilight years taking care of the couples' newborn infant. Baxter is young and full of energy, and also watchful of the new babe. He's so watchful, in fact, there's no need for baby monitors in this household. When the infant begins to cry, Baxter is at Mom's feet, pleading with her to tend to Baby's needs.

Of course Labs are more than just nursemaids to little children. They are rugged and athletic dogs who live to play, hike and swim. In fact, one chocolate Lab I knew named Cocoa drove her owner crazy whenever the two would go on a camping trip. Cocoa would find the closest body of water to camp and spend dawn till dusk demanding her master toss a stick into the water just so she could retrieve it, over and over again.

The Labrador Retriever is a very special breed, and is everything we love most about dogs all rolled into one superb package. If you are the kind of person who appreciates an active dog that's easy to train and loyal to a fault, this just may be the breed for you.

Audrey Pavia
Santa Ana, California

The Lab's kind temperament is the breed's most popular trait.

Chapter One
All About Labs

In their award-winning book *Labrador Tales: A Celebration of America's Favorite Dog,* authors John Arrington and Walt Zeintek beautifully describe the essence of the Labrador Retriever:

"Labs are Jeeps. And pickup trucks and sport utilities. Labs are never Lincoln Town Cars or Cadillac Eldorados. A Lab might be a Volvo Wagon, but never a Corvette. . .

"Labs are cabins in the woods, overlooking crystal blue lakes. Labs are cottages on the beach with waves crashing in the front yard. Labs are a walk through a state forest, public park or nature trail. Labs are seldom weekends in the city, five star hotels or casinos."

If you are reading this book, something inside you is drawn to the essence of the Labrador Retriever so accurately described by Arrington and Zeintek. Maybe you are captivated by the idea of adding one of these amazing dogs to your family. Or perhaps you already have a Lab in your life and are looking to soak up as much information as you can about the breed. Whatever the reason for your fascination, keep in mind that

the Labrador Retriever is no ordinary dog. Of course, if you live with one, you already know that.

If you selected this book because you are looking for a very special dog—a companion to you and a friend to your children—look no further than the Lab. This incredible breed, born of a working heritage, is the most popular dog breed in America. And it's no wonder. Labs personify what we love most about dogs: they are loyal and gentle, playful and hard working. When it comes to dog breeds, they are the cream of the crop.

A Brief History

The history of the Labrador Retriever starts around 15,000 years ago, when dogs first became domesticated. Anthropologists believe that wolves and humans came together over a common interest: food. The most likely scenario is that wolves began hanging around human camps in search of leftover scraps. Humans, intrigued by the boldness of this canine scavenger, began willingly offering food to wolves. In time, a relationship developed between the two very social species. One or two orphaned wolf pups were probably adopted by a group of humans, and it is thought that this closeness led to the pups becoming extraordinarily tame. Since these wolves grew up treating their human counterparts as members of the same family, the domesticated canine was born.

Throughout human history, dogs helped people survive in a harsh world. Providing more than just companionship, early domesticated dogs aided humans by herding and protecting livestock; hunting; and even serving as beasts of burden by hauling the belongings of their nomadic masters for thousands of miles.

From this place in time, we find the origins of the ancestors of today's Labrador Retriever. We don't know exactly how and when each stage happened, but at some point, the generic dog became the purebred Lab.

While we will never know exactly how it occurred, experts in canine history have proposed a number of theories. One notion is that it started in the late 1500s when European fishermen settled in what is now the Canadian island province of Newfoundland. It is believed the fishermen brought the ancestors of the Labrador Retriever along with them. The dogs were good hunters brought along to help capture game. They were also small enough to fit in the fishermens' dories, and they must

have been good swimmers to survive the watery working environment surrounding Newfoundland.

Another theory is that the Labrador Retriever descended from the dogs of Basque shepherds who immigrated to Canada from Portugal. This theory makes sheep-herding dogs the ancestors of today's Lab.

Whatever the early origins of the Labrador Retriever, experts agree that the breed's official beginnings hail from the 1830s when the 2nd Earl of Malmesbury began importing dogs from Newfoundland to England. The Earl recognized the Canadian dogs' considerable stamina, skill in the water and devout loyalty as traits that would be valuable to the landed gentry, those who treasured hunting as their favorite sport. According to the story, the Earl first saw the breed in a harbor in Dorset, England, and became intrigued as he watched them playing in the ocean and retrieving the fish tossed away by fishermen. The Earl started importing the breed from Canada, and he and others who brought the dogs to England bred them both to each other and to other types of hunting dogs.

The Earl of Malmesbury is also credited with naming the Labrador Retriever breed. Before the Earl dubbed them Labs, they were called a number of names, including St. John's Newfoundland, Lesser Newfoundland and St. John's dog. The word *labrador* means *worker* in both Spanish and Portuguese, and so Labrador Retriever seemed an appropriate name for this hard-working dog.

It wasn't until 1903 that the Kennel Club, England's premiere purebred dog registry, officially recognized the Labrador Retriever as a breed in the U.K. A few years later, American sports enthusiasts began importing British-bred Labrador Retrievers into the United States. The Countess Lorna Howe and the Honorable Franklin B. Lord are credited with introducing the Lab in the United States, having brought the breed to America to work as a retriever. Before long, the breed's popularity as a hunting dog soared. In 1917, the American Kennel Club (AKC) officially recognized the Labrador Retriever breed and began accepting Lab registrations.

In 1931, the Labrador Retriever Club, Inc. was formed to promote and preserve the Labrador Retriever in America. One of the club's primary goals was to organize field trials where Labs would be judged on their ability to retrieve waterfowl. The Labrador Retriever Club was recognized by the American Kennel Club as the parent club for the Labrador Retriever, and it still holds that position today. The club is responsible for maintaining the AKC Labrador Retriever standard which serves as a blueprint for the breed.

Today, the Labrador Retriever is the most popular dog breed in America, a claim it has held since 1991. Still used as a hunting dog by sportsmen, the breed is also cherished for its

For many dog lovers, the Labrador Retriever is the ultimate canine companion.

companionship. Over the years, America discovered one simple fact about the Labrador Retriever: this dog makes a wonderful pet.

Lab Truths
• Newfoundland, not Labrador, was the original home of the Labrador Retriever.
• Unlike in the U.S., Labs in England must earn a working certificate before they can become conformation champions.
• Most guide dogs and search-and-rescue dogs are Labrador Retrievers.

Who Is The Lab?

Probably the single most incredible thing about Labrador Retrievers is their ability to be so many different dogs all rolled into one. The Labrador Retriever is a working dog, bred to aid humans in retrieving game in the field. Labs can hunt alongside their masters for hours on end, day after day, using their keen senses and significant strength to get the job done. This same dog is also one of most dedicated companions in the canine world, a gentle dog who is trustworthy around children and intensely devoted to its master. Labs can be trained to aid the handicapped and taught to find disaster victims in a pile of rubble. Labs can seek out drugs stashed in suitcases and find bombs hidden in buildings. They can hike for hours, camp in rugged terrain and veg out on the couch, all in the same weekend. In essence, the Labrador Retriever is the consummate dog.

Lab Disposition

Ask Labrador Retriever owners what they love most about their dogs, and most of them will say "that Lab personality." The Lab's temperament is easily the breed's most popular trait, and it's not hard to see why. Labrador Retrievers are easy to train, love to have fun, and adore their humans above all else.

It's no accident that virtually all Labs manage to be born with these amazing personality traits. For decades, aficionados of the Labrador Retriever have bred dogs for these exact characteristics. In fact, the breed's standard—the blueprint breeders use when trying to create the ideal Lab—calls for a nature that is kindly, outgoing and eager to please. Any temperament other than this is considered a severe fault among responsible Labrador Retriever breeders, and Labs with such faults

are eliminated from breeding programs.

Consequently, Labs are known for their wonderful personalities and rightly so. Few dogs are as happy and human-loving as the Labrador Retriever.

Of course, no breed of dog is right for every person. If you prefer to spend your weekends watching TV instead of hiking, camping or playing a game of catch at the local park, then you probably won't be happy with a Labrador Retriever. Labs are vital, active dogs with boundless energy and a temperament that screams out, "Exercise me!" If you prefer a dog who will lay curled up at your feet most of the time and be content to just snooze the day away, a Labrador Retriever will drive you absolutely crazy. Instead of an active dog like the Lab, you'd be better off with a more mellow breed. You'll find plenty of other books on *those* kinds of dogs at your local book store.

The Lab Look

Aside from personality, there are other characteristics that set the Labrador Retriever apart from other dogs. These are physical characteristics that make the Lab *look* like a Lab.

For starters, the Labrador Retriever is a medium-sized dog. He's larger than a Dachshund yet smaller than a Saint Bernard. Most fully-grown male Labs weigh between 65–80 pounds. Female Labs come in at 55–70 pounds. The males stand around $22^1/_2$ to $24^1/_2$ inches at the top of the shoulder,

Labrador Retrievers are fun-loving dogs who require plenty of exercise.

with females a bit shorter at approximately 21¹/₂–23¹/₂ inches.

The shape of the Labrador Retriever's body is also distinctive and helps set him apart from other medium-sized dogs. Labs are strongly built, somewhat stout and athletic. Their body type is conducive to a dog bred to work in the field all day retrieving game.

The head of the Labrador Retriever is also an important factor in what makes a dog a Lab. The Lab's head is wide, with a slightly pronounced brow. The dog's lips fall in a curve toward the throat, and the muzzle is short and on the wider side. The ears hang close to the head and are set low on the skull. The eyes—one of the Lab's most cherished traits—are kind, friendly, alert and intelligent.

To the casual observer, the Labrador Retriever has a somewhat ordinary looking coat. It's not thick

and plush like the Siberian Husky's, nor is it long and flowing like the Afghan's. But although the Lab's coat may seem like typical short dog hair, it's actually an amazing cloak developed over hundreds of years to help the Lab do his job on land and in the water.

If you look closely and study a Lab's coat, you'll see that it's straight and dense, with a soft, weather-resistant undercoat that protects the dog's skin from water, cold weather and the kind of brush and bramble found in the field.

The color of the Lab's coat is also of great interest to those who love the breed. Labs come in three different colorations: black, yellow and chocolate. The black is just that: a jet black color that gleams in the bright sunshine. Yellow Labs range from an orange-red to light cream, with many having darker shading on their ears, back and underparts. As for chocolate, it can vary in shade from light to dark brown, and is the least common of the three Lab colors.

Of course, the Labrador Retriever is more than just how he looks when he's standing still. Any dog bred to work must be able to move well, too. When a Labrador Retriever starts moving, his stride is free and effortless. Labs that are well bred move straight forward when they trot; they never pace or weave.

Lab Personality
• Great with children
• Easy to train
• Good watchdog
• High energy level
• Happy and friendly

The Breed Standard

In February 1994, the Labrador Retriever Club drafted a revised breed standard for the Labrador Retriever. The American Kennel Club approved that standard, and the document went into effect the following month. Dog show judges use this standard to evaluate Labs presented to them in the show ring, and breeders use it to determine which dogs they will mate to help further the breed. Theoretically, the standard represents the ideal Labrador Retriever—a dog that doesn't exist in real life, but one that breeders strive to create.

The following is the current breed standard for the Labrador Retriever.

General Appearance

The Labrador Retriever is a strongly built, medium-sized, short-coupled, dog possessing a sound, athletic, well-balanced conformation that enables it to function as a retrieving gun dog; the substance and soundness to hunt waterfowl or upland game for long hours under difficult conditions; the character and quality to win in the show ring; and the temperament to be a family companion. Physical features and mental characteristics should denote a dog bred to perform as an efficient Retriever of game with a stable temperament suitable for a variety of pursuits beyond the hunting environment.

The most distinguishing characteristics of the Labrador Retriever are its short, dense, weather resistant coat; an "otter" tail; a clean-cut head with broad back skull and moderate stop; powerful jaws; and its "kind," friendly eyes, expressing character, intelligence and good temperament.

Above all, a Labrador Retriever must be well balanced, enabling it to move in the show ring or work in the field with little or no effort. The typical Labrador possesses style and quality without over refinement, and substance without lumber or cloddiness. The Labrador is bred primarily as a working gun dog; structure and soundness are of great importance.

Size, Proportion and Substance

Size—The height at the withers for a dog is $22\frac{1}{2}$ to $24\frac{1}{2}$ inches; for a bitch is $21\frac{1}{2}$ to $23\frac{1}{2}$ inches. Any

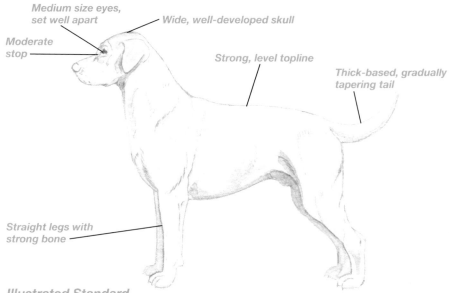

Medium size eyes, set well apart

Wide, well-developed skull

Moderate stop

Strong, level topline

Thick-based, gradually tapering tail

Straight legs with strong bone

Illustrated Standard

Color: Black, chocolate, yellow (varying shades)
DQ: Deviation from the height prescribed in the Standard; thoroughly pink nose or one lacking in any pigment; eye rims without pigment; Docking or otherwise altering the length or natural carriage of the tail; any other color or a combination of colors other than black, yellow or chocolate

variance greater than $1/2$ inch above or below these heights is a disqualification. Approximate weight of dogs and bitches in working condition: dogs 65 to 80 pounds; bitches 55 to 70 pounds.

The minimum height ranges set forth in the paragraph above shall not apply to dogs or bitches under twelve months of age.

Proportion—Short-coupled; length from the point of the shoulder to the point of the rump is equal to or slightly longer than the distance from the withers to the ground. Distance from the elbow to the ground should be equal to one half of the height at the withers. The brisket should extend to the elbows, but not perceptibly deeper. The body must be of sufficient length to permit a straight, free and efficient stride; but the dog should never appear low and long or tall and leggy in outline.

Substance—Substance and bone proportionate to the overall dog. Light, "weedy" individuals are definitely incorrect; equally objectionable are cloddy lumbering specimens. Labrador Retrievers shall be shown in working condition well-muscled and without excess fat.

Head

Skull—The skull should be wide; well developed but without exaggeration. The skull and foreface should be on parallel planes and of approximately equal length. There should be a moderate stop—the brow slightly pronounced so that the skull is not absolutely in a straight line with the nose. The brow ridges aid in defining the stop. The head should be clean-cut and free from fleshy cheeks; the bony structure of the skull chiseled beneath the eye with no prominence in the cheek. The skull may show some median line; the occipital bone is not conspicuous in mature dogs. Lips should not be squared off or pendulous, but fall away in a curve toward the throat. A wedge-shape head, or a head long and narrow in muzzle and back skull is incorrect as are massive, cheeky heads. The jaws are powerful and free from snippiness—the muzzle neither long and narrow nor short and stubby. **Nose**—The nose should be wide and the nostrils well-developed. The nose should be black on black or yellow dogs, and brown on chocolates. Nose color fading to a lighter shade is not a fault. A thoroughly pink nose or one lacking in any pigment is a disqualification. **Teeth**—The teeth should be strong and regular with a scissors bite; the lower teeth just behind, but touching the inner side of the upper incisors. A level bite is acceptable, but not desirable. Undershot, overshot, or misaligned teeth are serious faults. Full dentition is preferred. Missing molars or premolars are serious faults. **Ears**—The ears should hang moderately close to the head, set rather far back, and somewhat low on the skull; slightly above eye level. Ears should not be large and heavy, but in proportion with the skull and reach to the inside of the eye when pulled forward. **Eyes**—Kind, friendly eyes imparting good temperament, intelligence and alertness are a hallmark of the breed. They should be of medium size, set well apart, and neither protruding nor deep set. Eye color should be brown in black and yellow Labradors, and brown or hazel in chocolates. Black, or yellow eyes give a harsh expression and are undesirable. Small eyes, set close together or round prominent eyes are not typical of the breed. Eye rims are black in black and yellow Labradors; and brown in chocolates. Eye rims without pigmentation is a disqualification.

Neck, Topline and Body

Neck—The neck should be of proper length to allow the dog to retrieve game easily. It should be muscular and free from throatiness. The neck should rise strongly from the shoulders with a moderate arch. A short, thick neck or a "ewe" neck is incorrect. **Topline**—The back is strong and the topline is level from the withers to the croup when standing or moving. However, the loin should show evidence of flexibility for athletic endeavor. **Body**—The Labrador should be short-coupled, with good spring of ribs tapering to a moderately wide chest. The Labrador should not be narrow chested; giving the appearance of hollowness between the front legs, nor should it have a wide spreading, bulldog-like front. Correct chest conformation will result in tapering between the front legs that allows unrestricted forelimb movement. Chest breadth that is either too wide or too narrow for efficient movement and stamina is incorrect. Slab-sided individuals are not typical of the breed; equally objectionable are rotund or barrel chested specimens. The underline is almost straight, with little or no tuck-up in mature animals. Loins should be short, wide and strong; extending to well developed, powerful hindquarters. When viewed from the side, the Labrador Retriever shows a well-developed, but not exaggerated forechest. **Tail**—The tail is a distinguishing feature of the breed. It should be very thick at the base, gradually tapering toward the tip, of medium length, and extending no longer than to the hock. The tail should be free from feathering and clothed thickly all around with the Labrador's short, dense coat, thus having that peculiar rounded appearance that has been described as the "otter" tail. The tail should follow the topline in repose or when in motion. It may be carried gaily, but should not curl over the back. Extremely short tails or long thin tails are serious faults. The tail completes the balance of the Labrador by giving it a flowing line from the top of the head to the tip of the tail. Docking or otherwise altering the length or natural carriage of the tail is a disqualification.

Forequarters

Forequarters should be muscular, well coordinated and balanced with the hindquarters. **Shoulders**—The shoulders are well laid-back, long and sloping, forming an angle with the upper arm of approximately 90 degrees that permits the dog to move his forelegs in an easy manner with strong forward reach. Ideally, the length of the shoulder blade should equal the length of the upper arm. Straight shoulder blades, short upper arms or heavily muscled or loaded shoulders, all restricting free movement, are incorrect. **Front Legs**—When viewed from the front, the legs should be straight with good strong bone. Too much bone is as undesirable as too little bone, and short legged, heavy boned individuals are not typical of the breed. Viewed from the side,

Labs come in three color varieties: black, yellow and chocolate. Different shades exist within the yellow coloration.

the elbows should be directly under the withers, and the front legs should be perpendicular to the ground and well under the body. The elbows should be close to the ribs without looseness. Tied-in elbows or being "out at the elbows" interfere with free movement and are serious faults. Pasterns should be strong and short and should slope slightly from the perpendicular line of the leg. Feet are strong and compact, with well-arched toes and well-developed pads. Dew claws may be removed. Splayed feet, hare feet, knuckling over, or feet turning in or out are serious faults.

Hindquarters

The Labrador's hindquarters are broad, muscular and well-developed from the hip to the hock with well-turned stifles and strong short hocks. Viewed from the rear, the hind legs are straight and parallel. Viewed from the side, the angulation of the rear legs is in balance with the front. The hind legs are strongly boned, muscled with moderate angulation at the stifle, and powerful, clearly defined thighs. The stifle is strong and there is no slippage of the patellae while in motion or when standing. The hock joints are strong, well let down and do not slip or hyper-extend while in motion or when standing. Angulation of both stifle and hock joint is such as to achieve the optimal balance of drive and traction. When standing the rear toes are only slightly behind the point of the rump. Over angulation produces a sloping topline not typical of the breed. Feet are strong and compact, with well-arched toes and well-developed pads. Cow-hocks, spread hocks, sickle hocks and over-angulation are serious structural defects and are to be faulted.

Coat

The coat is a distinctive feature of the Labrador Retriever. It should be short, straight and very dense, giving a fairly hard feeling to the hand. The Labrador should have a soft, weather-resistant undercoat that provides protection from water, cold and all types of ground cover. A slight wave down the back is permissible. Woolly coats, soft silky coats, and sparse slick coats are not typical of the breed, and should be severely penalized.

Color

The Labrador Retriever coat colors are black, yellow and chocolate. Any other color or a combination of colors is a disqualification. A small white spot on the chest is permissible, but not desirable. White hairs from aging or scarring are not to be misinterpreted as brindling. *Black*—Blacks are all black. A black with brindle markings or a black with tan markings is a disqualification. *Yellow*—Yellows may range in color from fox-red to light cream, with variations in shading on the ears, back, and underparts of the dog. *Chocolate*—Chocolates can vary in shade from light to dark chocolate. Chocolate with brindle or tan markings is a disqualification.

Movement

Movement of the Labrador Retriever should be free and effortless. When watching a dog move

The Labrador Retriever breed standard calls for a dog with a kind, outgoing and tractable nature.

toward oneself, there should be no sign of elbows out. Rather, the elbows should be held neatly to the body with the legs not too close together. Moving straight forward without pacing or weaving, the legs should form straight lines, with all parts moving in the same plane. Upon viewing the dog from the rear, one should have the impression that the hind legs move as nearly as possible in a parallel line with the front legs. The hocks should do their full share of the work, flexing well, giving the appearance of power and strength. When viewed from the side, the shoulders should move freely and effortlessly, and the foreleg should reach forward close to the ground with extension. A short, choppy movement or high knee action indicates a straight shoulder; paddling indicates long, weak pasterns; and a short, stilted rear gait indicates a straight rear assembly; all are serious faults. Movement faults interfering with performance including weaving; side-winding; crossing over; high knee action; paddling; and short, choppy movement, should be severely penalized.

Temperament

True Labrador Retriever temperament is as much a hallmark of the breed as the "otter" tail. The ideal disposition is one of a kindly, outgoing, tractable nature; eager to please and non-aggressive towards man or animal. The Labrador has much that appeals to people; his gentle ways, intelligence and adaptability make him an ideal dog. Aggressiveness towards humans or other animals, or any evidence of shyness in an adult should be severely penalized.

Disqualifications

1. Any deviation from the height prescribed in the Standard.

2. A thoroughly pink nose or one lacking in any pigment.

3. Eye rims without pigment.

4. Docking or otherwise altering the length or natural carriage of the tail.

5. Any other color or a combination of colors other than black, yellow or chocolate as described in the Standard.

Approved February 12, 1994
Effective March 31, 1994

There are a number of things to consider when deciding to bring a Lab into your home.

Chapter Two
Before Buying

Few things are as exciting as adding a new dog to your life. When you bring a puppy into your home, you are beginning a very special relationship that will last you more than a decade. When you adopt an older Lab, you give a new lease on life to a dog in desperate need of your special love and care.

As joyful as new dog ownership is, you need to do your homework. Just as you would buy a house or a car by first giving careful thought to what you want and need, you should make an educated and informed decision when it comes to acquiring a dog also.

Is a Lab Right for You?

Labrador Retrievers are wonderful dogs. They have terrific personalities that are synonymous with the word *fun*. However, as great as Labs are, not everyone is suited to living with one.

Activity Level

Consider this: for hundreds of years, Labrador Retrievers were bred for one purpose—to retrieve game in the field. In olden days, hunters of upland game spent nearly all their daylight hours outside looking for birds. When they found their prey, they would bring the birds down with a gun blast and send their dogs—in this case, Labrador Retrievers—after the fallen fowl. The dogs who accompanied these hunters spent hour after hour, often day after day, traveling over large areas of land, searching for and retrieving shot birds. This work required a lot of running, swimming and jumping. It called for an incredible amount of athleticism, energy and stamina on the part of the dog.

Fast forward to today's modern world where the primary job of most Labrador Retrievers is household pet. While a number of people still use their Labrador Retrievers for hunting, the majority of Lab owners simply keep Labs for companionship. Yet, even though the Lab's job changed, his energy level hasn't. He remains the kind of dog who can run, swim and jump for hours a day.

If you are a parent, you know firsthand that a living creature with boundless energy must have an outlet. In the case of small children, scream- ing, running and playing seems to do the trick. In the case of high-energy dogs, work and plenty of exercise keeps them from almost literally exploding with vigor.

If you take those energetic kids and turn them loose on a playground, you will have found a safe and healthy way for them to expend their energy. Likewise with a high-energy dog: if you run with him, play with him and provide him with lots of exercise, you have found a good way to dissipate all that pent-up energy.

But—and this is a big *but*—if you take those same energetic kids and lock them in an apartment all day with no outlet for their urges to play, chances are they will destroy the place. And the same holds true for high-energy dogs. When Labs find themselves with boundless, unspent energy and no proper outlet for it, they often do things like eat the sofa, tear up the rug, and bark until the cows come home.

So, if you don't plan to do lots of outdoor stuff like hike, run, swim, and play with your dog, then you should not get an active dog like the Labrador Retriever. People with sedentary lifestyles drive Labs crazy— and vice versa. And don't think you can train your Lab into being a couch potato. The high-energy level of the Labrador Retriever was bred into him over many generations. You aren't going to get rid of it simply by telling your dog that he has to do what you want him to do. If you think he is

going to lay on the rug with you and do nothing but gaze at the football game every Sunday when the sun is shining outside and crisp autumn air is wafting through the window, you've got another thing coming.

On the other hand, if you are the kind of person who enjoys a lot of out- door activities that can easily include a dog, then a Labrador Retriever will fit nicely into your lifestyle. Just be honest about what it is you really do with your spare time. If you *want* to start running, hiking and swimming, and hope that a dog will motivate you to do that, it would be unwise to get a Lab for this reason. If it turns out you aren't going to do all that stuff after all, you will have already added a dog to your life who *must* do those things, or else!

Is the Lab a Good Match?
• Do you enjoy activity and the outdoors?
• Do you have time to provide plenty of exercise?
• Are you or someone in your family home often?
• Do you like a dog who follows you around?
• Do you have the space for a medium-sized dog?

Space Considerations
Because Labrador Retrievers are not overly large dogs, you may wonder if you need a big backyard in order to keep a Lab happy and well exercised. Actually, it's not so much the size of your yard—or whether you have one at all—that determines

Because Labs are such energetic dogs, they do best with owners who enjoy outdoor activities.

whether or not you should have a Lab. The important thing is whether you have time to give a Lab the amount of exercise it needs.

For example, there are more than a few Labrador Retriever owners who live in apartments in New York City. They don't have anything that even resembles a backyard. In fact, the closest they get to having their own outdoor space is a fire escape. However, don't assume that the Labrador Retrievers who live with these owners feel claustrophobic. As long as the dogs' owners give them two or more hours of active time outdoors every day, these dogs do fine.

Of course, not too many people enjoy the kind of schedule where they can provide two or more hours of outdoor exercise to a Lab—especially in areas where the winters are cold and the sun sets early. If you live in an apartment and want to own a Labrador Retriever, you must make

considerable sacrifices in time and energy to keep your very active dog from feeling cooped up.

On the other hand, there are people with large backyards for their Labrador Retrievers, yet the dogs still don't get enough exercise. *How could that be?* you wonder. Well, most dogs won't exercise themselves when left alone in a backyard. They have a tendency to sit by the back door and gaze longingly inside, hoping for human companionship. Don't think that just because you have a big yard you won't have to spend as much time exercising your Lab. You'll need to take advantage of that big space by going outside and playing a game of fetch with your dog, or taking a dunk with him in your swimming pool. (By the way, you will need a *fenced* yard to keep your Labrador Retriever safe from traffic and other hazards.)

Since the amount of time you spend exercising your Lab is more important than how much outdoor space you have, you may still want to consider one more space-related concern: Labs are the kind of dogs that follow you around the house like your shadow. They will not lay in a corner all day watching you putter around the house. They want to be there with you, helping you do whatever it is you have to do.

If you live with a Lab in a very small apartment or condo, you might find yourself tripping over your dog on a constant basis. Labs have a substantial physical presence, and their propensity to always be under foot means you will constantly be stepping around—maybe even on—your dog. If your kitchen is so small that there won't be room for you and your dog at the same time, you might start feeling a little crazy.

Personality Match

While the Labrador Retriever is an intensely active dog with a big need for exercise, he's also a good breed for novice dog owners. Never had a dog before? Not good at giving orders? Prefer a canine companion who will listen—not challenge you—when you tell him to do something? If so, you will get along well with a Lab.

You may be thinking *Aren't all dogs like that?* The answer is unequivocally no. A number of dog breeds were created to work apart from their masters, which means they developed very independent natures. Siberian Huskies, for example, were bred to pull sleds over the frozen tundra. Their masters were in close proximity, but it was up to the dogs to make important decisions like which areas of ground were safe to cross. Today, Siberian Huskies still tend to think on their own. Try telling a Siberian Husky what to do, and you'll experience their famous independent nature.

Labrador Retrievers, on the other hand, were bred to work closely with their masters. Retrieving dogs obey constant orders—that's the only way they can possibly do their jobs. Consequently, retriever breeds like the Lab are genetically programmed to pay close attention to the wishes and commands of their human masters—a great trait in a companion dog!

Dog owners who are learning the ins and outs of training and handling a dog do well with Labs. Just by virtue of the dog being a people-loving Lab, the owner already has the dog's attention. This isn't true of many other more independent working breeds like those found in the terrier and hound families, for example, and in breeds like the Siberian Husky, Alaskan Malamute, Shiba Inu and other similar nordic breeds.

Because Labs are such tractable dogs, they are also great with kids. This is not to say that the other breeds mentioned here aren't necessarily good with children, but Labs are *exceptionally* good with youngsters because they are so easy going and willing to please. Labs intrinsically love kids, and they can easily learn how to behave properly around those noisey and diminutive humans.

Even if you owned dogs before and have no kids in your home, odds are you will still find the Lab's tractable personality a joy. While some people relish the challenge of a dog who isn't easily trained, just about everyone can appreciate a dog who does what he's told, when he's told, without question. And that, of course, is the Lab.

Of course, Labs aren't born knowing what to do to please us humans. They must be taught. Otherwise, you will end up with a 65-pound spoiled brat on your hands. If you have no interest in taking a dog to obedience classes, then a Lab is not a good breed for you. Labs need training—in fact, they crave it—and if you own one, you must provide these crucial "Lab lessons in life."

There's one more personality trait you need to possess to enjoy living with a Lab: a tolerance for dirt. If you can't bear the thought of loose dog hair, muddy paws or yucky dog slobber, then you may want to consider getting a stuffed toy Lab instead of a real one. Real Labs come with all those messy things and more.

Spending Time

Along with a Lab's boundless energy and willing nature is a tremendous need for family. Labrador Retrievers live to spend time with their beloved humans. They want to be with you always, in everything you do. Labs make really great shadows.

Labs are very sociable dogs who crave interaction with people.

Before you bring a Labrador Retriever into your life, make sure you have the time to spend with a dog. You can't expect a Lab to stay home alone all day while you work and all evening when you go out to dinner with your friends. You also can't leave a Lab alone in the house for the weekend while you stay in a five-star hotel somewhere, relaxing and enjoying the view. And you certainly can't expect to pile the whole family into the car for a day at the beach while you leave your Lab home to guard the place (a bad idea for another reason: people-loving Labs make lousy guard dogs).

If you subject your Lab to this kind of solitude, he will suffer terribly from loneliness, and will probably express his pain in a woefully destructive way.

Does that mean you need to spend every waking moment with your Labrador Retriever? Are you never to go out to dinner again, or get away for a vacation without the dog and the kids? No, not at all. But you do need to think of your dog first whenever you are making plans to be away from home.

For example, if you and your spouse work, and the kids are off at school all day—meaning your dog is home alone for a good eight hours at a clip—you need to make time to spend with your dog when you *are* available. It could work like this: once you get home from work, take your Lab out for a game of fetch, and then keep him with you for the rest of the evening. Let him follow you around the house, hang around you in the kitchen and sit near the family while you eat dinner. After dinner, as you help the kids with their homework, allow your Lab to loiter around the room and watch the proceedings. When you relax in front of the TV before bedtime, make sure your dog is in the middle of the room with your kids around him. Let him know he's most definitely an important part of the family.

Your together time with your Lab shouldn't end here, however. Don't toss him out in the backyard alone for the rest of the night. Have him sleep in your room with you, or in one of the kids' rooms, so he receives as much family time as possible.

On weekends, plan activities in which your Lab can participate. If you want to go out for a romantic dinner with your spouse on Saturday night and leave the kids at Grandma's for an overnighter, that's fine. Your Lab can handle it—provided you spent the day with him, either puttering around the house or playing out in the park.

People who work and live alone face the greatest challenge when it comes to spending time with a dog. Single people often like to visit with their friends and co-workers after a hard day's work, and partake in social activities on the weekend. People with this lifestyle can still own a dog—even a demanding one like a Lab—provided they do whatever they can to spend as much time as possible with their pet. This means cutting back on after-work socializing (or hiring a dogwalker to come and spend time with their dog on those days that don't end until 10 p.m.), finding social activities that include their dog, and making a general effort to spend every spare minute with their dog so he will have the benefit of human company.

Make Sure It's Right

Before you bring a dog into your life, you need to do some serious soul searching. Sit down and ask yourself the following questions:

• Are you willing to take responsibility for a dog and its needs for the next 10–15 years, regardless of what life brings you?

• Do you have the time, money and patience to take care of a dog?

• Can you give the dog enough attention and exercise?

• Can you live with shedding and drooling for the next 10–15 years?

• If you plan on getting a puppy, do you have the time and patience to deal with the trials and tribulations of puppyhood?

• Can you resist the urge to get a dog impulsively, and instead work to make a responsible decision?

Where to Get Your Lab

Labrador Retrievers are wonderful dogs at just about any stage of their life. Lab puppies are so cute, fuzzy and fun that it's almost unbelievable. Adult Labs are soulful, soothing and unwaveringly loyal.

You may have already decided that a puppy is what you are looking for,

Responsible breeders put a lot of time and effort into breeding healthy puppies, and so are the best source for a young Lab.

that dastardly chewing stage, and have mellowed with time.

Whether you decide to get a puppy or an adult dog, there is a right way to go about making your acquisition. Carefully choosing the source of your new Lab can mean the difference between a wonderful, happy relationship with your dog, and a heartbreaking disaster. Adding a dog to your family is a serious commitment, and the decision on where to get one is an important part of the process.

The Problem with Puppy Mills and Pet Shops

If you watch television news shows, you have by now heard of something called a *puppy mill*. Brought to the general public's attention in the early 1990s by the news media, puppy mills are facilities that breed dogs like livestock. These dog farms, as it were, are located primarily in the Midwest and are readily identified by their practice of keeping dogs in small cages with virtually no exercise, minimal shelter and very little human contact. Female dogs are bred repeatedly, and churn out litter after litter of puppies, which are then shipped all over the country to pet shops, where they are sold.

There are several problems with puppy mills. First, many consider them to be inhumane. The way the

since Lab puppies are so incredibly adorable and there are many good reasons to start with a pup. If you get your pup at 8 or 9 weeks of age (don't take one younger than this because pups under 8 weeks are too young to leave their mothers), you will be keeping company with the dog during its most impressionable stages. Whatever a dog learns in his youth will stay with him for the rest of his life. Many Lab owners like the idea of molding their dog from the very start, helping him become the kind of dog with whom they want to live.

On the other hand, there are plenty of benefits to starting out with a dog that is already fully grown. Most adult dogs are housetrained, so there's no need to worry about accidents on the carpet. Puppies can also be a handful, too. They have boundless energy and can get into all kinds of trouble with their sharp little teeth and propensity to chew. The majority of adult dogs have successfully outgrown dogs are kept, in close quarters with little opportunity to live a normal life with exercise and human companionship, is reprehensible. Second, dogs in puppy mills are indiscriminately bred to one another without any thought to genetic illness or incompatibility. Third, the young dogs that result from puppy mills are not properly socialized as they should be from birth, and can subsequently develop behavioral problems down the line.

You probably know someone who purchased a puppy from a pet shop at some point in his or her life. The dog most likely turned out fine, and went on to live a full life as a cherished pet. On the other hand, you may also know someone who bought a puppy from a pet store, but had to return or euthanize it, because it had a serious health problem. Purchasing a puppy from a pet store is fine if the shop is reputable. However, many puppies in pet shops come from commercial sources where profit is the priority and the puppies' health is lower on the list. Pet store puppies can also be exposed to some contagious diseases or be put under heavy stress in less reputable pet shops. Again, this most likely won't be a problem if you purchase a pet store puppy. Just make sure that you purchase from a reputable store. After all, do you want to take the chance that the adorable puppy you fell in love with has to be returned or euthanized? Anyone who's been through this situation can tell you how traumatic it is.

Another potential problem with pet store puppies is that they can be difficult to train if they've spent most of their lives inside cages. They learn to relieve themselves in close quarters, and so may have trouble learning when you ask them not to do so in the house.

Buying from a Breeder

The alternative to buying a puppy from a pet shop is securing one from a responsible breeder. Responsible breeders don't just breed dogs—they do it in a way that takes the breed's welfare in account, along with that of the individual dog.

Reasons to Buy from a Breeder
• Early socialization of puppies
• Health and temperament screening of parents
• Help choosing the right puppy
• Less costly than buying from pet shop
• Lifetime assistance with your dog

Take your time shopping for just the right puppy.

Responsible breeders are heavily involved with the breed they represent. The majority show their dogs and belong to a national breed club. They study the pedigrees of the dogs they breed together to make sure the resulting puppies will be as free of genetically-linked disease as possible and more closely resemble the breed standard than poorly-bred puppies.

Responsible breeders guarantee the health of their puppies, carefully socialize them before sending them to new homes, and help puppy buyers choose the one in the litter best suited to them. They also provide expert help to the new owners for the entire life of the dog. And, what's more, responsible breeders generally charge a lot less for their puppies than do pet shops. You can't beat that!

Hopefully, you are now convinced that buying from a responsible breeder is the best route to take when shopping for a Labrador Retriever puppy. But how do you find one of these breeders? Actually, it's pretty easy. The Labrador Retriever Club can provide you with a list of reputable breeders in your area. Simply call or write to them, or visit the club's web site, and you'll get all the help you need to find a breeder in your area (see Chapter 9 for contact information on the Labrador Retriever Club).

Resist the temptation to look in the classified section of your newspaper for a breeder. Most people who advertise pups for sale in classified ads are "backyard breeders"; average pet owners who simply put two dogs of the same breed together to create a litter of puppies to sell. The careful thought and planning that goes into responsible dog breeding is not part of the scenario.

Once you have the names of a few breeders near you, call them and inquire about their breeding operations. Here are the important questions you should ask and the types of answers you should receive:

• *What is your involvement with the Labrador Retriever breed?* The breeder should be involved with field, obedience or conformation. Involvement in these activities indicates the breeder is serious about the breed.

• *How many litters of Labrador Retrievers have you bred?* Responsible breeders usually do not breed more than one or two litters a year, but bred enough litters over time to have garnered significant experience in the breed.

• *Where do you raise your puppies?* The answer to this question should preferably be "in my home." Puppies raised indoors tend to be better socialized than those that grow up outside in a kennel.

• *Do you evaluate the temperament of the puppies in your litters?* This is important. A knowledgeable breeder will know the personalities of each puppy and help you choose the one best for your situation.

• *Will you take back the dog at any time in its life if I can't keep it for some reason?* All responsible breeders answer "yes" to this question.

• *Can I call you with any questions or problems I may have with the dog once I take him home?* The answer should unequivocally be "yes."

• *Do the parent dogs have hip clearances from the Orthopedic Foundation for Animals (OFA)?* The breeder should have certificates from OFA showing that both dogs are free from hip dysplasia, a genetically-linked disease common in Labs. (OFA gives five ratings: poor, fair, good, very good and excellent. The better the rating, the lower the risk of dysplasia in the offspring.)

• *Do the parent dogs have current eye clearances from Canine Eye Registi. Fudt. (CERF)?* Labs are prone to progressive retinal atrophy and retinal dysplasia, eye diseases thought to be genetically linked. Dogs used for breeding must receive certification every year by a veterinary ophthalmologist to show they are free from eye disease.

• *Are both parent dogs free of other diseases commonly seen in the Labrador Retriever?* A number of illnesses in purebred dogs are thought to be genetically linked. Making sure the parents of your puppy are free from illness helps ensure your chances of getting a healthy dog (see Chapter 6 for a listing of diseases most common in Labs).

• *Would it be possible to meet the mother and father of the dog I'm considering?* You can tell a lot about your dog's likely temperament by meeting the dog's parents. The female should be owned by the breeder and there-fore easy to see. The sire may be owned by a different breeder. Ask for that breeder's phone number, and call to see if you can meet the dog. If not, interview the breeder over the phone about the dog's health and personality.

• *Can you provide references and telephone numbers of other people who purchased puppies from you?* Call these references and find out if they were happy with the dog and services they received from the breeder.

What to Expect: When responsible breeders sell their puppies, they keep the dogs' best interests in mind. This means that responsible breeders *screen* potential puppy buyers to make sure they will provide a dog with a good home.

When you contact a breeder and say you are interested in a Labrador Retriever puppy, not only will you ask questions of the breeder, but the breeder will also quiz you. The breeder will want to better understand your lifestyle and prospects as a responsible dog owner.

Some of the questions the breeder will ask you may include:

• *Are you married or single? Do you have any kids? How old are they?*

• *Do you own or rent? Do you live in a house? Does it have a fenced yard?*

• *Have you ever had a dog before? If so, what happened to it?*

Don't take offense when a breeder asks you these questions. Such queries are designed to help the breeder understand if you can provide the right home for a Labrador Retriever puppy. Based on your answers, you may discover your situation best suited for a smaller, less active breed. Or, you may learn you are the perfect person to own a Lab. Either way, the screening process will prove educational for both you and the breeder.

Once you and the breeder mutually approve each other, the breeder will want to meet you and show you a litter of puppies—provided there is a litter. Responsible breeders often wait until they find sufficient homes for puppies before they actually breed their dogs. They may tell you that you'll need to wait a few months before the puppies are born, but may invite you over to meet some adult dogs that they have bred. Don't let that scare you. Buying a puppy should not be an impulse decision. If you want a puppy right away and absolutely can't wait, ask the breeder to recommend someone with a current litter available. If this is not possible, you will have to wait. In the end, you'll find your wait more than worthwhile. Don't give into the impulse to go to a pet shop or less reputable breeder just to get a dog *today*. You may regret the decision down the road.

Since all Lab puppies are equally cute, it's a good idea to ask the breeder for advice on which pup is best for you.

Picking Your Puppy

When you meet the litter of puppies for the first time, you will most likely be overwhelmed with emotion. Labrador Retriever puppies are cute—*very* cute. You will probably find yourself sitting on the breeder's floor with 10 or 12 adorable little fur balls crawling all over you. How can you possible decide which one to pick?

One of the reasons you went to a responsible breeder for your Labrador Retriever was so you could get help with this decision. Breeders know their puppies very well, and have temperament tested them to determine their personalities. The breeder will assess *your* personality and talk to you about the kind of dog you want. Based on what you say, the breeder will suggest the puppy most suited to you in the litter.

Before you arrive at the breeder's house, think about what you want to do with your Lab. Do you want him to go hunting with you? How about jogging? Do you want a dog with whom you can compete in the exciting sport of flyball? Or would you prefer a quiet Lab, one that will go on long walks with you at the beach, play with the kids in the backyard or just hang around and keep you company?

Sometimes, puppy buyers fall in love with the "wrong" puppy in a litter. They are taken with the feisty little male who knocks over his brothers and sisters, and demands all the attention for himself. Or, they prefer the shy little guy in the corner, the one who would rather sit quietly while the rest of the litter plays. However, what the inexperienced puppy buyer doesn't realize is that the cute little tough guy in the first scenario is going to be a handful when he grows up. He'll need a strong owner who can handle the challenges and difficulties of training a dominant dog. If you tend to be a pushover, a dog like this will be a real headache for you, especially when you try to train him. He also won't go for quiet walks on the beach, or calmly hanging around the house, but instead will be a good candidate for competitive sports. Conversely, if you are looking for a Lab to do flyball, agility or some other event, that quiet, shy little puppy most likely won't be up to the challenge.

While the breeder generally offers the last word on which puppy in the litter is best for you, there are a few things you can look out for yourself. Seek an inquisitive puppy that seems comfortable with its surroundings.

Ask the breeder for a toy, and toss it to see if the puppy will go after it and maybe even return it to you. Walk around and call the puppy to see if it will follow you. If it does, this is a tractable puppy who loves people and will probably make a great companion.

Whatever you do, don't get hung up on your puppy's gender. Both male and female Labs make wonderful pets if they are spayed or neutered—which your dog should be unless you intend to show your dog in conformation classes and become seriously involved with the breed. The only time you should concern yourself with gender is if you already have another dog at home. Dogs of opposite sexes (spayed and neutered) tend to get along better, especially if one of the dogs is of a dominant personality type.

Choosing an Older Dog

All puppies are adorable and a barrel of laughs. But with all the good stuff that puppies bring there comes some difficulties, too.

For example, puppies need housetraining. This means getting up in the middle of the night for a few weeks to take the little guy out for a potty break. What fun. It also means being on constant alert to make sure the little one doesn't piddle in the house.

Puppies are also notorious chewers. The teething stage puppies go through early in life can be disastrous to a household. If you've ever had a puppy, you know that shoes, kids' toys and even furniture are all fair game to the relentless jaws of a teething puppy.

Adult dogs, on the other hand, often come housetrained. They have outgrown the chewing stage in most cases, and are a lot less rambunctious than puppies. Also, adult dogs have generally grown into the kind of dogs they are going to be, both personality and health wise. There are few surprises when you get an adult dog. What you see is what you get.

These are all good reasons to acquire an adult dog instead of a puppy. But there is one more reason even more compelling than those mentioned above: most adult dogs needing homes are desperate for a family to take care of them. No longer cute little babies, these older dogs often face a difficult time finding homes simply because most people prefer puppies instead.

So, if you are considering adding a Labrador Retriever to your family, think seriously about rescuing an older dog.

Breed Rescue - How it Works

Okay, you are open to the idea of providing for an adult Lab in need of a home. But how do you go about finding one? And how do you know this will be a good dog that will get along with everyone in your family?

The best way to go about adopting an adult Labrador Retriever is to enlist the help of the Labrador Retriever Club. This AKC parent club for the Labrador Retriever maintains a national network of breed rescue

clubs. Located around the country, these breed rescue clubs are made up of individuals involved in the Labrador Retriever breed and in the rescue of Labs in need. Whenever a Labrador Retriever needs help, these rescue volunteers spring into action to assist the dog in whatever situation it's in. This could be an abusive or neglectful home, life on the streets or internment at the local pound. Once rescued, the dog is taken to a foster home and evaluated for health and temperament. Here it stays until a suitable permanent home is found.

Your first step then, in adopting an older Lab, is to contact the Labrador Retriever Club (listed in Chapter 9). The club will put you in touch with a rescue group in your area. You can contact the rescue

Purebred rescue groups are a good source for an older Lab that needs a home.

coordinator for your area club to begin the adoption process.

When adopting a dog through a breed rescue group, you can expect certain things to happen. First, the rescue coordinator will ask you a number of questions to determine if a Lab is the right dog for you. The coordinator will also try to determine the canine personality type best suited for your household and needs.

While each rescue group employs somewhat different procedures, the basic intent is to match you with the right dog. Good rescue groups provide plenty of help to new adult dog owners, and will give you lifetime assistance with your dog. They will also take the dog back without hesitation in the future if you are unable to keep it for any reason.

Rescuing a Labrador Retriever through a breed rescue group is relatively inexpensive. You will pay an adoption fee to help offset the cost of caring for the dog while it was in foster care. Since the dog you get will already be inoculated and spayed or neutered, the adoption fee is a small price to pay in return. Also, the money from adoption fees helps the group rescue more dogs.

The benefits gained by adopting a dog from a rescue group as opposed to a pound or animal shelter are that, in most cases, you will receive much more assistance from the rescue group in selecting the right dog and solving any problems that occur once you've taken the dog home. Most animal shelters—particularly those

run by a county or city—simply don't have to resources to provide that kind of aid to adopters.

Reasons to Adopt an Adult Lab
- You are saving a dog's life
- You will avoid the hassles of puppy-hood
- Less costly than buying a puppy
- Your dog will be forever grateful

Adopting From the Pound

The alternative to adopting a Labrador Retriever from a rescue group is to go to a private animal shelter or city- or county-run pound. There is a difference between these different types of facilities, and understanding them can help you make an educated choice.

Government Facilities: Chances are, the county, city or other municipality in which you live operates a government-funded animal shelter designed to provide temporary care for homeless pets. Most such facilities are low on money and staff. The dedicated people who work there are up to their elbows in abandoned dogs and cats, and have all they can do just to keep the place going.

Because there are so many more pets in this country than there are homes for them, government-run shelters are nearly always filled to the brim with animals. They can house only a specific number of animals at once, so the dogs and cats in these shelters have a limited amount of time during which they can be adopted. As little as five to seven days is

Providing a home for an older dog in need can be a very rewarding experience.

great certainty that you saved that animal's life.

Private Shelters: Over the past several decades, a number of private animal shelters were established throughout the country. Generally run by non-profit animal welfare organizations, these shelters operate mostly on private donations. Some of these facilities are considered "no-kill" shelters, meaning that the pets they take in are not euthanized unless they are gravely ill or suffering from a serious aggression problem. Adoptable pets are kept for an unlimited amount of time until they find suitable homes.

As you might imagine, no-kill shelters are very busy places. The homeless animal population in this country is staggering, and people are anxious to take unwanted pets to shelters where they won't by put down. It's often difficult to get one of these shelters to take in an animal you have found or are trying to place, simply because they have no room.

Other private shelters *do* euthanize pets that are adoptable in order to make room for the scores of waiting animals in need of a roof over their heads. These shelters typically keep the animals longer than a county- or city-run pound, giving the pets more time—and a greater opportunity to be adopted—before they are put to sleep.

Some private shelters are not much different from their government-run counterparts. They are low on resources and don't provide much

common in many urban areas. If an animal is not adopted during that time, it is usually euthanized.

Government-run shelters are usually strapped for money, rarely having the resources to provide pre-adoption counseling and after-adoption assistance. If you adopt a Lab from one of these shelters, don't expect much help with your decision and any problems that may arise once you bring your dog home. On the other hand, if you adopt a dog from a public shelter, you will know with in the way of adoption counseling and after-adoption help. Conversely, there are other private shelters with extensive programs in place to help adopters choose the right dog and help that dog settle into life with a permanent family.

If you choose to adopt a Lab through a private shelter, find out what kinds of assistance the shelter will give you with your decision. Do they have adoption counselors to help you choose the right dog? Does the shelter offer free or low-cost obedience classes for adopted dogs? Do they provide assistance with any behavioral problems that may arise later when the dog comes home to live with you?

If you want such assistance, ask a lot of questions before you arrange a visit to determine if it's the sort of shelter you are seeking. You can get a good sense over the phone as to the programs each shelter offers.

Finding a Shelter: If you want to adopt your dog from a public pound, all you need to do to find your local government shelter is to look up "animal control" in your telephone book. Your area's animal control agency will direct you to the nearest public shelter.

Finding a private shelter requires a little more leg work. One good way to locate a private shelter is to contact a local veterinarian. Most veterinarians know the private shelters in their area and can recommend one for you to try.

Be aware that whether you pursue a public or private shelter, you may not find a Labrador Retriever that needs adopting on the day you visit. Know, however, that sooner or later, a Lab will come in. Ask to have your name put on a waiting list for a Labrador Retriever so the shelter can contact you if one is surrendered or abandoned.

Picking That Older Dog

Hopefully, when you begin the process of adopting an older dog, you will be in a situation where a rescue group coordinator or an adoption counselor can help you pick the right dog for you. In these cases, the dog's temperament and health will have been evaluated before the dog was offered for adoption. You should ask certain questions about the dog before you make your decision.

These are the most important questions you should ask when considering an older dog:

• *What is the dog's history?* The purpose of this question is to find out why the dog ended up without a home. The reason will give you some insight into his background and what kinds of problems he may have.

• *Does the dog have any behavioral problems?* This question should help you get an idea of the dog's difficulties, if any. The dog's behavioral problems may be as mild as pulling on the leash or something as serious as showing aggression towards children. Use caution when adopting a dog with a serious behavior problem.

While adopting a dog from a shelter can be somewhat of a gamble, the rewards are often tremendous.

Most adult dogs in need of adoption could benefit from basic obedience training, but problems like aggression or destructiveness require the services of a professional trainer, and your time and money. In fact, most experts in canine behavior recommend not adopting a dog with *any* signs of aggressiveness, since this is a difficult—and dangerous—problem. Reputable shelters don't offer these kinds of dogs for adoption.

• *Is the dog housetrained?* Many of the adult dogs you'll find available for adoption came from home situations where they learned to go to the bathroom outdoors and not in the house. For this reason, the adult dog you are inquiring about may be housetrained already. However, do not assume that this is automatically true. Ask the shelter staff or rescue group if the dog is reliably housetrained. Be aware, too, that even if the dog was housetrained in its previous life, time spent in a kennel may have undone that housetraining. In this case—or in the case of a dog that was never housetrained—you will need to teach the dog from scratch, just as you would a young puppy. Dogs already taught but simply in need of a refresher course will pick up the training relatively fast.

• *What is the dog's medical history?* In situations where the dog was surrendered by its owners, you should find out if the dog experienced any health problems. Be cautious about adopting a dog with a chronic medical problem, like allergies or hip dysplasia. If you can pay for the veterinary care involved in treating a dog with these problems, then by all means, give a home to a dog that needs this help. But make sure you know what you are getting into before you agree to take the dog home.

• *Has the dog been spayed or neutered, and given its vaccinations?* A reputable shelter or rescue group will take care of these needs before putting a dog up for adoption. Be aware that if these procedures have not been performed, you will need to lay out the time and money to get them done yourself.

Making the Decision

Choosing an adult dog is a little different from choosing a puppy from a litter. Puppies grow up rather different from the alternately rambunctious and sleepy creatures we see when they are only 8 weeks of age. With adult dogs, though, what you see is what you get—for life.

When evaluating the personality of an adult dog you are considering for adoption, keep in mind what you would like to do with the dog once you bring him home. Are you looking for a companion for your children? Do you want a dog you can hunt with? Are you hoping for a dog that will accompany you on your jogs around the neighborhood? Or do you want a pet that can participate in agility, tracking or some other competitive event?

The job you lined up for your Labrador Retriever should be an important factor in picking your dog. Give the shelter staff or rescue group as much information as you can on what you want to do with your dog so they can help match you with just the right Lab.

As you look at a dog and consider it, remember to think about whether that dog seems right for your lifestyle. If you want a Labrador Retriever, you should have your heart set on a dog that will be an active canine companion. If you want a dog that does something specific—like hunting or competition—get help from the shelter staff or rescue group in determining if the dog you are considering has the aptitude for the job.

A Check by the Veterinarian: Whether you are bringing home a young puppy or an adult Labrador Retriever, one of the first things you should do once you take possession of your dog is bring it to the veterinarian for a check up.

The reasons behind this action are simple: you want your veterinarian to verify that the dog is indeed healthy, and you want to establish a relationship between your dog and your veterinarian.

When you take your dog for his first visit to the vet, bring the dog's health care records provided by the breeder, previous owner or rescue group. This will give the veterinarian a look into the dog's background. Also bring a stool sample that is not more than 12 hours old so the veterinarian can check to see if your dog is infected with worms.

Whether your Lab is a puppy or an adult, the veterinarian will examine him for infectious disease and congenital problems. The veterinarian will also weigh the dog, listen to his heart and lungs, feel his major organs through his skin, and check for fleas and ticks. A check of the dog's mouth and teeth, eyes and ears will also take place.

After examining your dog thoroughly, your veterinarian will discuss a preventative care program with you. This will include inoculations, heartworm medication and spaying or neutering.

If your new Lab is a puppy of around 8 or 9 weeks of age, you won't have to worry about your dog's initial shots—the dog's breeder will have inoculated the pup against distemper, parvovirus, parainfluenza and hepatitis (the health care records the breeder gave you will indicate this). Your veterinarian will then tell you when your puppy is due for the next series of shots.

If your Lab is an adult dog, your veterinarian will ask if you know the dog's vaccination record. If you don't, the veterinarian will probably start your new pet on a program right away. You will also want to take some time to discuss spaying or neutering

your Lab with your vet, assuming the dog hasn't already had this important surgery.

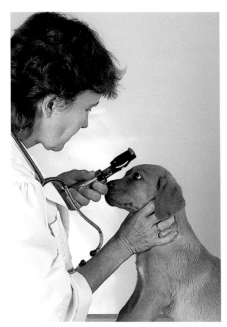

Whether your new Lab is a puppy or adult, have the dog examined by a veterinarian soon after you take him home.

Bringing your Lab home will be exciting for both of you, but make sure you're prepared for your new friend.

Chapter Three

In the Beginning

The day you bring your new Labrador Retriever home will be exciting for both you and your new dog. You can anticipate years of fun and companionship, and your dog can eagerly explore his new digs.

But before you allow your new dog to actually set his paws in your home, you need to do some preparation. Adding a dog to your life is a big commitment, and you'll want to make certain you are completely ready for that joyful day when it comes.

Dog-Proofing Your Property

An important step in preparing for your new Lab is the act of dog-proofing your house and yard. This is especially important if you are acquiring a puppy, since young dogs are more likely than older ones to get into trouble.

Before your Lab comes to live with you, inspect your entire house from a dog's point of view. Look around for theses following potential problems:

• *Things that break easily.* Labs are notorious for their wagging tails. Always happy and full of life, Labs love to swing their long tails at every opportunity. The only down side to this wonderful expression of joy is that those tails can damage glasses, vases, nicknacks and other breakables that are typically stored at tail-level. Consider rearranging the decorative items in your house so they are out of reach of your Lab's tail.

• *Stuff to chew on.* Dogs—especially puppies—have a tendency to chew and swallow the strangest objects, like socks, kid's toys, jewelry, books, and audio cassette tapes. And believe it or not, Labs have even been known to chew on and swallow rocks! If your new dog is so inclined, as many dogs are, he will make a beeline for these items. Be sure to pick up any stuff lying around before your Lab makes his grand entrance, and get into the habit of keeping these items in their rightful place once your dog comes to live with you.

• *Items that are off-limits.* Low kitchen cupboards and bathroom cabinets are favorite storage areas for household cleaners and other toxic substances. Make certain that your cupboards and cabinets close securely and can't open easily with a probing paw. Also, take care to keep caps and lids securely fastened on toxic items.

The days of tossing your kitchen trash into an open pail are over now that you are becoming a Lab owner. Get yourself a good, secure trash can with a lid, and try to keep it hidden away in a kitchen cabinet, if possible. Otherwise, your Lab will end up helping himself to your leftovers the moment you are out of sight.

The inside of your house isn't the only area that needs inspecting. Your outdoor areas must be inspected with a fine-toothed comb to make sure your Lab will be safe when he's out in the yard. Here's what you need to check for:

• *Garden plants.* A number of plants are poisonous to dogs if swallowed. Get a list of poisonous plants that grow in your area from your veterinarian, and get rid of any growing in your yard before your new dog comes to live with you.

While the majority of yard-proofing is for your dog's protection, you will also want to protect your garden from your dog. More than one Lab has been known to dig up a beautiful flower or vegetable garden on a whim. Protect the special areas of your yard with wire fencing that your dog can't penetrate.

• *Possible escape routes.* Labs are homebodies who prefer to stay in close proximity to their owners.

However, there are situations that can lure even the most home-loving Lab out into the big, bad world. A stray dog running down your street, a wild rabbit hopping around on your front lawn, a group of children playing on the sidewalk—these distractions can result in your Lab making a break for it so he can join in the fun. To make sure your Lab can't get out of your yard, walk around the perimeter of your property looking for gaps in the fencing, areas where your dog can climb up and over the fence, and spots where your dog can dig underneath the fencing. Rectify any situations you discover before you let your new Lab loose in the yard.

Canine Equipment

Once your home and yard have been dog-proofed, your family has discussed the doggy rules of the house, and you have familiarized yourself with how you will keep your dog comfortable on his first night in your home, it's time to go shopping. Your new Labrador Retriever will need all kinds of goodies to make him feel at home. You can purchase the bare minimum of supplies you'll need, or you can have a ball shopping for all the latest fun stuff on the market for dogs.

You have a number of choices for where to buy your dog's supplies. Pet stores and pet supply chains stock a large selection of dog products from which to choose. Mail

Shop for basic items before your dog's arrival so he'll have everything he needs once he comes home.

order catalogs can provide even more variety at discounted prices. And the Internet is becoming loaded with pet supply retailers that allow you to shop for dog products online.

The outlet you choose for your Lab's supplies is a matter of personal preference. Any one of the above-mentioned retailers can get you what you need.

The Basics

If you are on a tight budget and want to provide your dog with just the essentials, here is what you'll need to buy:

Leash and Collar: In order to keep your Lab secure and under control when you are out in public, you will need a collar and leash for your pet. If your new Lab is a young puppy, you'll need to purchase a collar small enough for his neck, and a leash light enough to accommodate his weight. As your pup grows, you will have to buy new collars and leashes in bigger sizes to fit him. If your new Lab is an adult, simply buy him a collar and leash suitable for his size and weight.

When you go shopping, you'll find plenty of collars and leashes available in a huge selection of colors, styles and materials. Rolled leather is always a good choice because it looks good and is less likely to damage the fur on your dog's neck. Rolled leather typically comes in buckle-collar designs, with a matching leash. Flat leather collars are also popular because they are durable and look good.

Another option for collars and leashes is nylon. Less expensive than leather, nylon collars and matching leashes come in a huge variety of colors and patterns. You'll see everything from solid neon colors to paisley designs. Many dog owners enjoy the range of options available in nylon collars and leashes, and so prefer to go with this type of material. Nylon collars offer both buckle and elastic slip-on designs.

You have probably seen plenty of dogs wearing metal choke chain collars. Choke chains are actually meant for training, and shouldn't be worn by a dog except during training sessions. Dogs that are properly trained in obedience class don't need to wear choke chain collars when they are walked.

Although your Lab shouldn't wear a choke chain around the house or every time he goes on a walk, he will probably need one of these collars for use during his obedience training. When you enroll your Lab in obedience class, talk to your instructor to find out if a choke chain collar for training purposes is recommended.

Bowls: You'll find a wide variety of food and water bowls on the market. Many are inexpensive and purely functional, while others strive to be decorative and also get the job done. Your budget and personal tastes will dictate which type of bowl you'll buy, but as you shop, keep in mind that you need one deep enough to hold the food and water without easy spillage (yet be sure the bowl isn't too deep if your new dog is just a little puppy). Stay away from food and water bowls that come in one-piece combinations; the food will be in such proximity that it will often foul the water.

You can choose among plastic, metal or ceramic when selecting dog bowls. Ceramic is always a good choice because it's easy to clean and harder for the dog to tip over. Metal bowls can be good too as long as they come in a non-tip design. Plastic is the cheapest of the three materials, although some dogs are allergic to it and break out in a rash on the chin.

Dog Crate: You may not realize it yet, but a dog crate can be both you and your dog's best friend. A dog crate will help you housetrain your dog, provide a place for him to go when you need to confine him, and double as a travel carrier when you go on trips with your pet. A crate will also provide a place of quiet and security for your Lab, and he will grow to love it.

When you go shopping for a dog crate, you'll generally find two different types on the market: plastic airline travel crates and wire mesh crates. Advantages exist to both crates, although the airline travel style is most popular because it provides the dog with privacy and a sense of security, is safer for car travel, and is lightweight and easily cleaned. Wire crates, on the other hand, offer plenty of ventilation, are often collapsible for easy transport and are more attractive than their plastic counterparts.

Whichever type of crate you decide to purchase, make sure you get one big enough for your Lab to comfortably turn around and lie down in. If your new dog is a puppy, avoid the temptation to buy a crate big enough to accommodate him as an adult. The reason for this is simple: if the crate is too big, if won't be effective as a housetraining tool.

Dog Bed: Your new Labrador Retriever will need a place to sleep. Commercially-made dog beds are good choices for this because they provide warmth and protection from the hard ground that your dog needs to feel comfortable.

Dog beds are primarily designed for use indoors, and come in a large variety of styles. Large cushions stuffed with fiberfill are a favorite of many Labs, although some prefer the basket-and-cushion style. Or, if you plan to use your dog's crate as his bed, you can purchase a cushion designed specifically for the size crate you've purchased.

If you are on a tight budget and would rather use an old blanket as your dog's bed, this can work as long as you place the blanket on a rug or carpet that already provides some cushion from the hard floor. Also, make sure your dog is not inclined to chew up the blanket and swallow it. Some dogs think old blankets are something to gnaw on, and if your dog ingests parts of the material, he could end up with a serious digestive problem.

Once you've purchased a dog bed, find a location for it in your home that is safe and comfortable for your dog. Keep it out of drafty areas and direct sunlight. Choose a spot in your home where human family members tend to congregate, like a living room or family room. Your dog will feel most comfortable sleeping in an area where you spend considerable time.

Dog House: Some people also like to provide their dog with an outdoor home he can call his own. Dog houses are good investments if your dog will spend a lot of time outside in the yard. A good dog house will provide shelter from inclement weather and a place of security for your dog when he's outdoors.

In the past, a dog house was a shelter made of wood that you would put together at home in your workshop. These days, a number of companies offer very well-made commercial dog houses in a variety of different styles and materials.

Whatever type of dog house you choose, make sure your selection is completely waterproof and insulated. Situate the dog house in a part of your yard that is sheltered from wind, rain, snow and sun. Put a soft cushion, clean straw or other type of dog bed inside the house to entice your Lab to think of it as home.

Food: You've probably noticed the scores of different kinds of dog foods on the market. These range from inexpensive supermarket brands to the more costly products sold in pet shops and pet supply stores. Knowing which brand to buy for your particular dog can be tricky, but there are factors to help you make your decision.

First off, find out exactly what food your new Lab is already eating and continue feeding it to your dog while he acclimates to his new home. If you want to change the food later on, you can do so by gradually changing over during a period of four to seven days to avoid stomach upset.

If you are buying a young puppy from a breeder, the breeder will tell you the brand of dog food preferred. The breeder may even send your dog home with a few days' supply of this food. If your breeder experienced good luck with this food, you should seriously consider keeping the product as your dog's diet.

When deciding which food to ultimately give your Lab, your veterinarian is your best source of advice. Discuss your dog's diet with the veterinarian and find out which food the veterinarian recommends. Keep in mind that even though supermarket brands are easier on your wallet than the premium products available in pet supply stores, you get what you pay for when it comes to dog food. Give your dog the best food you can possibly afford (for more information on what to feed your dog, see Chapter 6).

Identification

Before your new Labrador Retriever even sets foot in your house, make certain you have an identification tag ready to go on the dog's collar. This tag should contain your name, address and phone number. This is important, because if your dog should somehow escape from the house or yard, or in some way become separated from you, an identification tag can mean the difference between finding your dog and never seeing your Lab again.

Eventually, you may want to consider having your dog affixed with permanent identification in the form of a tattoo or microchip. Tattoos are often given on the dog's inner thigh where there is less hair and where they can easily be seen. Some owners include the dog's American Kennel Club registration numbers. Others affix their social security number, drivers license number or a number assigned by a canine tattoo registry. In any of these cases, the dog's owner can readily be traced if the dog is lost by you and found by a stranger or picked up by animal control.

Your veterinarian can provide your dog with a tattoo or give you a referral to someone who places tattoos on dogs.

Microchipping is another form of permanent and unalterable identification for your dog. The way it works is that your veterinarian implants a computer chip under your dog's skin. The chip contains an identification number and is readable with a scanner. Many animal control agencies and shelters use these scanners to pass the instrument over dogs that are deemed lost. If your dog is implanted with a microchip, the scanner will indicate the dog's identification number, which can be traced back to you through one of several microchipping agencies that register owner information (see Chapter 9 for a list of these agencies).

Even if you opt for permanent identification like a tattoo or microchip for your dog, you should still keep a collar with an identification tag on him at all times.

Dog Toys

Toys for your dog aren't luxury items—they are necessary for your dog's health and mental well-being, especially if your dog is expected to spend time alone without his human family.

The best kinds of playthings to buy for your Lab are durable and safely-made toys. If your new Lab is a puppy, you should select chew toys as your first choice. Puppies need to chew, and providing your dog with a safe toy for this purpose will reduce the likelihood that he will gnaw on your shoes and furniture when the urge to chew strikes.

The safest chew toys to buy for your Lab are nylon or rawhide products made specifically for this purpose. Be careful that you don't scrimp when it comes to chew toys—cheap, poor quality chew toys will break apart in your Lab's strong jaws, and could easily be swallowed, causing all kinds of medical problems. When you shop for chew toys, choose sturdy products that will last your pet a long time.

In addition to chewable playthings, you may want to buy your dog some toys he can enjoy when he's in the mood to run around instead of sitting and chewing. These toys will not only provide him with a reason to exercise, but playing with them will also give you an opportunity to bond with your dog.

Some of the most popular dog toys include balls, rope and squeaky toys. Rubber balls are good choices for both puppies and adult Labs, and can result in hours of chasing and fetching. Rope toys are wonderful for tossing around and carrying, and squeaky toys are great fun. If your Lab is fully grown, you may want to consider a flying disc that you can toss and your dog can fetch.

Your Lab will have definite preferences in the kinds of toys he likes to play with.

Another ideal toy for a Lab is a hard rubber object with a hollow center. You can fill the center with cheese or peanut butter and watch your dog spend time slowly getting the food out.

Exercise Pen

Another item you may want to consider purchasing is an exercise pen, or ex-pen for short. Ex-pens are portable barriers you can set up inside your house or outdoors wherever its needed. You can make the space within the ex-pen as large or as small as you want by adding on or taking away sections.

The great thing about ex-pens is they are portable and easy to set up anywhere you want. You can put an ex-pen in your living room to confine your puppy while you are in the kitchen cooking, or you can put it in the backyard to keep him from getting into trouble while you mow the lawn. Uses for ex-pens are virtually limitless, and an ex-pen is a handy item to have.

Grooming Tools and Products

One of the nicest things about owning a Lab is you won't have to spend too much time grooming your dog. Labs do shed, however, and you will need to brush your dog at least once a week. You should also give him baths and toenail trimmings on a regular basis.

To accomplish these tasks you can purchase a rubber curry brush or a rubber grooming glove; a wire-bristle slicker brush; a shedding blade; a toenail clipper; and a mild shampoo and conditioner made just for dogs. You should probably add a canine toothbrush and toothpaste to the list, since your dog's veterinarian will most likely recommend that you brush your dog's teeth every day.

Shopping Checklist
Necessities for your dog:
- Leash and collar
- Food and water bowls
- Identification tags
- Dog toys
- Crate
- Brush and comb
- Dog shampoo
- Dog bed *(optional)*
- Exercise pen *(optional)*
- Dog house *(optional)*

Knowing the Rules

A day or so before your dog comes home to live with you, sit down with your family and talk about all the rules and arrangements that will be put into effect once the dog arrives. If you think you don't need any special rules or arrangements just because a Labrador Retriever is coming to live with you, think again! Dogs are like children; they need to know the household parameters. Likewise, the rest of the family needs to know what's okay and what's not okay when it comes to the new dog.

Here are some examples of what to discuss with family members:
• *Dog safety rules.* Determine the dog-related rules that family members

must obey in order to keep your new Lab safe and sound. Stress the importance of keeping backyard gates and front doors closed at all times so the dog won't get out. Explain why it's necessary to keep objects the dog could chew and swallow out of the dog's reach. Talk about other possible hazards to your dog's safety, and remedy these problems before your Lab comes to live with you.

Rules Your Dog Should Know

- No jumping up on people
- No digging holes in the garden
- No barking at passers-by
- No begging
- No biting, even in play
- No chewing on objects except dog toys

• *Doggy access.* Talk about the parts of the house in which your Labrador Retriever will have access. Will he have free run, or will there be places that are off limits? (Keep in mind, that when you first get your dog, you should confine him to one room or area so he feels secure. As he gets more comfortable and is reliably housetrained, you can gradually give him full run of the house.)

• *Dog behavior rules.* Discuss the rules your Lab must obey. For example, you should not permit your Lab to jump up on people; dig holes in the garden; bark incessantly at passersby; beg at the dinner table; bite anyone in the household, even in play; or chew on any object other than a chew toy. Make sure everyone in the family understands that the dog is to

obey these rules at all times, without exception. In order for your Lab to become a good companion and family member, everyone in your home must consistently enforce these rules.

The First Night

The first night your Lab spends in your home will be an uncertain one for both you and your dog. If your new Lab is a puppy, he will miss his littermates terribly, and will feel insecure in this strange, new environment. If your new Lab is an adult, he will feel a little more self-confident than a pup, but he will still need some time to adjust to his new home.

Your Lab's first night in his new home will be a scary one for him. Provide him with the security of his own bed near where you'll be sleeping.

You can take a number of steps to help your dog feel comfortable in his new surroundings as you begin to establish the routine you intend to follow with your pet.

For puppies. If your new Labrador Retriever is a young puppy, his first night away from his mother and littermates will be an anxious one. Most likely, he's never been away from his mom and siblings for any length of time, yet suddenly he will find himself alone in the dark surrounded by the unfamiliar.

It's only natural for a puppy in this situation to cry for his mother. It's your job to help him learn to get used to his new life and adjust to the absence of his canine family. You can accomplish this in a few different ways. First, figure out exactly where you will keep the dog's crate on a permanent basis, and then put the crate in this spot. Next, spend some time in that room playing with the pup until he seems tuckered out. Take him out for a bathroom break, and then put him to bed with one of his old toys from the breeder's house, or an unwashed item of your clothing. You may want to turn a radio on for him (preferably a talk station) and leave it close to his crate, since the sound of voices may prove soothing to him. Consider leaving a treat or chew toy to occupy him.

Be prepared to hear some crying. If you located the crate in the same room where you sleep, you can just get up and reassure the puppy that you are there. It may take a few nights, but eventually, he will get used to being without his mother and siblings. If you located the crate in another room, you can still go and reassure the pup, but do not take him out of the crate to soothe him. Otherwise, he will learn that crying means he can come out and be cuddled—and neither one of you will ever get much sleep.

The tricky part of this situation is trying to distinguish the puppy's cries of loneliness from his cries of "I need to go to the bathroom." Expect that your puppy will need to relieve himself every two hours or so, and plan to take him out that often, whether he's crying or not. You'll need to do this until the puppy learns to cry only when he must go to the bathroom.

For adults. Unlike puppies, adult dogs don't experience separation anxiety from their mom and siblings on their first night in a new home. Depending on the circumstances surrounding your adoption of an adult Lab, however, the dog may feel uncertain. Abandoned dogs or those passed around from home to home become insecure and have trouble making themselves feel comfortable right away in a new environment.

To help an adult Lab feel secure in your home, treat him much the same way you would a puppy. Place his crate or bed in the same part of the house where you intend for him to sleep on a regular basis, and provide him with an article of your clothing or something that reminds him of his previous home. Be sure to take him outside and play with him just before bed time to tire him out, and then put him to sleep with a treat or chew toy to occupy him for awhile.

The primary difference between a puppy's and an adult dog's first night is that the adult dog is unlikely to whimper because he misses his mommy! However, if your adult dog is not crate-trained and you put him in the crate for the first time, he is going to cry to get out. Be sure to gradually crate-train your dog before you confine him for long periods of time (see Crate-Training later in this chapter for advice on how to do this). In the meantime, confine him to one room with his crate open so he doesn't associate his first night in an unfamiliar place with being locked in a crate. Or, if you intend to keep your dog in your bedroom with you while you sleep, simply put his bed or crate in the room with you when you bed down for the night. (Don't let him sleep in bed with you unless you plan to make this a nightly occurrence for the rest of his life.) In this scenario, your Lab is likely to take comfort from your presence and won't feel the urge to cry or whimper.

Another way to ensure your dog's comfort on his first night in his new home is to not make an abrupt change in his diet when he has his first meal with you. Find out the type and brand of dog food your new Lab ate in his previous home and continue to feed him this product so it doesn't upset his digestive system. If you intend to eventually switch him over to a different food, do so very gradually over a period of a week, increasingly mixing the old food with the new one. This will give his body a chance to acclimate to the new diet.

Making Introductions

If your new Labrador Retriever will not be your only pet, you will need to make some introductions when your dog arrives at his new home. The approach you take in introducing your new dog to your other pets depends on what kind of animals are already living in your home.

Dogs. If your home already includes a resident dog, you need to carefully introduce your new Lab to your existing pet to help ensure that the two will get along.

Before you bring your new Lab home, set up a time when your Lab and your resident dog can meet on neutral territory. This is especially important if both dogs are adults. A fully-grown dog might accept a puppy with little resistance, but may object to another adult dog on what he perceives as his turf. Introducing the two dogs in a place with no territorial significance to either one of them will facilitate their friendship without any complications of turf ownership. (If your adult dog shows any aggression toward a young puppy, seek advice from a trainer before allowing the two to spend time together.)

When planning that first meeting, select a venue in which your resident dog is not familiar. Don't introduce the two dogs at your local park if this is a place you regularly take your resident dog. Instead, go to a park well outside your neighborhood, or to a friend's yard where your resident dog rarely or never visits. (If either one of your dogs is a young puppy under six months of age, avoid introducing the dogs in a park where you might expose your puppy to a contagious disease.)

Have a friend or family member convene with you at the scheduled meeting place with your resident dog. Meanwhile, take your new Lab there in a separate car or on a separate walk. Keep both dogs on a leash and allow them to slowly approach each other. The two will probably sniff each other and perform some other doggy rituals, hopefully without any aggression. Let the dogs spend time with each other while you and your friend chit chat nonchalantly. Take them for a walk together, and let the dogs get used to each other's presence. Once they seem comfortable together, you can then take your new Lab home for good. Chances are, your resident dog will accept your new Lab with minimal fuss. Be prepared for some growling and jostling for position that will probably occur; but as long as the dogs aren't seriously fighting, there is no need to interfere. Eventually, they will work things out together. (In the event that your dogs can't seem to get along, eliminate any contact between them, and get in touch with a dog trainer or certified animal behaviorist for assistance.)

Cats. If you are a cat owner, you made a wise choice in selecting a Labrador Retriever for a pet. Unlike some other breeds with a strong predatory or chase instinct, Labrador Retrievers are bred to possess a trait called a "soft mouth." This is a good trait in a dog that lives with cats because it means the Lab is unlikely to harm the kitties in the household.

On the other hand, just because Labs tend to be gentle doesn't mean they don't need to be carefully introduced to cats and taught to respect them. Labrador Retrievers are big dogs, and if they are not taught to

When introducing your new Lab to resident pets, be sure to exercise both caution and sensitivity.

treat cats with high regard, they can make a cat's life pretty miserable.

When introducing your new Lab to the resident cat, realize that unless your cat has grown up with dogs, he will not be very happy. The best way to start the relationship is to allow the two to get used to each other by keeping them separated by a door. Keep the cat and dog in separate rooms for a few days, allowing them to sniff each other under the door until they become accustomed to the sound and smell of one another.

After awhile, you can allow the two to meet face to face. As a precaution, trim your cat's front claws before the meeting in case he decides to take a swipe at your Lab's face.

If your Labrador Retriever is an adult dog, you need to proceed with caution to make sure the dog won't harm the cat. That means, when the moment of truth comes, put your Lab on a leash and allow your cat to enter the room with the dog. If your dog begins to whine or pull toward the cat, give him a first correction in the form of a sharp tug on the leash and a loud "No!" You want to teach your Labrador Retriever to leave the cat alone, and this means discouraging any attention the dog is paying in the cat's direction. If you hope that the two will someday become friends, this will happen on the cat's terms only. The cat can learn to like the dog provided the dog leaves him alone.

If your new Lab is a young puppy, you should wait until your pup is at least nine weeks old before introduc-ing him to the cat. By this age, the puppy will be old enough to learn not to hassle the cat. If he repeatedly bothers the cat, gently discourage this behavior. Be sure not to yell at or show harshness to a young puppy because it will scare him. Instead, tell the puppy "No" in a firm but gentle way. Make him sit so he focuses on you instead of the cat, then encour-age him to play with a ball or other toy instead of your feline.

For the next several days, allow the dog or puppy and the cat together in the same room only when the dog is leashed and under your control. Con-sistently correct the dog every time he shows inappropriate interest in the cat. Labs learn quickly, and before long, your dog will get the idea.

It's a good idea to never leave a dog alone with a cat unsupervised until you are completely certain the dog will not show any aggressive behavior toward the cat—and in the case of a young puppy, that the cat will not scratch the puppy or hurt him in any way. Supervise the two together for a few months just for safety's sake.

Small animals. If you have children, chances are a few small animals—a rabbit, guinea pig or hamster—may already share your home. Add a Labrador Retriever to the mix, and you create quite a menagerie!

Labs are known for their gentle-ness with other creatures, but this is no reason to think that it's okay to let your Lab loose with one of these small animals. You should follow an introduction process here just as you would with another dog or a cat. This is for the safety and well-being of your small pet as well as for the education of your Labrador. (If your Lab is a puppy, wait until he is at least nine weeks old before making the introductions.)

The first time your Lab meets your small pet, make sure the rabbit, hamster or guinea pig is safely within the confines of its cage. Keep in mind that small animals are easily frightened, especially by large animals who are potential predators. Put your dog on a leash and allow the dog and the small pet (in its cage) time together in the same room. If your Lab shows any kind of assertive interest in the small pet, correct him and tell him "No!" The objective here is to teach your dog not to bother the small pet, while also allowing the small pet to get used to the dog's presence.

These training/introduction sessions should take place for several days until your Lab gets the message. In the meantime, don't allow your dog any access to the small pet when you are not around.

Can your Lab and your small pet someday become friends? This is a distinct possibility, especially if your Lab meets your small pet as a young puppy. Keep in mind, however, that your dog can easily kill or injure a small animal without meaning to, so never leave the pair alone unsupervised, no matter how gentle your dog seems.

Birds. Your Lab was bred with a fascination for feathered creatures, so if you have a pet bird in the household, take particular care of your winged pet. Never leave your Lab unsupervised with your bird, even if it is in its cage. An over-enthusiastic Lab could potentially knock the cage over and literally scare your bird to death.

Meeting Friends and Neighbors

Plenty of people will want to meet your new Labrador Retriever, particularly if your dog is a puppy. Friends, neighbors and relatives will all demand to make your new dog's acquaintance.

While it may be tempting to invite everyone you know to come over and meet your dog on its first day at home, you may want to refrain from introducing your new Lab until after he's comfortable with his new surroundings, especially if he is a young puppy. Wait until he is at least nine weeks old before you start making introductions. Then, invite people over one at a time or in small groups so your pet can meet them.

Be sure to apprise all guests of the rules of behavior your dog is expected to follow. Don't allow your dog to jump up on people when they come into the house, for example, and discourage guests from feeding table scraps to your Lab in an effort to befriend him. Instead, encourage guests to play a game of fetch with your new family member, or take him for a walk if they are in the mood to do so.

Socializing Your Puppy

Imagine the world through the eyes of a puppy: everything is new and exciting, vast and intriguing. All that you take for granted in life are complete unknowns for a young dog who has never been away from his mom and littermates.

If your new Labrador Retriever is a puppy, you will help this young creature explore the world and learn to understand it. Being a puppy owner is not unlike being a parent: you are responsible for guiding and shaping a young mind in both situations. As a puppy owner, that young mind is purely canine, and will develop rather rapidly. The way you handle your puppy now and the life experiences you give him will influence his personality for years to come.

Why It's Important

Puppies are like human children in many ways. Both are full of energy, both require a lot of attention, and both are pretty darn cute (usually).

But puppies and children are also similar in another very significant way: each has varying stages of development that determine how they will view life when they become adults. Human children learn how to love and be loved; they learn how to ride a bike and use roller skates; and they learn how to read, write and do arithmetic.

Puppies, on the other hand, learn to accept humans as pack members; they learn to follow commands; and they learn to be independent from their mothers.

Of course, it's much more complicated than this, but basically, that is how growth development works. And when it comes to young dogs, each stage of puppyhood comes with a different focus.

Much of a puppy's serious development takes place while he is still with his mother and littermates. For example, for the first 20 days, the puppy learns to use his muscles and recognize his mother and siblings. From 21–35 days, he learns the rules of pack behavior, and he discovers the joys of human interaction. Once he hits five weeks of age, he starts learning to venture forth and become an independent soul from his canine family.

Most puppies are sent to their new homes at the age of eight or nine weeks. Nine weeks is a better age to take a puppy home because the puppy is past his initial fear period, which tends to occur at eight weeks. This is the period when the puppy is easily frightened, and whatever scares him during that time will leave a lasting impression. If you can, ask your Lab's breeder to keep the puppy with his mother until he is at least nine weeks old so he feels safe and secure during this most vulnerable period. The breeder will have been working on socializing him ever since he was born, and can continue the process at this crucial point in his life.

Assuming your puppy comes to live with you at the age of nine weeks, you will need to contend with the remaining stages of puppy development. From 9–12 weeks of age, your

It's important to provide your Lab puppy with as many new experiences as you can.

puppy needs exposure to certain stimuli and activities so he can learn that these elements are part of his environment and adjust to them.

Stuff to Show Your Puppy
- Cats
- Children
- Strangers
- Other Dogs
- Bicycles
- Horses
- Rabbits
- Birds

Fun Places

Labs are active dogs who love to do fun things with their owners. While your dog is still a young puppy, take him out to different places where he can learn all about life and the different types of environments that exist.

Some places to which you might consider taking your puppy are a local playing field, especially during a game so he can get used to the sights and sounds of crowds; a beach that allows dogs, although try to do it at a time of day when there aren't a lot of other dogs around; and a local stable or farm where he can meet some horses and livestock, and take in the sights. Remember, you won't need to stay there too long since a half an hour at a time is more than enough exposure for your pup.

Because your pup's immune system is not as strong as that of an adult, you must use caution when taking your puppy out for socialization. Avoid bringing him to places frequented by many other dogs (like a park or public street). Instead, go to a remote beach or an area where other dogs are less likely to be.

Places to Take Your Puppy
- Beach
- River
- Lake
- Park
- Street fair

Baby Training

Nine to 12 weeks is a good time to introduce your puppy to the concept of training. You can start by getting him used to wearing a buckle collar. He can also get accustomed to wearing a leash at this age. Attach a lightweight leash to his collar and let the puppy walk around with you at the other end of the leash. Don't try to control which direction he goes in just yet—let him go wherever he wants with you following behind. Do this for a couple of minutes each day.

You can also teach your young Lab some basic commands. Labs are naturals when it comes to obedience training, so you should have no trouble with this one.

To teach him to sit, put one hand on his chest and the other hand on his rump. Say "Sit" and then gently push his bottom down so he is sitting. At the moment his butt touches the ground, praise him enthusiastically.

He doesn't have to stay in that position—just the fact that he moved into the sitting position for even a few seconds will help make your point. Do this a few times a day to help him get the idea.

Another important command to start teaching your Lab at a young age is "Come." Take your puppy out in the backyard and say "Blackie, come!" as you run in the opposite direction. Chances are, your little Lab will come charging after you. When he does, stop in your tracks, stoop down and give him lots and lots of praise. Do this a few times and then quit for the day. Try it again tomorrow.

Handling Sessions

Whatever your puppy learns now will stay with him for the rest of his life. Since you plan to brush him, trim his toenails and do other assorted things to his body throughout his life, now is a good time to practice.

Take a few minutes every couple of days to brush your puppy with a soft brush while you talk to him and tell him what a good boy he is. Handle his feet and gently squeeze his toe pads so he gets used to having his feet touched. Pick up his ear flaps and look inside. Rub his ears and look at his eyes as if you were examining them for problems. Run your hands all over his body and feel him as if you were looking for lumps.

Although this might sound silly, it will amaze you how much more comfortable your adult Lab will be at the veterinarian's and groomer's office if you perform this simple ritual a couple of times a week when your dog is a pup.

Children

One of the most important things you must teach your young puppy is that children are okay. This is important whether you have kids of your own or not. Dogs who grow up with virtually no contact with children often grow up to fear or dislike kids. This presents a real problem because children are everywhere in our environment, and will often seek out dogs to interact with whenever they can.

If you have children of your own who can help you socialize your puppy, then you are in luck. Teach your kids to be calm and quiet around your puppy so they don't scare him. Have them hold the puppy, cuddle him and play with him. If your children treat the puppy with gentleness and respect, your Lab will grow up to adore the youngest members of our society.

If you don't have kids of your own to socialize your puppy, you will need to borrow some. Neighbors' kids are great for this purpose, as are nieces, nephews and the children of friends. Have one or two kids come over at a time just to play with the puppy and pet him. Tell the children they should be quiet and calm since loud noises and running around will frighten the puppy. Most kids understand the notion of fear and will cooperate when you explain the puppy is easily scared. After finding a couple of kids who are particularly good at this,

Give your Lab lots of exposure to well-behaved children when he's young. This will help him grow up to love kids.

have them come over once a week for a few weeks to help your puppy get used to them.

Other Stuff

One of the most fun things about having a puppy is showing the world to it, one step at a time. Throughout your Lab's life, he will deal with different kinds of objects and beings. Because you want him to react appropriately and non-aggressively (and non-fearfully), you should start introducing him to as many of these things as you possibly can—one thing at a time and on a gradual basis—while he is still young and impressionable.

Aside from taking your puppy to new and exciting places, also create new situations for him to experience. Go up and down stairs with him, and walk over plastic bags laid on the ground. Let him watch while you mow the lawn and start up the car. Take him outside when an ambulance or bus roars down the street, and let him stay in the room while you vacuum or mop.

You may see your puppy react with fear in some of these situations. But you can help your dog get over his apprehension by not by picking him up and coddling him, and by acting unafraid and enthusiastic yourself about what's going on. For example, if you are vacuuming the living room and your puppy seems afraid of the vacuum cleaner, start talking to him in a happy voice and acting like vacuuming is the most fun activity in the world. Your dog will eventually take your cue and learn to see the vacuum cleaner as nothing more than a noisy—but harmless—machine.

Crate-Training Your Dog

The idea of keeping a dog in a crate may seem inhumane to you, as it does to many dog owners who never tried this method of confinement before. Somehow, people have the notion that a *crate* is synonymous with a *cage*, and that putting a dog in one is tantamount to keeping him in jail.

Nothing is further from the truth. If you take the time to train your dog properly, he will view his crate as a safe and secure hideaway rather than a prison to which he's been banished.

If your Labrador Retriever is a puppy, now is the best time to teach him all about the crate and how wonderful it is. Since a crate can help housetrain a puppy, you will want to start working your youngster with a crate right away. In fact, the breeder who sold you your puppy may have already started teaching your new dog all about the crate.

If your Lab is an adult dog, it will take longer and require more patience to crate-train him. It can be done, however, as long as you are consistent and unwavering in your training methods.

Start out by purchasing a crate suited to your dog's size (see the section on buying a dog crate earlier in this chapter). Decide where you want to keep the crate on a regular basis. Since your dog will sleep in it at night, you may want to put it in your bedroom or in another area close to your room so your dog can hear and smell you during the night. This will help him feel secure and allow him to spend as much time with you as possible.

Introduce your Lab to his crate by leaving the crate door open and tossing a treat into the crate. As your dog runs inside the crate to retrieve the treat, give him a word or phrase command you have selected to use as one to prompt your dog to go in his crate. Some people say "Blackie, crate!" Others say "Blackie, bedtime!"

or "Go to bed!" The choice is yours. Just make sure the command you select doesn't use too many words.

Toss a treat into the crate several times until you notice that your dog doesn't seem reluctant to enter the crate and stay in it. If you can, do this for several days to ensure your dog is truly comfortable before moving onto the next step.

Once your dog is okay with the notion of being inside the crate, begin feeding him his regular meals in it. Place his bowl deep inside the crate and have him finish his meal there. Do this a few times until you feel certain he's completely comfortable with being inside the crate for a prolonged period.

Next, it's time to close the door of the crate with your dog in it. Do this while your Lab is still eating his meal. If he's like most Labs, he probably won't even notice the door is closed until he's finished his dinner. Once he sees it's shut, he may start pawing at the door and whining to get out. Don't give in if he does this. Tell him "No!" or "Quiet!" and wait until he is silent in the crate before you release him.

Continue this last step until your dog finishes his dinner quietly in the crate and waits patiently to be let out. Once you achieve this level of comfort in your dog, you can then put him in the crate a few times a day for several minutes at a time. Gradually lengthen the amount of time he spends in the crate.

You will eventually want your Lab to sleep in his crate at night, but it's important not to confine him in it throughout the evening until you have acclimated him to the crate with this gradual method. Otherwise, the crate will traumatize him and he will never feel comfortable in it.

While crates are most handy during housetraining time, you will find the crate valuable throughout your dog's life. It offers an ideal place to confine your dog when company is coming over or you are unable to supervise him in a particular situation. Crates are also valuable for traveling since they protect both you and your dog on car rides. Not only can you confine your dog to the crate while you are driving to keep him from getting into trouble while you concentrate on the road, but having him in a crate could save his life and yours in the event of an accident.

Once you arrive at your destination, you can use the crate to confine your dog whenever you need to, such as when you are checking into a hotel room or when you are in the hotel room.

When using the crate at home, avoid leaving your dog inside for many hours at a time, except at night when you are sleeping. The crate should be used for short periods only, when you can't supervise your dog. If you need to confine your dog for several hours, limit him to one small part of the house.

If properly trained, your Lab will come to think of his crate as his own private retreat.

Housetraining Your Lab

The bad news is that Labs aren't born knowing to go to the bathroom outdoors instead of inside the house. The good news is that it's easy to teach them.

Various people tried different methods to housetrain dogs over the years, but the one that seems to work best involves use of a crate. By using a crate in your Lab's house-training lessons, you will take advantage of your dog's primitive denning instinct, which tells him "Don't go to the bathroom where you sleep."

Before you begin housetraining your Lab, read the sections on crates and crate-training elsewhere in this chapter. Once you have purchased the right size and type of crate for your dog's needs, and have taught your dog to gradually get used to the crate, you are ready to start house-training.

The key to housetraining your Lab is to help him understand that all elimination should be done outdoors. The way you do this is to set him up for success. Give him plenty of opportunities to go to the bathroom where he should, and eventually he will get the idea.

The other habit you want to teach your dog is to go the bathroom on command. This training comes in handy when it's pouring rain outside or when it's the middle of the night. Instead of standing around for ten minutes waiting for your dog to go t o the bathroom, you can use a verbal command to get him to go right away.

When you begin housetraining your dog, you will need to keep him confined during the times he is not under your direct supervision. This means keeping him in a bathroom or kitchen, or other small space with an easy to clean floor, or better yet, inside his crate where he can't get away from any mess he might make.

The next step is to take your dog outside as frequently as possible to give him the opportunity to go to the bathroom outdoors. If your Lab is a young puppy, you will need to take him outside every two hours since puppies can't hold their urine for longer than this. If your dog is an adult, you can lengthen this time to every four hours—although the more you can take him out, the better.

When you bring your dog outside for housetraining purposes, you don't want to play with your pet or distract him from the business at hand, which is going to the bathroom. Instead, put him on a leash (even if you are just going into the backyard) and take him out to the same spot every time. Let him sniff around, and when he begins to eliminate, say the words you've chosen to use as his verbal command to eliminate. (Some popular phrases include "Go potty," "Do your business," and "Make it.") After you give the command, verbally tell him he's a good boy. Don't bend down and start petting him because that will distract him.

What should you do if your Lab ends up going to the bathroom inside the house? Never hit him with a rolled up newspaper or rub his nose in his "accident." These archaic methods accomplish nothing other than creating fear and distrust in your dog. In fact, if the accident took place more than a few seconds before you notice it, your dog won't even associate the punishment with the deed, and he will not understand why he's being reprimanded.

If you find a mess in the area where your dog was confined, don't bother yelling at him or correcting him in anyway. Instead, reevaluate the situation. You probably need to keep your dog in a smaller space (a crate, preferably), or start taking him outside more frequently. Remember that the act of going to the bathroom outdoors is a habit that you must create in your dog. The less you allow your Lab in a situation where he goes in the house, the sooner the outdoor habit will take hold.

What happens if you catch your dog in the act? Should you punish him then? No, but you can let him know he's not going where he should. Give your dog a verbal correction like "No!" to make him stop what he's doing, and then immediately take him outside. When he continues to finish his business outdoors, praise him for doing the right thing.

It will take a few weeks to teach your puppy to eliminate outdoors and on command. Within five months, he should be completely reliable in the house. (If not, check with your veterinarian to determine if your dog has a medical problem.)

If your Labrador Retriever is an adult dog, it may take longer to housetrain him. Be patient and accompany your dog whenever he goes out so you can verify he is going to the bathroom.

Training your dog properly is beneficial for the owner as well as the pet.

Chapter Four

Obedience Training Your Lab

Nearly everyone has heard of obedience training. For hundreds of years, people have employed this practice to teach dogs to perform certain behaviors on command.

Fortunately, the Labrador Retriever is one of the easiest breeds to obedience train. Their tractable nature and willingness to please make them naturals for this type of schooling.

The Importance of Training

If you are like most dog owners, you may wonder if you really need to obedience train your Labrador Retriever. You may ponder the importance of your dog knowing how to sit, stay and come when called. After all, won't he learn these behaviors on his own? And if he doesn't, is it really such a big deal?

In order to comprehend the importance of obedience training to *every* dog regardless of breed, you need to understand what happens when dogs do not receive a formal education in following commands. The consequences are immediate to that dog and his family, and to society as a whole.

Knowing Who is Leader

Dogs are pack animals who instinctively look for a leader in every situation they encounter. The most effective way to solidify this perspective in your dog is to obedience train him.

When a dog is comfortable in his position within the family and sees his human friends as in charge, he is most likely to be a well-behaved and valuable member of his immediate family and the community as a whole. The obedience-trained dog listens to commands, refrains from aggressive behavior and treats humans with respect.

If you obedience train your Labrador Retriever, you will teach your dog that you are the leader of the pack and that he should take his behavioral cues from you. You, your dog and your neighbors can all benefit from this.

A Job to Do

Another strong argument for obedience training your Lab is this: Labs are working dogs who aren't truly happy unless they have a job to do. In days gone by, that job consisted primarily of hunting in the field with an owner, helping the family put food on the table. These days, obedience training is an excellent substitute for that former duty.

Because Labs are such active dogs, both mentally and physically, obedience training gives them an activity to occupy their minds and bodies. Labs enjoy the task of learning and are less likely to become bored with life if they participate in regular sessions of obedience training.

Good Companionship

If for no other reason, Labs should be obedience trained simply because a trained Lab is a pleasant Lab. When your dog is well-behaved and obedient, you will want to spend time with him, and so will the rest of your family. He'll be welcome at your friends' homes, he'll be a joy to take camping or to the park, and he will be well respected within your community. On the other hand, if your dog runs around like an out-of-control lunatic when you take him places, runs off at the first opportunity and won't come back when you call him, and jumps all over everyone he sees, people will not want to be around him.

Statistically speaking, obedience-trained Labs are more likely to stay in their homes than end up surrendered at animal shelters as a result of behavioral problems. The time you invest in obedience training your Lab now will pay off in the end with a happy, well-adjusted dog who is a permanent member of your family.

Reasons to Obedience Train

- Your dog will feel more secure
- You'll have more control over your dog
- Your dog will be welcome in more places
- Your dog will have more freedom
- Your dog will be less likely to develop behavioral problems

Methods of Training

Dogs were once trained mainly by using coercion. In order to get a dog do what you wanted, you used plenty of punishment to force the dog to bend to your will. The result was often fearful dogs who didn't really enjoy their training, but instead did as they were told simply to avoid punishment.

Today, most dog trainers are much more enlightened. Through years of study, experts in animal behavior discovered that positive reinforcement is more effective when training dogs—and other animals, including humans—than brute force. Plus, it's more humane, and results in happy, confident dogs.

When applied to dog training, positive reinforcement works on a simple principal: encourage the dog to do what you want, and when he does it, reward him. For dogs, the most effective rewards come in the form of treats and praise. Many trainers who use positive reinforcement also use corrections simply to let the dog know when he made a mistake, but the primary tool of learning is the reward.

Labrador Retrievers are especially receptive to positive reinforcement, and the training methods described in this book are based on the theory of positive reinforcement. When considering a trainer or obedience class for your dog, make sure positive reinforcement is that trainer's or instructor's method of choice.

Creating a Training Routine

Dogs are creatures of habit, and they love routine. You should not only establish a routine for when your dog eats and goes to the bathroom, but you should also establish one for his training.

Start With Classes

The best way to begin your Lab's obedience training is to take him to formal obedience classes. Although you will eventually take over your dog's training yourself, it's a good idea to start out in a class situation. In a class setting, your dog will gain the opportunity to socialize with other dogs and learn to concentrate on his training in a somewhat distracting environment. In addition, you will learn the important methods of teaching your dog basic obedience commands and will get help from the trainer or instructor when you need it. Once your Lab graduates from beginning obedience, you can continue with more advanced classes or do more work with him on your own.

You can also opt for private training where you and your dog work one on one with a dog trainer in private sessions. This training is more expensive than group classes, however, and doesn't afford your dog opportunities for socialization like a class setting does.

Start your Lab in obedience training as soon as you possibly can. If your dog is a young puppy just eight

Taking your Lab to obedience class allows you to train him and socialize him at the same time.

or nine weeks of age, he is too young to take to a formal puppy kindergarten class. Young puppies don't have the attention span required for an obedience class, and are at risk of catching an infectious disease from other dogs because of their tender age. You can start practicing basic obedience with your small puppy at home, however, by teaching him some of the lessons mentioned in Chapter 3.

By the age of 12 weeks, your Lab puppy will have developed enough concentration to learn beginning obedience in a class setting, and will also have acquired two sets of the vaccinations he needs to protect him from many of the contagious diseases to which dogs are susceptible. If you enroll your puppy in a puppy kindergarten class, make sure the instructor takes puppies as young as 12 weeks, and that all dogs are required to have proof of vaccinations before being admitted into the class.

Be aware that some veterinarians may discourage you from taking your puppy to obedience class until the dog reaches 16–20 weeks of age. Many vets are concerned about the puppy's possible exposure to contagious disease before his immune system is properly prepared to fight off these problems. On the other hand, if your puppy doesn't receive early socialization with other dogs and basic obedience training at a young age (the optimum time for this is 8–14 weeks), you will miss a very important training window in your

Lab's development. You can proceed with caution, enrolling your puppy in a class where you are certain the other pups received vaccinations, or you can opt to wait until he is older, working with him at home. The choice is ultimately yours.

Training at Home

You will most likely attend obedience class once a week. On the day of the class, your Lab will spend a concentrated amount of time learning one or more obedience commands. But this shouldn't be the only day in the week that he works on his obedience. Take 15 to 20 minutes each day to practice what you learned in class that week.

When training your dog at home, keep several points in mind to achieve the best results:

Use positive reinforcements. Labs thrive on attention. Whenever your dog does what you've asked— whether it's a "sit" on command or a refrain from jumping up on company because you've told him no to—be sure to reward him. You can start out with treats and praise, eventually phasing out the treats and giving verbal praise exclusively. Your dog will learn faster this way, and you'll have fun doing it.

Use correction when necessary. Even though you are using positive reinforcement to train your dog, occasional corrections let your dog know when he's made a mistake. Make your corrections consistent and brief. The word "No!" and a quick jerk on the collar is more than enough of a message for most Labrador Retrievers. Never correct out of anger, and always reward your dog as soon as he does what you want.

Be consistent. One of the biggest training mistakes that dog owners make is inconsistency. In order for your dog to learn, his actions must elicit the same response from you every time. For example, if you let him ignore you some of the time when you call him, he will learn that it's okay to ignore the "Come" command. You will end up with a dog who simply doesn't come when he's called, or only comes when he feels like it. Instead, insist that he obey the commands you give him, each and every time.

Practice. Obedience training is an ongoing process for your dog. In beginning obedience classes, he will learn the fundamentals of canine compliance. For the rest of his life, you will need to reinforce these commands by using them in everyday situations and conducting short practice sessions one or more times a week to help keep them fresh in his mind.

Important Elements in Training
- Be consistent
- Give lots of praise
- Make it fun
- Keep it short
- Backtrack if necessary

Basic Obedience Exercises

Experts in dog training recognize five basic obedience commands that all dogs should know: sit, stay, down, come, and walk calmly on leash. Dogs who reliably perform all of these commands when asked are usually controllable, well-mannered canines and a joy to live with.

It's not difficult to teach your dog these five basic commands. If you enroll in obedience class, your instructor will show you how to teach your dog each of these exercises. You may want to get a head start on teaching your dog at home by showing him these commands before enrolling him in class. If you prefer to train your Lab at home on your own,

The sit is one of the most important and basic of all obedience commands.

you can teach your dog these commands yourself.

Sit

The *sit* command is one of the most basic and valuable obedience commands for your dog to learn. If your Labrador Retriever knows how to sit on command, you will exert considerable control over him. The *sit* command is especially useful if your dog is getting hyper or is doing something he shouldn't, like jumping up on guests or running around the house like a maniac. When you tell him to "Sit!" you are forcing him to control himself, settle down and pay attention to you.

To teach your dog to sit, put a leash on him and get one of his favorite treats. With the leash in one hand, hold the treat with the other hand above his head just out of reach. Keep the treat close enough to his nose that he can smell it, but not so close that he can reach it. Then, move your hand toward the back of your dog's head. As you do this, use your Lab's name and tell him to sit ("Blackie, sit!"). Your dog will instinctively sit as he attempts to keep his eyes focused on the treat. Keep him in that position for a couple of seconds, then say "Okay" and praise him physically by giving him the treat and petting him while you tell him what a good dog he is.

In the event your dog won't sit down when you hold the treat over his head, but instead backs up, you'll need to use a different method to get him to sit so he will understand the command. You can accomplish this by physically putting him in the sit position as you say the word "Sit!" Do this by placing one hand on the front of your dog's neck and the other hand on his back. Push his body down with the hand on his back, slowly sliding it toward his rump. Remember, you are saying the word "Sit!" while you do this, and keeping your dog in this position for a couple of seconds after his rear end makes contact with the ground. Then say "Okay" and reward him with a treat and by petting him while you tell him how good he is.

Practice your Lab's sit a few times each day, gradually increasing the amount of time you ask your dog to hold his position before you release him by saying "Okay" (to let him know that he doesn't have to hold the position any longer) and then praising him. Eventually, he will perform the sit command without expecting a treat.

Stay

The stay is a particularly valuable obedience command because it gives you a significant amount of control over your dog's actions in just about any situation. You can use this command to get your dog to stop whatever he is doing and stand still, which means keeping him from running away, darting out into traffic or tearing after a cat or rabbit when he's off leash.

In order to teach your dog to stay, he must first know how to sit on command since you build on the sit exercise by incorporating the stay command into it. This is known as the sit-stay command.

Put your Lab on a leash and tell him to sit. While you stand in front of your dog, present an open, flat hand with the palm side out to your dog's face. As you do this, say your dog's name and the word "Stay!" If your dog is sitting quietly, take a step back and stand there for 10 seconds. If your Lab takes a step toward you during that 10 second period, move him backwards and put him in the sit position once again and start over.

Eventually, your Lab will get the idea and will stay still as you back away, holding the position for 10 seconds. Once this happens, say "Okay!" and praise your dog by petting him and telling him he's wonderful. Practice this a few more times, and then do it every day until your dog really has the hang of it. When he's reliable at 10 seconds, step further away from him after you give the stay command, and increase the amount of time to 20 seconds. Continue to increase both the distance between you and your dog and the amount of time your dog is expected to hold the position until your dog really has the stay command down. You can then try doing this off leash (in an enclosed area), gradually increasing the time and distance once again until your dog is reliable at the stay.

After you teach your dog the following down command, you can work on the down-stay exercise where your dog will be lying down when you give the stay command.

Down

If you like the control you get over your Lab with the stay command in conjunction with the sit, you will really appreciate the down command and what it can do when it comes to keeping your dog in one place when used in conjunction with "Stay."

Teaching your Lab the down command is not difficult if you already taught him to sit. Start him in the sitting position and hold a treat in front of his nose. As you lower the treat to the floor, say your Lab's name and

Teaching your dog the down command will give you more control when you want him to stay put.

the command "Down!" Your dog will move his head toward the ground in an attempt to reach the treat. Gently push his front end down with your other hand so that his entire body is resting on the ground. Continue to hold him in this position for a couple of seconds and then say "Okay!", praising him and giving him the treat. Practice this several times daily until he readily lays down when you give him the down command. Gradually ask him to hold the position for longer and longer periods of time until he really has it figured out. When he's reliable at this, add the stay command after you put him in the down position, using the same method of teaching that you used when showing him how to stay at the sit. Eventually, your Lab will perform the down-stay so well that you can literally walk away from him and still keep control over him from a distance.

Come

Another very important command for your Lab to learn at an early age is the "come" command. When your dog learns to reliably come when called, you can retrieve him from just about situation where you don't have control with a leash.

To teach your Lab to come, fit him with his collar and leash. Get some treats together, and stand in front of him holding the leash. Show him a treat and then say his name followed by "Come!" When your Lab moves in your direction, back up. If he continues to move toward you, praise

him verbally and hand him a treat. Do this repeatedly over several days and pretty soon you won't even need the treats. Your dog will respond to the voice command alone.

Once your Lab is reliable coming to you on a short leash, begin the process again using a leash that is 20–30 feet long (a clothesline works well for this).

Find a fenced-in area—preferably your backyard—and allow your Lab to go loose with the leash dragging behind him. Get his attention by showing him that you have some treats, then call him using the come command. If your Lab comes racing to you, tell him how wonderful he is and give him a treat. However, if he ignores you, pick up the leash and reel him in while you say "Come!" Praise him verbally when he gets to you, but don't give him a treat. Save those for when he comes to you without your having to use the leash. Once he does this consistently, you can practice this without the leash, but still within a fenced area.

After you teach your Lab to come when called, consistently reinforce it for the rest of his life. Don't allow your dog to ignore your command to come, or else he won't pay any attention when you give it.

Walk Calmly on Leash

Teaching a dog to walk on a leash is something most people do as soon as they acquire a puppy. But learning to walk calmly on a leash properly is something that many dogs never learn.

Teaching your Lab to come whenever you call is important for his safety.

If you ever walked a dog that pulled you along like he was a competitor in the Iditarod dog sled race, you know how annoying this habit is. Once pulling on the leash gets started, it's difficult to correct. The best approach is to teach your Lab to walk on a leash properly from the very beginning. While you can simply encourage young puppies to accept the leash and enjoy taking short strolls, older puppies and adult dogs should receive consistent training on how to walk calmly on leash.

To teach your Lab to walk properly on a leash—that is, beside you and not pulling ahead in front of you—put his collar and leash on and take him to an outdoor area with only minimal distractions. Make sure you bring along a good supply of treats.

Find a moment when your dog is relatively relaxed, and position your-self in front of him, with the leash in hand. Hold a treat in front of his face and start to back up, calling him and asking him to follow you. When he walks toward you, tell him he's a really good dog and hand him the treat. If for some reason he doesn't follow when you ask, keep encouraging him until he gets the message. Practice this several times until you can tell he caught on.

If at any point your dog pulls in another direction with obvious disregard for your presence, give a sharp jerk on his collar. When he turns to look at you, praise him for refocusing his attention on you, show him the treat again, and encourage him to follow. If he does, make a fuss over him and give him the treat.

Once he's got the hang of this, move on to the next step. Perform the same exercise, only this time, turn your back and walk forward instead of walking backwards, allowing him to move up to your left side. Take a few steps, and if he stays with you with his attention focused on you and you alone, tell him he's doing great and give him the treat. If he gets ahead of you and starts pulling, begin backing up until your dog hits the end of the leash. The jerk on his collar will cause him to stop and look at you in surprise. When he's focused on you, walk forward again. If he pulls again, repeat this correction until he realizes that whenever he walks next to you he gets a treat and praise, but when he pulls on the leash, he gets a jerk on his collar.

Consistency is incredibly important when teaching your dog to walk properly on a leash. If your dog's tendency is to pull when you walk him, don't take him on walks until after you train him to stop doing this. If you allow him to pull you at all, he will get into the habit and your walks together will become increasingly unpleasant. Your dog will ultimately suffer in this situation because neither you or anyone in your family will want to take him outside for a stroll.

Mandatory Commands

The five basic commands every Lab should know:
Sit
Stay
Down
Come
Walk Calmly on Leash

Dogs who walk calmly on leash are a joy to take for a stroll.

Teaching Manners

Have you ever spent time around an ill-mannered dog? It's not a pleasant experience. Dogs who don't know their P's and Q's do things like jump up on you and nearly knock you down, stare at you and drool when you are eating, bark incessantly at every person and animal they lay their eyes on, and even, in some cases, go so far as to bite you—or at least threaten to.

You will want to make sure your Labrador Retriever is not guilty of these offenses, so he is liked and welcomed by your family and friends. To ensure this, you'll need to teach your Lab how he's supposed to behave in human society. Remember, if you don't show him, no one will!

Your Lab is never too young to learn to mind his manners. Start teaching him these lessons as soon as he comes to live with you. You will probably have to work with your Lab on these rules for much of his first year since it can take that long for a Lab to fully mature and gain control of his impulses. Keep in mind that, with patience and perseverance, your Lab will become a wonderful, well-behaved dog.

Mustn't Bite

Dogs who bite go beyond the definition of annoying. Biting is a dangerous and serious behavior that can hurt and traumatize people, and even result in you being sued or your dog being confiscated by the authorities.

The time to teach your Lab never to bite is when he is a young puppy.

Puppies are mouthy little creatures; they are always biting each other in play. But, if you allow it, your Lab puppy will start to take your hand in his mouth, too, and will sink those sharp puppy teeth into your skin. Not only does this hurt, but it also sets a bad precedent by teaching your puppy that it's okay to bite people.

Instead of permitting your puppy to gnaw on your hand (or any other part of your body), you must correct him every time he tries. Whenever he takes your hand in his mouth, tell him "No bite!" in a sharp tone and then refuse to play with him for at least several minutes. Do this each and every time he gets mouthy with you so he learns this behavior is not okay.

If your Lab is already an adult, you can still teach him that it's not okay

Puppies must be taught from a young age never to mouth or bite humans.

to bite people, even in play. Give him the same sharp reprimand of "No bite!" whenever he gets mouthy and refuse to give him any attention for several minutes afterwards.

Dogs that bite or threaten to bite out of aggression have a serious problem that must be dealt with immediately. Contact a professional dog trainer right away for help if your dog bites you or a member of your family, or acts as if he might.

Mustn't Jump Up

When a dog as big as a Labrador Retriever jumps up on you, you know it. The sheer force of 60-plus pounds hurled at your chest is unmistakable. This habit is irritating enough if you are a strong, healthy adult, but if you are a child or elderly person, being jumped on by a Labrador Retriever is downright dangerous. That's why it's important to teach your Lab from the very beginning that it's *not* okay to jump up on people.

For most people, the hardest thing about teaching a Lab not to jump is the guilt. After all, your dog is happy to see you—or whoever—and is trying to show his enthusiasm. But what your dog doesn't understand is that he can hurt people, or at the very least annoy the heck out of them with his jumping. He'll make more friends in life if he's the type to sit and wait for attention instead of demanding it by throwing his body at every human he meets.

The key to teaching your Lab not to jump up on people is to teach him to do something else instead. The best alternative to jumping up is to sit politely, inviting a friendly pat or word. First teach your dog to sit on command. You can then work on teaching him to sit instead of jumping up when he greets someone.

Teaching your Lab not to jump up requires you to establish a training period of a few weeks. Set up times when your Lab will wear his collar and be loose in the house so he can greet you freely when you come through the door. Make sure you have nothing in your hands during these moments so you will exert control over the situation.

When your Lab jumps up on you as you walk through the door, grab his collar and say "No jump!" as you push him down. Command him to sit and hold him there, praising him for keeping his rump on the floor.

Using this technique, your Lab will eventually learn he's not allowed to jump up on you. But, in order for him to learn that he can't jump up on other people, too, he will need to receive the same lessons from the rest of your family members. Each person should practice teaching him "No jump!" until he learns that every person in the family is off limits.

Of course being the friendly and boisterous dog that he is, your Lab will probably still want to jump up on guests that visit your home. When you know company is coming over, put a leash on your dog and tell him to sit as the guests enter. Ask your visitors to refrain from petting your dog or paying any attention to him at all unless he is sitting calmly in front of them. If he tries to jump up on your company, tell him "No jump!" as you pull him back with the leash. Do this consistently with the help of your visitors and your Lab will eventually get the message.

Mustn't Bark Excessively

When it comes to barking, Labs do their fair share. While not known for being ferocious guard dogs, Labs will sound the alarm if they think a possible intruder is afoot. The problem arises when your Lab starts to see certain people and animals as unwelcome individuals in or near his territory, and begins barking his brains out and driving you and your neighbors crazy.

Most people like it when their dog barks to let them know a stranger is approaching the house. What people don't like, however, is when their dog barks incessantly for 10 minutes and refuses to shut up, or spends half an hour yapping insanely because a squirrel is sitting on the front lawn.

Teaching a dog when it's okay to bark and when it isn't is tricky. The good news is Labs are smart dogs that are quite capable of understanding the difference between "appropriate barking" versus "excessive barking," as long as you teach them.

You want your Lab to understand that it's okay for him to bark a few times when a stranger is on your property, but that he must stop once he has alerted you.

The way to help your dog comprehend the nuances of the right amount of barking, enlist the help of a friend. Ask your helper to come to your front door and knock or ring the bell. When your dog hears someone approaching the house, or at the sound of the knock or door bell, he will start barking. Grasp him by the collar and say his name and then the command "Quiet!" If he stops barking, praise him with pats and happy words. If he ignores you and continues to bark, close his mouth by putting your hand around his muzzle and tell him "Quiet!" once again. When he stops barking, tell him what a good dog he is.

You and your helper will need to practice this numerous times over several days before your Lab gets the point. Since Labs are so trainable, you probably won't have to do more than this to get your dog to quit his excessive barking. If he doesn't respond, however, you must use a more forceful technique.

Fill a squirt gun or spray bottle with water. Have a helper knock on the door or ring the doorbell, and repeat the action of grabbing your dog's collar and closing his muzzle as you tell him to be quiet. If he stops barking, tell him he's a good dog. If he ignores you and continues to bark, squirt him on the neck with the water. The spritz will most likely distract your dog, and he'll probably stop barking. As soon as he shuts up, tell him he's a good dog so he gets the idea.

This same training technique will work in your front or backyard too.

Have friends and neighbors "set up" your dog by walking past your yard. Teach your dog the meaning of "Quiet!" using the same methods as you did indoors.

Keep in mind that these techniques for eliminating excessive barking are only useful in a situation where your Lab is barking to alert you to the presence of strangers. If your dog is barking incessantly because he is suffering from separation anxiety, boredom or loneliness as a result of long periods of isolation, you will not be able to train him to stop barking. Instead, address the cause of the problem as outlined in Chapter 5.

Dogs who are rewarded for begging soon develop pleading for food as a habit.

Mustn't Beg

It's hard to find a dog anywhere who doesn't beg for food. The act of begging is probably what brought humans and dogs together in the first place, so it's not surprising to discover nearly every dog has this instinct.

As old as the tradition of begging may be for the domestic dog, it's a behavior you would be wise to discourage in your Lab. Begging dogs are displeasing to most people, particularly guests. Some dogs even go so far as to turn from beggars to outright thieves, snatching food from the hands of children and getting incredibly bossy about partaking in human meals. Also, given the fact that too many table scraps can lead to obesity in your dog, there really is no reason to permit your Lab to beg for human food.

You can begin your Lab's training in "no begging" by never, ever feeding him from the table or giving him a nibble of what you are eating. If you want to give him a treat of people food now and then, place it in his bowl after your finished eating instead of feeding it to him directly from your hand. This will help prevent him from getting into the habit of begging. He will undoubtedly give begging a try now and then just to see if he can get away with it, but if you never give in, he will eventually give up.

If you've already allowed your Lab to develop the habit of begging at the dinner table or whenever people are eating, you can work on training him to stop. Before you can do this, however, you must teach your dog the basic obedience commands of down and stay. When he is very reliable at performing these exercises, you can start training him not to beg.

As you prepare to sit down to a meal or have a snack on the couch, take your Lab by the collar and walk him to a corner of the room. Tell him "Down! Stay!" and then walk away from him and begin your meal. If he gets up and begins to walk toward you, go back over to him, take him by the collar, and walk him back to his corner. Again, give him the "Down! Stay!" command and return to your meal. You may need to do this several times during each meal to keep your dog from begging, but if you do it consistently and never allow him to beg or break the down-stay, your Lab will eventually get the message.

Learning about your Lab can be fun and educational.

Chapter Five

Understanding Your Lab

You and your Lab will spend a significant amount of time together over the next decade or so. Evenings, weekends and whatever other free time you can find is time you can, and should, spend with your dog.

Given all this togetherness, its imperative you understand the way your dog looks at the world and perceives his surroundings. Without this knowledge, you will not understand why your dog acts like he does, and how to change certain behaviors, if need be. You also cannot effectively communicate with your Lab without a basic understanding of his special canine language.

Learning the language of the Lab is not only important to your relationship with your dog, it's also loads of fun. You will find the feeling you get when you successfully communicate with a member of another species—namely, your dog— immensely rewarding.

How Your Dog Sees the World

Canines and humans have a couple of very important things in common. Both species are mammals, which means both nurse and care for their young until the babies are old enough to take care of themselves. Also, both canines and humans are genetically programmed to live in complex social groups, with distinct hierarchies and strong emotional attachments.

The social bonding that both humans and canines crave makes the two species compatible. It's the sociable nature in dogs and people that draws these two creatures together.

The Pack

When it comes to sociability, humans are very complex. We live in villages and neighborhoods, cities and towns, states and countries, all elaborate places we call home. It is here that each person finds a place to make a living, raise a family and live out our lives.

Canines, on the other hand, do things a bit differently. Instead of living in cities and countries, many canines—including wolves, the ancestors of today's domestic dogs—live in packs. Each pack operates with a leader and a social order among the members that determines the pecking order within the group.

The domestic dog—namely, your Lab—inherited this basic need for pack life from his wolf ancestors. But since dogs don't live in the wild like wolves do, and instead share their existence with humans, this pack perspective is extended to the dog's human family.

What all this means, essentially, is your Lab thinks of your family as his pack, with a leader and subordinate members. It's important your Lab see *you* and all other humans in the group as above him in rank. Not only will this ensure that the Lab will follow your commands and respect your authority, but it will also give him the kind of environment he needs to feel emotionally secure.

Becoming Alpha

So now that you know being the leader—or alpha member—in your Lab's eyes is of the utmost importance, how do you go about achieving this position of importance?

The answer lies in training. If you start your relationship with your Lab with basic training exercises, like sit,

down, come and stay, you will help establish yourself as the leader with your dog.

Since packs consist of other members besides the leader, each with their own dominant or subordinate position, other members of your family can also use training to help your Lab see them as higher up in the social order. While your Lab will probably identify only one of you as the ultimate alpha, he will see other members of the family as above him in rank and will follow their commands and respect their authority in all or most situations.

Labs tend to be submissive dogs who are more than willing to accept the leadership of their human companions without a challenge. However, if you fail to convince your Lab that you are in charge, and your Lab has a dominant personality, you may find yourself with a dog who growls when you try to move him from your favorite chair, steals food from your hand while you watching TV, or simply ignores you when you give him a command.

If your Lab has a submissive personality and feels a void in the area of human leadership, he could possibly become a cowering ball of insecurity with problems like separation anxiety, submissive urination and other difficult behaviors.

If you follow the instructions in Chapter 4 for obedience training your dog, and consistently reinforce your dog's training throughout his life, you should have no problem with your dog seeing you as alpha. If for some reason your dog challenges you and tries to take over the role of alpha himself, contact a dog trainer for help before the situation gets out of hand.

Communicating With Your Lab

Dogs are amazingly intelligent animals and are capable of learning the meaning of 300 or more human words. Commands like "Sit" and "Stay" are only a small portion of the human vocabulary you can teach your dog. In fact, you won't have to consciously teach your dog most of

Training your dog is a good way of helping him see you as alpha.

these words—simple habits like saying "Do you want to go for a walk?" just before taking your dog out for a romp in the neighborhood will help him pick up on the meaning of the phrase without much effort.

While you will find teaching your dog simple words and phrases relatively easy, showing your dog exactly what you want and when you want it can be a little trickier.

Likewise, learning to decipher exactly what your Lab wants *you* to know will also take some schooling in the art of canine communication.

Canine Body Language

While dogs have vocal chords they use them to get certain messages across, they primarily use body language to communicate with each other and their human friends.

Likewise, dogs are incredibly astute at reading the body language of other dogs, and even that of humans. Given the dog's reliance on this form of communication, it behooves all dog-loving humans to learn to understand the nuances of this subtle canine vernacular.

Submissiveness: One of the first forms of body language you will notice in your Labrador Retriever is that of submissiveness. Dogs often use this body language when they greet owners or friends. Some dogs also express submissiveness when they meet other dogs.

A submissive dog will put his ears back flat against his head. He will crouch down and show a "smiling" expression on his face. His tail will hang down, possibly tucked between his legs, and probably be wagging. A submissive dog will sometimes lie down on his back with his feet in the air and his ears flat against his head. He may even urinate.

When your Lab demonstrates a submissive posture, he is basically saying "Okay, you are in charge. I defer to your authority." This is good to see in your Lab because it shows that he considers you his leader.

In extreme cases of submission brought on by fear, a dog may cower and urinate as a way of trying to avoid the aggression he anticipates from another dog or a dominant human. Dogs lacking in confidence or those that have been severely abused will demonstrate this level of submissive fear. If your Lab shows this kind of behavior, get advice from a dog trainer on how to help your dog become less fearful.

Dominance: The flip side of submissive posturing is a dominant stance. A dog expressing dominance will stand tall with a raised head and a high tail. The dog's ears will move forward and he will look directly into the eyes of whoever he is feeling dominant over, whether it's a human or another dog.

A dog may also mount the dog—or leg of the human—he is trying to convince of his dominant position. While the behavior of mounting is usually thought of as a sexual maneuver, it is also commonly used by dogs who want to express dominance. This is why female dogs or

neutered males with dominant tendencies will often mount other dogs, much to their owner's surprise.

Another less subtle way of showing dominance among dogs is growling and snapping. In order to send the message of "This object is mine" or "I'm not getting out of the way," a dog will emit a throaty growl or clack his jaws together as the precursor to a bite.

If your Lab greets or approaches anyone in your family with a dominant posture, or tries mounting this person, you may want that family member to practice obedience commands with your dog so he gets the message that this person is dominant over him, and not vice versa. If your Lab resorts to growling or snapping at anyone, seek the help of a dog trainer right away. Aggression is a very serious problem that demands the services of a professional.

Aggression: While growling and snapping are often a sign of dominance in many dogs, other kinds of aggressive behavior can result from intense fear or territoriality.

Fear Biting

Dogs who are extremely frightened may sometimes show aggression such as a snapping, snarling and biting. Dogs who become aggressive out of fear are called "fear biters" and try to defend themselves from a perceived enemy. Dogs who exhibit this behavior were often not well-socialized as puppies, were poorly bred or were abused by a human being. You can tell fear aggression from dominance aggression because fear aggression is usually accompanied by a cowering posture and tucked tail.

Aggression from fear is a very serious problem and one you should not take lightly. If you suspect your dog is a fear biter, contact a dog trainer immediately.

Territoriality

Territorial aggression is unmistakable, and something that nearly everyone has witnessed in a dog at one point or another. Dogs who are territorially aggressive will bark and snarl at whoever they perceive as an intruder on their property. This kind of behavior is usually reserved for postal carriers, delivery persons and other strangers who get too close to the dog's home or yard.

Although Labs love tug of war, this is a bad game to play as it encourages aggressiveness.

Labs are not typically very territorial dogs, although they will bark at strangers who come to the door or approach the backyard. It's not long before these same territorial defenders will kiss the face of the "intruder" once the dog realizes the stranger is friend and not foe. However, don't take chances with people's safety. If your Lab behaves territorially toward someone, isolate your dog until he is calm, or keep him away from the stranger completely to make sure that no one gets bitten. Be sure to reprimand your dog with a firm "No!" if he continues to behave aggressively toward a stranger even after you have accepted this person willingly into your home.

Playfulness

Labs are big clowns, and it shouldn't take long before you see your dog demonstrating his special message for "Let's play!"

The most common way that dogs tell other dogs and humans they want to play is with the "play bow." This form of canine body language consists of the dog dropping his front end to the ground while his back end sticks high in the air. His tail will be wagging furiously, and you may hear a high-pitched bark.

Another way that some dogs send out an invitation to play is by bumping their rear ends against the legs or body of the person or dog. As the dog squats in a sitting position, he repeatedly thumps his rump against his desired playmate in the hopes of engaging a game of tag or fetch.

Games *Not* to Play
With Your Lab

The following games can encourage aggressive or disobedient behavior, and so shouldn't be played:

• Chasing
• Tug of war
• Biting
• Wrestling

Speaking to Your Dog

Now that you understand the signals your Lab sends to you and other dogs, how can you best communicate with your dog so he will understand you?

Because dogs rely so much on body language for communication within their own species, they are also very adapt at judging the subtle visual cues that humans put forth subconsciously. Your dog will inherently know when you are happy, or sad, angry, or delighted, from the expressions on your face, the sound of your voice and the way you hold your body.

Helping your dog understand the specifics of what you want from him requires conscious thought, however. The act of training your dog calls for a basic understanding of how dogs—and other mammals—learn.

In Chapter 4, you discovered how to teach your Labrador Retriever the commands he must know in order to function well in your family and in human society. It's also crucial to

know what motivates a Lab to learn.

Labs are born wanting to please their human companions, which is one of the reasons why they are such popular dogs. Once your Lab knows that all he needs to do is obey your commands in order to please you, he'll bend over backwards to do so at every opportunity.

Another great motivator for Labs is food. Most dogs will do just about anything for a treat, and Labs are no exception. Young dogs in particular are the most likely candidates for using food rewards, at least in the beginning of their training, since their attention spans can be rather short.

Whether you use praise or food as a reward when teaching your Lab, remember that consistency and practice yield the best results. Labs are fast learners, and if you are a good teacher, you'll be amazed how quickly your dog catches on.

Problem Behaviors

Labs are fun, easygoing dogs, but they can still develop problem behaviors. These problems are usually the result of poor socialization when the dog was young, improper care from an unknowing owner or personality quirks with which the dog was born.

The vast majority of adult dogs surrendered to animal shelters across the country are turned in because of behavioral problems. Many people don't have the knowledge or desire to help uncover what is causing their dog to misbehave. It's often easier to get rid of the dog than to figure out what is causing the problem and solve it.

The Lab, however, is a very malleable dog who deserves a chance to overcome any behavioral problem he may have developed (the only exception to this might be aggression, where human safety is at stake).

Several of the most common behavior problems seen in dogs in general are also seen in Labs. Some are simply mere annoyances. Others are serious problems that jeopardize the Lab's place within his human family. Each problem comes with a symptom, a cause and a cure. Try to solve your Lab's behavior problem yourself using these suggestions. If you are unsuccessful, contact a professional dog trainer for help.

Nuisance Barking

While dogs mostly communicate with body language, they also discovered that barking is an effective communications tool. Dogs bark when they feel happy, lonely, protective, and bored.

Barking isn't normally a problem in and of itself, unless the dog gets carried away and won't stop, driving you, your family and your neighbors to distraction. When barking becomes excessive, it is known as nuisance barking, and requires measures to get the problem in check.

The first thing you need to do is to consider when your dog barks excessively. Does he bark only when you leave him out in the backyard alone? Does he bark non-stop after you leave the house? Does he bark whenever someone comes to the front door? Does he go crazy barking when school lets out and kids start walking past your house on their way home?

The Lonely Bark: If your dog is barking excessively when he's home alone, he is most likely carrying on because he is lonely, anxious and bored. If he barks when people approach your house and walk past on the sidewalk, he is barking out of protectiveness. Either way, you have a problem on your hands that you need to solve.

Labs are very sociable dogs and need plenty of companionship. Spend as much time as you can with your dog to avoid behavioral problems.

Dogs who bark when they are left alone are having trouble handling the isolation that often comes with being a domestic dog in today's modern world. Because dogs are highly social pack animals, they have an intrinsic need for companionship. Spending hours all alone can make a dog anxious, lonely and bored. The result is an annoying and repetitive bark that basically says "Hey! I'm anxious, bored and lonely! Someone pay attention to me!"

In the case of dogs with severe separation anxiety, barking will also be accompanied by destructiveness. If you come home to find your neighbors complaining and your furniture destroyed, you can bet you have a dog with separation anxiety.

Because it's not practical for you to quit your job and stay home to keep your barking Lab company so he'll shut up, there are other things you should try to help thwart his barking:

Exercise. A tired dog is a good dog, generally speaking, so giving your dog a good workout before you leave for work in the morning can do wonders to tire him out. He'll spend a few hours snoozing away after you've taken him out for a morning run or game of catch, and will have less time and inclination to bark.

Companionship. Since loneliness and separation anxiety are common causes for nuisance barking, one way to help deal with the problem is to provide your dog with some companionship to help ease his feelings of isolation. You can do this in a few different ways. Try hiring a dog walker or pet sitter to come to your house once or twice during the day to visit with your dog, play with him and take him out for a walk. Not only will the visit help him feel less lonely, but it will also provide him with some exercise to make him feel better.

Another solution is to take advantage of one of the new doggy day care centers springing up all around the country. These day care centers for dogs provide your Lab with exercise and the companionship of humans and other dogs to help ease your pet's loneliness.

You may also want to consider adding another dog to your household to help keep your lonely Lab company. However, don't run out and get another dog just as a companion for your first dog. A second dog means added responsibility and expense, and you must really want to have two dogs in your life before you go out and get another one.

Mind Game. For dogs who bark out of sheer boredom when left alone, a toy or puzzle that will keep them busy for hours can help. One favorite trick is to get a thick, hallowed-out bone and fill it with cheese spread or peanut butter. It will take your dog hours to get all of the filling out of the inside of the bone, and the time he spends doing this will be less time he can spend barking. You can also give your vocal friend a sturdy chew toy or a hollow rubber toy filled with cheese or peanut butter that he can work on for hours while you are gone.

The Territorial Bark: When a dog is barking to protect his property, it's pretty obvious. Territorial dogs run along fence lines or charge at barriers when a perceived intruder approaches. These dogs will usually not stop barking until they "chase away" the intruder. Since the alleged intruder is usually just someone walking by on the street, the dog is convinced his barking was effective because the intruder always ends up leaving.

Another type of territorial barking occurs inside the house, when you are at home or when you're away. The well-meaning but misguided territorial barker will sound off when anyone approaches the front door, and often won't quiet down even when his owner asks him too. These dogs are convinced they must drive away whomever delivers the mail, tends to the landscaping, tosses the daily newspaper, or rings the doorbell.

When you're home. If your Lab goes crazy barking whenever anyone approaches your house, you will need to work with him to teach him that such carrying on is not appropriate. Start with a simple command of "Quiet!" whenever he starts barking at the doorbell or postal carrier. Most Labs will learn quickly that you don't want them to wake up the neighborhood every time someone comes to the door.

If your Lab needs a little more persuading, try distracting him and correcting him at the same time whenever he starts barking. You can accomplish this with the help of a squirt gun filled with water. Keep it handy, and when your dog starts barking furiously at the postal carrier or the newspaper delivery person, tell him to stop. If he ignores you, squirt him to startle him. Do this consistently every time he starts barking inappropriately, and he will soon get the message. (See Chapter 4 for more details on training your dog not to bark at visitors.)

It will also help to keep your dog well-exercised at all times, especially when you are going to be gone for the day. If your dog is tired out, he'll have less motivation to bark furiously at everyone who walks by your house.

When you're not home. If your Lab is a territorial barker and does most of his dirty work when you are not home, you face a tougher problem. Your first plan of action is to eliminate some of the stimuli that gets your dog barking when you aren't around. Close your blinds and curtains during the day so your Lab can't easily see what's going on outside your house. Or, try keeping him in a part of your home where he is less likely to hear the comings and goings of the entire neighborhood. If he does his barking outside in the backyard, keep him confined inside the house when you're not home.

If it's noise that triggers your dog's barking attacks—such as another dog in the neighborhood who is also barking all day—try drowning out the sound. Do this by playing a white noise machine, or a radio or television. Your dog has very sensitive hearing and will probably still hear things outside that will trigger his urge to bark, but he'll be less likely to go on a barking rampage if outside sounds are diluted by a noise machine or a TV or radio.

Persistent barkers who won't quit their carrying on even after you try these methods are candidates for an anti-barking citronella collar. These collars are designed to squirt harmless but distasteful citronella into the air every time the dog starts barking. Because the dog soon learns his barking results in stinky citronella being released from the collar, he will eventually stop. Using citronella collars properly can be difficult at first, so contact a dog trainer for help when you first attempt this.

Destructive Behavior

A woman once left her Lab alone in the car for 10 minutes while she went into the grocery store to pick up a few things. When she returned, she found that her dog had torn apart all of the leather upholstery in her car. What would possess a dog to do such a crazy thing? And how could an owner ever forgive such behavior?

Dogs who behave destructively usually do so when they are left alone, and for good reason. Separation anxiety is not just a problem that plagues toddlers left alone by their mothers with babysitters—it's also a phenomenon seen in dogs who are incapable of being left alone without going wild with fear.

Dogs who suffer from separation anxiety express their terror at perceived abandonment by chewing, pawing, digging, ripping and tearing at whatever they can find around them. These dogs also tend to bark, whine and howl in an effort to get their owners to come back.

Dogs suffer from different degrees of separation anxiety. Some will only bark and howl all day while others will tear their surroundings apart. Others will simply find one object to chew on until they've turned it into dust, while another will dig a hole in the backyard the size of the Lincoln Tunnel. Whatever method of expression your dog chooses, the message is the same: "I become terrified when you leave me alone."

Separation anxiety is a serious problem for many dogs, and often results in a self-fulfilling prophecy for the pet: the dog becomes so destructive at the prospect of abandonment by his owner that the owner ends up surrendering the dog at the pound. It's a tragic situation that doesn't have to end that way as long as the dog's owner is willing to make the effort to help the dog solve his problem.

If you own a Labrador Retriever who behaves destructively when you are not home, chances are your dog is suffering from separation anxiety. You can try the following methods to help your dog get over this problem:

Obedience training. Dogs who suffer from separation anxiety are generally insecure, nervous pets who lack confidence in themselves and

When left to their own devices, Labs are capable of getting into all sorts of trouble.

their surroundings. Formal obedience training can do wonders for these dogs because it helps them feel more secure in their place within the family pack, and gives them an outlet for their energy. Enrolling your dog in obedience classes and practicing obedience routines with him at home will make him more confident and less likely to freak out when left home alone.

Crate him. Dogs who are insecure when left alone often feel better if they are confined during their owner's absence. Try crating your dog before you leave the house, giving him a chew toy to gnaw on while you are gone. It's a good idea to exercise him first to help tire him out and give him a chance to relieve himself. (Make sure your dog is properly crate-trained before you do this. See Chapter 3 for instructions on crate training.)

More exercise. Before you leave your house for an extended period of time, take your dog out for a run or a game of ball in the yard or park. Exercise is a good way to keep anxiety at bay, and if your dog is tired when you leave, he'll be less likely to freak out when your gone.

Distract him. The worst part of separation anxiety for your dog is the time immediately after you leave. Try giving him a favorite chew toy or a hollow rubber toy filled with cheese or peanut butter as a distraction. If your dog is concentrating on the toy for the first few minutes after you walk out the door, he may successfully get past the worst part of his anxiety.

Companionship. Dogs who suffer from separation anxiety can't handle being left alone for long periods of time. Hire a petsitter, dog walker or neighbor to come in and visit with your dog a couple of times a day when you are gone. Or, take your dog to a doggy day care center and leave him there while you work. He'll find plenty of companionship in both human and canine form at these facilities.

When you are home, try to spend as much time as you can with your dog. Let him sleep in the bedroom with you at night, and spend every possible waking minute that you can with him. Remember that dogs are pack animals who feel terrible loneliness and isolation when kept away from the family they love. Help your dog get as much quality time with you as he possibly can.

If you are away from home a lot and your dog is forced to spend considerable time on his own, you may want to think about getting a second dog to keep him company. Don't do this, however, unless you are willing to take on the added responsibilities that owning a second dog will bring.

Practice coming and going. Dogs are quick to recognize the signs of an owner about to leave the house. When you pick up your keys, put on your jacket or grab your purse, your dog knows he will soon be all alone.

If your Lab suffers from separation anxiety, these signs will cause him to start getting emotionally worked up. You can help desensitize him to such triggers by practicing leaving for very short periods of time after going through your usual parting ritual. For example, pick up your keys, put on your jacket, and walk out the door as usual. But instead of being gone for six hours, come back into the house after a minute or two. Do this repeatedly through the day for several weeks, gradually increasing the amount of time you are gone, and

your dog will discover he can actually survive without you for awhile.

Another important aspect of changing your dog's view of your departure is to minimize the importance of comings and goings. Don't make a big fuss over your dog before you leave the house, or when you return. Instead of hugging him and kissing him and saying "Mommy will be back soon, I promise!" act like leaving is no big deal.

The same should apply to coming home. Don't carry on like you haven't seen your dog in a week. Simply walk into the house as nonchalantly as you can, and don't pay attention to your dog right away. If your dog is crated or confined, don't let him out immediately. Instead, putter around the house for a few minutes before acknowledging him. You'll feel like a meanie ignoring those whines of joy

Chewing is a natural behavior for puppies, and must be directed to appropriate objects like chew toys.

and that frantically wagging tail, but just remind yourself that you are doing this for your dog's own good!

If the above methods don't work to help your dog recover from his separation anxiety, seek the help of a professional dog trainer or certified animal behaviorist. In severe cases, behavior modification along with certain medications administered by a veterinarian can help dogs learn to cope with separation anxiety.

Natural Behaviors

The follow antics, while natural to Labs, cause trouble for humans if not controlled:

• Digging
• Begging
• Barking
• Jumping Up
• Play-biting
• Chewing

Digging

Digging is one of those inherent canine activities that all breeds tend to share. While Labs don't like to dig as much as terriers do, they nonetheless can dig big holes in their owners' gardens when the mood strikes them.

Labs dig up backyards for different reasons: they smell or hear a rodent living underground; they want to create a cool place to lie down on a hot day; they saw you doing it when you were planting the garden and it looked like fun; or it's something to do when they feel bored.

Problem diggers are those dogs who get these urges often—namely, every time they feel soft dirt under their toes. These dogs make their owners' backyards look like mine fields and drive their human companions crazy.

If you have a Lab who loves to dig, you can try a few things to control this destructive habit:

More exercise. If your Lab does most of his digging when he's alone, make a point of giving him lots of exercise before you leave the house for extended periods of time. If you wear him out before you leave, he'll have less energy to dig up the garden.

Correct him. Whenever you catch your dog digging, give him a firm reprimand of "No!" This lets him know this activity is not okay. As soon as he stops digging, hand him a toy or toss a ball to him to get him into the habit of using his energy in a constructive way.

Cool him off. If your Lab does most of his digging on hot days, give him a child's wading pool filled with water so he use this to cool off instead. Since Labs love water, he will probably prefer this to lying in the dirt. Also, make sure he has access to plenty of shade and cool water to drink.

Give him his own spot. If all else fails and you can't convince your dog to stop digging, create a place in your yard where your dog can dig to his heart's content without causing a problem. Protect the rest of your garden by placing bricks on the areas where he repeatedly digs, and put wire fencing around your plants and other areas. Meanwhile, encourage him to dig in the spot you designated for this activity. When you catch him trying to dig elsewhere, take him to his designated spot and say "Dig here!" until he catches on. Eventually, when he gets into the habit of digging in his allowed spot only, you can slowly remove the protection you placed around other parts of the yard.

Chewing

Unlike dogs who gnaw on everything in their wake because of separation anxiety (see previous section in this chapter), chronic chewers enjoy the feeling of their teeth sinking into new and strange objects. Most problem chewers are young dogs who will gnaw on whatever they can regardless of whether you are home or not. While dogs who chew because they are anxious will usually only do so when left alone, chronic chewers will chomp on whatever they can get even if you are sitting in the same room.

Chewing is a bigger problem in young dogs than older dogs because much of it is related to teething, which can last until about 10 months of age. Puppies and young adult Labs enjoy the sensation of chewing against their budding choppers, and will find whatever they can to gnaw on. Chewing is also a great way to release pent-up energy.

Don't try to stop your dog from chewing entirely—not that you should attempt to since this is a very natural and healthy behavior. The trick is to get your dog to chew on appropriate materials only instead of things like your best shoes and your oriental rug. The following methods can help give your Lab the right idea.

Provide chew toys. Your Lab will most likely chew on whatever is in his reach. If you provide him with a variety of chew toys to exercise his teeth, he'll probably not need to find his own items to gnaw on. Some favorite dog chew toys include rope toys, nylon chews, pigs ears, and bones. (If you opt to give your dog bones, make sure they are thick and won't splinter when he chews them.)

You will probably need to experiment to find the chew toys your dog likes best. Once you discover his preferences, keep those types of toys in tall supply.

Hide stuff. If your dog likes to chew on your leather shoes, your kids' toys and your hardcover books, keep these items well out of his reach. Remember, dogs will chew on whatever is convenient. If these items are left lying around, chances are he's going to sample them.

Don't make the mistake of giving your Lab an old shoe to gnaw on and then expect him to know the difference between this item and your new slip-ons. *All* shoes should be off-limits, and only designated dog toys should be allowed in his mouth.

Discourage bad chewing. Whenever you catch your dog chewing something he shouldn't, reprimand him with a firm "No!" and then hand him an appropriate chew toy instead. When he starts working on this new item, tell him he's a good dog so he gets the message.

If your dog chews on items like the area rug, your table leg or a corner of the wall, spray some perfume, after shave or bitter apple or orange on the spot to discourage his interest.

Soiling the House

Because Labrador Retrievers are such trainable dogs, problems with house soiling are not very common in the breed. Once a Lab learns he must go to the bathroom outdoors, he consistently does so unless a problem occurs.

If your Lab is soiling the house, consider the following possibilities:

Poor health. Your dog may suffer from a medical problem. House soiling in normally housetrained dogs is a sure sign of illness. Take your dog to the veterinarian immediately.

Too long indoors. While most Labs make heroic efforts to hold their feces and urine in for as long as they can, only so much is physically possible. If you are gone for long periods of time and you come home to find that your dog had an accident in the house, you are probably asking him to hold it for too long. Don't feed him immediately before you leave the house. Instead, allow him a couple of hours after eating to eliminate. Take him outside just before you leave to give him a chance to go. If you still find an occasional accident in your home, consider the possibility that your dog simply can't hold it in for too long. Four to six hours is usually the most a dog can comfortably refrain from going to the bathroom, but, depending on how much he's

eaten or drank that day, even that amount of time may be too long. This is especially true of older dogs and young puppies, both of whom find it more difficult to hold their bowels and bladders than do middle-aged dogs.

Aggression

Since Labs are happy and easy-going, it's unlikely you will have a problem with aggression with your dog, especially toward humans. If you do find your dog starting to behave in an aggressive manner, whether it's with you, your family or friends and strangers, you have a serious problem you will need to address right away.

Aggression towards other dogs is not a pleasant canine personality trait to handle, but the fact of the matter is that many dominant dogs behave aggressively toward other members of their species. If your dog wants to tear apart every dog he sees in the neighborhood, make sure you keep your dog properly restrained at all times for the protection of other dogs.

When it comes to aggression toward humans, a dominant canine personality combined with a lack of appropriate training is usually the culprit. In some cases, aggression is the consequence of a temperament defect caused by poor breeding. Whatever the source of your dog's aggression, it is a serious problem that you need to solve right away with the help of a professional trainer.

To avoid having to deal with this dangerous behavioral problem, take your dog to obedience classes so

Aggression toward humans should never be tolerated, and requires the help of a professional trainer.

you can establish a leadership position in your dog's mind. Most aggression problems result when the dog thinks he's the one in charge and then starts bossing everyone around. You can prevent this from ever entering his mind by making yourself the top dog in the relationship through obedience training.

Most canine aggression problems start slowly and progressively worsen. Recognize the early warning signs of aggression and seek help immediately if you see your dog do any of the following:

Growling. If your dog growls at you or anyone in your family under any circumstances, you have an aggression problem on your hands. If your dog has a dominant personality type and hasn't accepted your authority as pack leader, he will growl when you do things like take a toy away from him, lift his food bowl up off the floor, or move him from your favorite chair. The growl is his way of telling you to back off. Don't wait for his growl to turn into overt aggression. Contact a dog trainer immediately for help.

Snarling. If the growl is a warning to get away, the snarl is definitely one precursor to a bite. When a dog snarls, it curls its lips and bares its teeth to show you that if you don't back off soon, he'll bite you. If your Lab ever snarls at you, get help from a dog trainer right away.

Biting. The most obvious sign of aggression in dogs is biting. Don't tolerate any amount of biting, even in play. Dogs must learn from a young age that their teeth should never come into contact with human flesh.

If your dog bites anyone in your family out of aggression, you have a grave problem with your dog and one that needs the help of a professional trainer. If your dog bites a friend or stranger, you will most likely have to deal with the authorities, since many local government statutes require that dog bites be reported. Your dog may be taken away from you and even euthanized if officials determine the dog is truly dangerous. Do not let an aggression problem escalate to this level. Contact a trainer immediately if your dog shows any signs of aggression. (Be sure not to react by striking your dog in any way, since this can increase the aggression.)

Jumping Up

If there is one bad behavior that Labs are notorious for, it's jumping up on people. Although these dogs are well-meaning and only jump up to get closer to you, such behavior is still unacceptable. Not only is the act of jumping up annoying, but Labs are big enough to easily knock over a child or elderly person unintentionally. They can also mess up your clothes when they jump up and put their dirty paws on you.

Labs instinctively want to jump up on people, so you'll need to work hard with your dog to teach him this is unacceptable behavior. Even young puppies start jumping up as soon as they get the hang of it.

The most important aspect to teaching a Lab not to jump up is consistentcy. Do not allow your dog to jump up on you even when he is a tiny puppy weighing only a few pounds. If you do, your dog will grow up thinking it's okay to do this, and you'll have a hard time breaking him of this habit once he's older. Also, don't allow him to jump up sometimes and not others. If he's not allowed to jump up, he is *never* allowed to jump up—period.

To teach your dog not to jump up, start by reprimanding him every time he does it. Say "Off!" in a harsh voice and push him away from you. Do this repeatedly, and don't pet him until he is sitting. In fact, by teaching him to sit everytime he greets someone, you will find it easier to keep him from jumping up.

It's important that everyone in your family implement this training, not just you. Your Lab won't learn that jumping up is unacceptable if some people allow it while others do not.

If your dog tends to jump up on visitors who come to the house, prepare him for guests by putting him on a leash and correcting him when he starts to jump toward your visitors. Ask your visitors to ignore him until he stops jumping and has his feet on the ground where they belong.

Your Lab should have two best friends—you, and his veterinarian.

Chapter Six

Your Lab's Health

Labrador Retrievers tend to be healthy dogs with relatively few inherited diseases and strong constitutions. The best way to keep your Lab in tip-top shape is to provide your dog with regular preventive care and to watch for any signs of illness. You should also acquaint yourself with the conditions most often seen in Labrador Retrievers so you can recognize a problem if one occurs.

Finding a Veterinarian

When it comes to your Lab's health, your veterinarian is your dog's very best friend. The veterinarian you choose will provide your dog with basic preventative care throughout its life, as well as diagnose any problems your dog may develop. For this reason, you should choose wisely when picking your dog's veterinarian.

If you can, begin your search for a veterinarian before you bring your new Lab home because you will want to have your pet examined right away to determine its general health. (Many breeders recommend that puppies be checked by a veterinarian as soon as they go to a new home to verify the dog is in good health.)

If you purchased your Lab from a breeder who lives near you, ask the breeder for a reference to a veterinarian. Your breeder will know many veterinarians in your area, and will probably give you the best referral.

Another way to find a good veterinarian is to talk to other dog owners. Ask your dog-owning neighbors and the dog owners you meet in the park who provides their dog's health care, and if they are happy with the doctor they are using. Ask them whether or not they can recommend this veterinarian for your dog.

You can also find a veterinarian by looking in your local telephone book, although a personal referral is preferable to this method. If you find a veterinary clinic through the phone book, make sure you thoroughly inspect the clinic to determine the quality of care it provides.

Once you locate a veterinarian you are interested in, pay a visit to the clinic to view the facilities. The reason you should visit the clinic in person is to determine if it is clean and well-organized, and also to make sure the staff and attending veterinarians are accommodating to potential clients.

When you go to the clinic, make a point to talk to the staff. Explain that you are considering their services for your Labrador Retriever, and that you would like a tour of the facilities when the time is convenient. Ask to see the examining rooms and the infirmary where dogs are housed after surgery or in the event of serious illness. If the veterinarian who runs the clinic is available, ask to meet him. (If you already have a dog, take your pet with you and see how the doctor and staff treat this perspective client.)

While you are there, ask an office staff member how many doctors work at the clinic. The upside of a multi-doctor clinic is that the more veterinarians there are, the easier it is to schedule appointments. The downside is that you may not get the same veterinarian twice unless you specifically ask for an appointment with him and are willing to wait for one if necessary.

Also, request a schedule of fees for services like basic examinations, vaccinations and spay/neuter surgery while you are there. You want to make sure the clinic's costs are within your budget even though you realize that expert veterinary care costs money. But, trying to get away too cheaply on your dog's veterinary care can ultimately be penny wise and pound foolish.

Ask if the clinic provides 24-hour emergency care. If not, find out if patients are referred to an emergency hospital in the area. If the clinic refers after-hours emergencies to a different hospital, find out where that hospital is located and visit this facility as well. The staff at both the clinic and the emergency center should be friendly and willing to answer your questions.

When to Call the Veterinarian

Because your Lab can't talk to you to tell you when something is bothering him, it's up to you to recognize the signs of illness in your pet.

You should get to know your dog and learn its normal behavior patterns. If those patterns change—your dog starts eating less, going to the bathroom more frequently or has less energy than usual—it can signal that your dog is not feeling well. If you suspect your dog is sick, make an appointment with your veterinarian right away.

In some cases, your dog may need emergency treatment. If you spot any of the following symptoms in your Lab, take the dog to your veterinarian or emergency clinic *immediately*:

• *Heavy bleeding.* If your dog is injured and bleeding heavily (blood is spurting or oozing strongly) from somewhere on its body, apply pressure to the wound using a gauze or clean cloth to try and stop it. Rush your pet to the veterinarian whether or not you are able to slow down the bleeding.

- *Diarrhea.* If your dog has severe and watery or bloody diarrhea.
- *Abdominal distress.* If your dog is panting, salivating profusely, vomiting, straining to defecate and/or has a distended abdomen.
- *Inability to stand.* If your dog can't or won't stand up.
- *Straining.* If your dog is straining to defecate or urinate.
- *Injury.* If your dog has a wound that is deep or exposes the bone, or if a limb is broken.
- *Refusal to eat.* If your dog has a normally healthy appetite but suddenly won't eat.
- *Labored breathing.* If your dog exhibits rapid or raspy breathing .
- *Fever.* If your dog's rectal temperature is significantly above or below the normal canine body temperature range of 100 degrees Fahrenheit to 102.5 degrees Fahrenheit. You can take your dog's temperature by slowly inserting a human rectal thermometer, coated preferrably with a water-based lubricant, gently into the dog's rectum (don't force it). Don't forget to shake down the thermometer to below 96 degrees before inserting it.
- *Painful eye.* If one or both of your dog's eyes is tearing, partially or completely held shut, or if the dog is pawing at the eye.
- *Severe pain.* If your dog appears to be in great pain in any part of its body.
- *Weight loss.* If your dog experiences a noticeable and unexplained loss of weight in a matter of a day or so.

Preventative Care

All dogs need preventative care to live long, happy lives. Your Labrador Retriever is no exception. Throughout your dog's life, you monitor his general health at home and take him to the veterinarian for periodic health-maintenance when needed.

Good Nutrition

One of the most important steps you can take to keep your Labrador Retriever healthy is to provide him with good nutrition. A dog with a healthy diet is less likely to succumb to disease, and will probably live longer than his poorly-fed counterparts.

Most dog foods today are nutritionally complete, which means that all your dog needs to eat is a regular diet of these foods in order to stay healthy. Knowing which nutritionally complete dog food in particular to feed your Lab can be tricky, however. A variety of brands and types of foods abound in the marketplace, and it's enough to make any dog owner's head spin. With all these products on the market, how can you pick the one best suited for your dog?

Price vs. Quality

One of the first things you'll notice when you start looking at all the different dog foods is that some are much more expensive than others. In your local supermarket, you'll mostly see inexpensive brands commonly advertised on television. In addition to being less costly, such brands are convenient because you can pick them up at the grocery store when you do your regular shopping.

If you go to a pet supply store, however, you will see many more brands a lot higher in price. Some of these names will not be familiar to you because the companies that produce them do not do a lot of advertising. Because most of these foods are not available in your local supermarket, you will have to make a special trip to the pet supply store if you decide to choose one of these brands.

On the surface, it may seem as though choosing the cheapest and most convenient dog food would be the best way to go, given the options. However, there is more to dog food than what meets the eye.

The reason that grocery store brands and premium brands of dog food differ in price is because the type and quality of ingredients included in each type of food differ from one another. If you examine the labels on the dog food packaging, you'll see, for example, that many grocery store brands list vegetable products like ground corn and cereal high up on the ingredients list. The labels on most premium brands will show a higher amount of meat protein in the list of ingredients. The more expensive premium brands will show actual meats in the ingredients, rather than meat meals.

Many premium brands also use natural preservatives and colorings, as opposed to other less expensive brands where chemicals such as the preservative butylate hydroxyanisole (BHA) and food dyes like FD&C Red No. 40 are used. Dog owners concerned about additives to their pets' food often stay away from diets with these chemical dyes and preservatives because tests show these additives cause cancer in laboratory animals.

Because of the higher proteins and quality ingredients present in more expensive dog foods, most veterinarians advise clients to feed premium dog foods to their pets, despite claims from some manufacturers of less expensive dog foods that both types of food carry the same nutritional value.

Good nutrition is probably the most important aspect to keeping your Lab healthy.

When it comes to which type of food you should feed your Lab, ask your veterinarian for advice. He is the best person to help you decide among brands.

How Much, How Often?

The answer to the question of how much you should feed your Labrador Retriever will depend on your dog. Your Lab's age, weight, level of activity and individual tastes are the determining factor in how much he eats every day.

Good Routine: Before you figure out how much your dog should eat, think about when you want to feed him. Dogs enjoy routine in their lives, and your Lab's feeding routine will turn out to be one of his favorites. Feeding at regular times of the day will not only help your Lab feel more secure, but it will also encourage him to finish his meals as soon as they are given.

Because Labs are prone to a digestive condition called bloat, which can be deadly, it's best to feed your dog twice a day, in the morning and evening. Dogs that eat two smaller meals instead of one big one seem less likely to develop bloat.

Another way to avoid bloat is to have your dog rest for at least an hour after exercise before you feed him. Also avoid feeding him right before bedtime. The reason for this is that a meal just before your Lab beds down for the evening might result in his need for a bowel movement in the middle of the night.

When figuring out a feeding schedule for your Lab, remember it's a good idea to stick to the same time every single day. You'll quickly find that your dog will expect to eat at these times each day and will probably finish whatever you give him right away as a result.

Feeding Your Puppy: If your Labrador Retriever is a young puppy, his feeding requirements will differ significantly from an adult Labrador Retriever. The type and amount of food he eats will vary from the time he is young to when he is older.

If your Lab puppy comes to live with you at the age of eight or nine weeks, he's already weaned from his mother's milk and eats solid dog food. His energy needs during this time are great because he is developing at a fast rate, and so he needs plenty of nutritious food to help him grow. In fact, your puppy's greatest growth will take place between the ages of nine weeks to five months.

Young Labrador Retriever puppies need to eat frequent meals because they are growing so rapidly and because their little tummies aren't big enough to hold much food all at once. Four times a day is a good rule of thumb when feeding a puppy. Don't give your puppy free access to food at all times, but instead offer him separate feedings at scheduled intervals throughout the day.

The kind of food you give your puppy is important, too, since his dietary needs differ from that of a full-grown dog. He should receive food

Be sure not to overfeed your Lab puppy since obesity in puppies is especially dangerous.

made specifically for puppies. If you can, give him the same food he ate at his prior home, assuming this was a food made especially for puppies. Avoid switching foods on your puppy since this will cause stomach upset. If you must change the pup's diet, do so gradually over a period of a week or so to allow his body to adjust to the change.

When determining how much food to give your puppy at each feeding, follow the recommendations on the dog food label, or use the method of one cup of food for every 10 to 15 pounds of weight, divided up throughout the day. You can verify this amount with your veterinarian if you want to make certain it's appropriate for your dog.

Whatever you do, make sure your puppy isn't getting too much food

and becoming overweight. Obesity in puppies is dangerous, especially in larger breeds like the Lab. Too much weight on a puppy's body can cause a problem with bone development. Also, too much food can result in rapid growth and cause your Lab to develop osteochondrosis, a serious bone and joint disorder.

As your puppy grows older and his stomach becomes larger, he will start to accommodate fewer and bigger meals. By the time he is one year old, he should receive only two meals a day.

Feeding Your Adult: Labs are considered fully grown at the age of 12 to 16 months, and should receive a diet for adult dogs at this time. Foods designed for adult dogs are more suited to the metabolisms of fully-grown canines, and will keep them happy and healthy if properly fed.

Start out by feeding your dog the amount of food indicated on the dog food label, or use the method of one cup of food for every 15 to 20 pounds of adult weight. Offer your pet his food in at least two feedings a day to help avoid the possibility of your dog developing a condition called bloat (explained elsewhere in this chapter).

When you first start feeding your adult Lab the prescribed ration indicated on the packaging, keep a close eye on him to determine if he gains weight. If he does, you will need to either increase his exercise level or cut back on the amount of food you give him. Don't allow your Lab to become overweight. Excess weight is harmful to your dog, and can result in his lifespan being considerably shortened.

If you can't seem to get your dog's weight under control by increasing his activity level or reducing his food intake somewhat, try switching your pet to a "light" version of the food he eats, if there is one. Or gradually switch over to one of the brands that offer a light diet. If this doesn't work, talk to your veterinarian about the problem. The veterinarian may need to put your dog on a prescription weight reduction diet.

If you find your Lab grows thinner on the recommended daily ration of dog food you give him, he is most likely very active and needs more calories than he is receiving. Try lightly increasing his food intake until he gets as much as he needs to maintain a normal weight. If you can't seem to manage this on your own, contact your veterinarian for help.

When your Lab reaches the age of 7, you may need to switch him to a special diet for senior dogs. These diets are usually reduced in calories to help prevent older dogs from gaining too much weight. They also tend to contain less protein in order to help the older dog's body more easily metabolize the food, and more vitamin B than regular diets. Talk to your veterinarian about changing your older Lab over to a senior diet as he approaches 7 years old.

What About Treats?

Most dogs live for treats, and your Lab is probably no exception. Treats are excellent training tools, and are also fun to give your dog whenever you feel like seeing his face light up. But not all treats are healthy for dogs, and what you give your Lab when you want to reward him for good behavior or for just being a great companion can seriously affect his health.

Table Scraps: Labs are expert beggars; this is most certainly true. It doesn't take a Lab puppy too long to figure out that the sandwich you are eating or the bag of potato chips you are holding might make a tasty treat. Labs will stand in front of you and just stare at whatever you are eating, almost as if they are trying to will your food right into their mouths.

It's very tempting to break off a piece of whatever you are munching on and hand it over to your Lab. After all, you love him and want to make him happy. But there are two problems with giving into this temptation. First, your action will reward your dog's begging and you will soon have a big pest on your hands, one who will constantly bother you and your guests when eating. Second, you will end up with an overweight dog that is lacking the proper nutrition he needs.

Does that mean your Lab should never experience the joy of eating human food? Never to taste turkey on Thanksgiving or pot roast on Sunday evenings? Actually, you don't have to be *that* strict with your dog, but if you want to give him table scraps, you will need to do so wisely and in moderation.

It's crucial to your Lab's health that nutritious dog food, not table scraps and treats, make up a majority of his diet.

The first rule to remember is your Lab should not receive more than 10 percent of his diet in human food. That means you can give him occasional table scraps, but not in large quantity on a daily basis.

Next, pick and choose what you give your dog. Don't automatically dump your kids' leftover macaroni and cheese or mashed potatoes into your dog's dish. Instead, choose such healthy, low-fat table scraps for your Lab as cooked vegetables, lean meats, and low sugar and sodium foods.

Another important rule to remember is never feed your Lab table scraps by hand or while you are sitting at the table eating your dinner. If you get into the habit of handing him people food whenever he starts begging, you and your family and guests will find him forever haunting you when you are eating. Instead,

after you finish your meal, put whatever scraps you want to give your dog into his regular food bowl.

The Trouble With Table Scraps

The following are reasons **NOT** to feed table scraps too often to your Lab:
• High in fat and sodium
• Can cause obesity
• Encourages begging
• May contain ingredients harmful to dogs

Commercial Treats: When it comes to training rewards, commercially-made dog treats are most practical. These products usually come in the shape of a biscuit or cookie, are easy to handle, and are very yummy to your dog.

A large number of dog treats are available on the market, and you will find yourself baffled as to which to feed your dog. If you do some research, however, you'll see that dog treats fall into the same categories as dog food: there are supermarket brands and premium brands of dog treats, and even all-natural biscuits and cookies. The choice is yours depending on what your priorities are in terms of price and convenience.

Whatever type of treats you decide to buy for your dog, remember to feed them only in moderation. Too many treats—even healthy ones—can result in your dog becoming overweight.

Treats to Avoid: Certain foods are not good for your dog because of their high fat or salt content. When feeding table scraps, take a look at the ingredients and amount of fat and sodium in foods before you give them to your dog.

Also, avoid giving your Lab too many onions, as an excess of this food can result in an ailment called hemolytic anemia. Too much garlic can also be harmful because of the sulphur levels present in this food.

In addition, chocolate is a big no-no. Large quantities of this candy can cause cardiovascular shock or seizures in your dog because of a chemical called theobromine that is present. The caffeine present in chocolate is also unhealthy for dogs.

Do Not Feed

The following are not good for your dog:

- Chocolate
- Onions
- Garlic
- High-fat foods

Supplements

As you stroll through the local pet supply store, you will notice the many vitamin and mineral supplements available for dogs. Should you give some of these supplements to your Labrador Retriever?

Actually, the subject of vitamin and mineral supplements for dogs is somewhat controversial. On the one hand, some experts believe that if a dog receives a balanced diet of commercial dog food, he doesn't need supplements. In fact, they argue that giving vitamins and minerals on top of this balanced diet could actually harm the dog by causing vitamin toxicity.

Conversely, advocates of supplementing believe that commercial dog food loses much of its nutritional value during processing and is lacking in vitamins. They believe adding supplements to the food will replace whatever nutrients were lost when the food was processed.

If you aren't sure which camp you should be in, ask your veterinarian for advice. In most cases, vets won't recommend adding a vitamin and mineral supplement to your dog's diet unless your dog has special needs or is recovering from an illness.

Don't Forget the Water

While proper diet is an important part of keeping your dog healthy, nothing is more important than providing clean, cool, fresh water for your dog on a daily basis. Water makes up more than half of your dog's body weight, and is routinely lost during urination, digestion and respiration. In order for your dog's body to function properly, your pet requires as much water as he wants, whenever he wants it. This is particularly important on hot days.

Vaccines

Domestic dogs are subject to a host of dangerous infectious diseases, most of which can be warded off through regular vaccinations. Puppies are prone to these types of illnesses, and so need to receive a number of vaccines while they are young. Older dogs usually require only annual boosters to stay healthy because their immune systems are more capable of warding off infectious disease than those of puppies.

Young puppies raised by responsible breeders usually receive their first set of shots before they go to new homes. This initial vaccination contains inoculations against distemper, parainfluenza, hepatitis and parvovirus. Once the pups leave their littermates, they will no longer benefit from the immunities passed on through their mother's milk, and they will face exposure to more infectious diseases out in the world. Therefore, at the age of 8–12 weeks, they receive a second inoculation known as DHLPP, which contains vaccines for distemper, hepatitis, leptospirosis, parainfluenza and parvovirus. At 12–6 weeks, puppies also receive their first rabies inoculation. When a pup reaches 16 weeks of age, the veterinarian may opt to give the dog another DHLPP inoculation. Some vets follow up with a parvovirus booster at 18–20 weeks if the dog is in an area the veterinarian determines a high risk for parvo.

If your Labrador Retriever is a puppy within the ages of 8–16 weeks, it is your responsibility to make sure the dog receives the appropriate inoculations to protect against disease. Take your puppy to the veterinarian for an initial exam and the development of a vaccination and preventative health care program.

Unlike puppies, older dogs need only annual boosters to protect them from infectious disease. The DHLPP shot is given once a year to dogs over the age of 12 months, while a

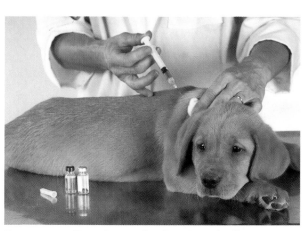

Your puppy will need several series of vaccinations before his immune system is fully equipped to fight off contagious disease.

rabies vaccine is administered every one to three years, depending on the type of vaccine and the rabies regulations in the state where you live.

While you are at the veterinarian getting these basic vaccines for your Lab, it is a good time to discuss other vaccines that may be relevant to your dog's particular situation. For example, your veterinarian may recommend placing your dog on a schedule to receive vaccinations for Lyme disease if you live in an area where Lyme disease is a problem. If your dog travels to dog shows and other canine events, your veterinarian may suggest your dog receive an inoculation against a contagious respiratory illness called kennel cough.

Vaccines for Dogs

Over his lifetime, your Lab will receive vaccinations for all or most of the following:

- Distemper
- Parainfluenza
- Hepatitis
- Parvovirus
- Leptospirosis
- Lyme disease
- Kennel cough

Deworming

Worms are internal parasites that can cause damage to a dog's internal organs. While many dogs live healthy lives with mild worm infestations, severe infestations can be life threatening, especially to puppies.

Most dogs are born with an intestinal parasite called roundworm. If your Labrador Retriever is a puppy, your veterinarian will most likely deworm him twice, and then check the stool to make sure all the worms are gone.

If your Lab is an adult, the dog won't need deworming unless you spot obvious signs of an infestation. (also, the dog may already receive protection from its heartworm medication, which may contain a dewormer.) Roundworms, hookworms and whipworms can possibly infect your dog, and will sometimes appear in the dog's stool upon microscopic examination. Tapeworms are sometimes visible to the naked eye. Other signs of worm infestation including vomiting, diarrhea, loss of weight and a dull coat. If your dog experiences any of these symptoms, ask your veterinarian to check the dog for worms.

Heartworm

Heartworm is a dangerous parasite that can cause fatal damage to your dog's heart, lungs and liver. Treatment for this disease can be dangerous to your dog, so prevention is key.

Heartworm is transmitted through the bite of an infected mosquito. Dogs living in areas with high mosquito populations are most at risk, although the disease is documented in many different regions.

To keep your dog from getting heartworm, you will need to give monthly treatments of a heartworm

Labs that are spayed or neutered live longer, healthier lives.

preventative, available only through your veterinarian. If your dog is over the age of six months, he should be tested for heartworm before receiving preventative medication to make sure the dog isn't already infested with the parasite. Dogs that are already infected with heartworm need special treatment to kill the existing adult worms safely before they can receive most heartworm preventatives.

Spaying and Neutering

Unless you plan to show your Labrador Retriever in conformation events or become seriously involved in field trials, you should spay or neuter your dog. Spaying and neutering provides many health benefits to your dog, including a decrease in the likelihood of cancer to the reproductive organs. It will also keep your dog from developing behavior problems associated with hormonal fluctuations, like aggression, roaming and inattentiveness to training (see Chapters 4 and 5 for more information on this).

Most veterinarians prefer to spay and neuter dogs at six months of age, although more clinics are starting to offer early spay and neuter services for puppies as young as eight weeks old. Discuss spaying or neutering your Lab with your veterinarian when you take your puppy in for its initial exam.

Fleas and Ticks

Sooner or later, every dog comes into contact with fleas and ticks. These external parasites generally live outdoors, where they lie in wait for a host. When your dog walks or brushes past one of these creatures, the flea or tick climbs on board your pet. It lives out part of its life cycle on your pet as it consumes your pet's blood.

Fleas and ticks are dangerous because they can not only weaken your dog if present in great numbers, but they can also spread illness like Lyme disease to your dog through their saliva. In addition, fleas multiply rapidly in number and can cause a nasty infestation in your home.

In recent years, some excellent and very safe products were released over-the-counter to deal with the problem of fleas. These preparations are easy to administer and do a great job of keeping fleas under control. Even if your dog shows no signs of flea infestations, veterinarians recommend you treat your pet monthly with a flea product as a preventative.

Ticks are different than fleas in that they fasten themselves to a dog's skin and stay there. For this reason, ticks are easier to spot and remove. To remove a tick, kill it by applying alcohol to the parasite with a cotton-tipped applicator. Using a tweezer, grasp the tick as close to your dog's skin as you can. Pull back steadily until the tick comes out of the dog's body. Don't touch the tick with your bare fingers since ticks can carry diseases dangerous to humans.

To keep your dog from picking up ticks while it is outdoors, apply a tick repellent to the dog's coat before going into tall brush or wooded areas.

Tooth Care

Humans aren't the only ones who need their teeth cleaned periodically. Dogs also tend to build up tartar and bacteria under and around their

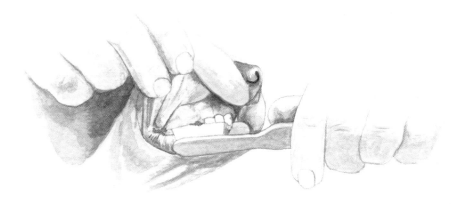

Brushing your Lab's teeth on a daily basis will help his mouth stay healthy longer.

gums. And just like humans, dogs with neglected teeth end up with diseased gums and ultimately, tooth loss. It's important to keep your Lab's teeth clean so the dog will keep them well into old age.

Another reason to keep your dog's teeth clean is to prevent bacterial infection in the mouth. Bacteria in the gums can ultimately find its way to your dog's bloodstream and heart, which can be fatal.

You can do a lot at home to keep your dog's teeth and gums in top shape. Give your dog large, unbreakable bones or hard nylon chew toys to keep his teeth in good order. You should also brush your Lab's teeth as often as you can. Do this by wrapping a piece of gauze around your finger and applying specially made canine toothpaste, available at pet supply stores, to the gauze. Rub each tooth with the toothpaste, getting as close to the gum as possible.

Even with regular at-home care, you will occasionally need to have the dog's teeth cleaned professionally (and under anesthesia) by your veterinarian to remove the plaque beneath the gum. The veterinarian will check your dog's teeth during your pet's annual exam, and will recommend that your dog receive a teeth cleaning if the dog needs one.

Foot Care

Because Labrador Retrievers were bred as hunting dogs, they have strong and resilient feet. However,

When clipping your Lab's toenails, be sure to avoid cutting into the quick.

even the toughest-toed Lab needs to have his toenails groomed.

How often you trim your Lab's nails will depend on how fast they grow and how quickly they wear down naturally on pavement or hard ground. You can do this yourself or take your Lab to a professional groomer or veterinarian. It's easier and less expensive to learn to do it yourself.

If you opt to do the trimming yourself, you will need a pair of dog toenail clippers on hand. You can use a scissors-style clipper or a guillotine-style clipper. Although both are good for clipping Lab nails, many people seem to prefer the scissors-style clipper.

Before you clip your dog's nails, take a trip to the drugstore and buy a tube of styptic powder. Styptic powder will come in handy in case you clip the nail too close and it begins to bleed.

Labs accustomed to having their paws handled since they were young pups are the easiest Labs to deal with when toenail clipping time arrives. If you have such a dog, you will have no problem using the clipper on your own without an assistant. If your Lab is the struggling type, however, you'll need to get someone to help you hold the dog while you do the cutting.

The easiest way to cut a dog's nails is to make the dog lay down on a table in front of you, if you can. Press down firmly on the paw pad to pop the nail out as far as possible so you can easily cut it.

Start the clipping process by first examining your Lab's toenails closely. Chances are they will appear dark in color, making it hard to see the vein that runs through the nail known as the quick. You need to know where the quick is before you start cutting so that you don't accidentally clip into it and cause bleeding. By taking a flashlight and holding it behind the nail, you will see the quick and will gain an idea of where to cut the nail.

A good rule of thumb is to trim the nail at the point where it begins to curve downward. This usually helps you avoid the quick while still trimming enough off the nail to make the clipping useful.

As you are trimming your dog's toenails, keep an eye out for any cuts, sores, blisters or foreign objects lodged in his paws. If you see anything stuck in there, you can try removing it with a pair of tweezers. If you see swollen, red areas on your dog's paws, call your veterinarian.

Ear Care

Because Labrador Retrievers have drop ears, they are prone to infections and inflammation of the ear canal.

While it's not necessary to clean your Lab's ears on a regular basis, you should examine them regularly to make sure they are healthy. If your dog's ears appear particularly grubby with wax and dirt, you can clean them with an ear cleanser made especially for dogs (available at pet supply stores) using a moistened cloth wrapped around your finger. Be sure to clean the folds in the ear as well as deep inside the flap. Keep an eye on the ear after you clean it since the dirt and wax build-up you noticed could be signs of a pending infection. If your Lab is scratching at its ear or the ear continues to become dirty quickly, your dog may have an ear infection that should be seen by your veterinarian.

You can help keep your Lab's ears healthy by being careful not to get water in them when bathing the dog. Also, inspect your Lab's ears after a day outdoors in the brush to make sure no foreign bodies are clinging to the hair near the ear canal. Foreign objects that work their way into the ear are a common cause of infection.

Coat Care

If you aren't the type of person who likes to spend time grooming a dog, then you certainly picked the right breed. You won't need to spend anywhere near the time and money that Poodle owners, for example, do in order to properly care for your Lab's coat. Yet, you will still need to attend to your Lab's grooming needs at least once a week.

Labs need grooming for several reasons. First, despite their short coats, they do shed like other hairy animals (including humans!). Second, regular grooming will keep your dog's coat healthy and make him look good. And, just as importantly, grooming time provides you with an opportunity to examine your dog's body closely and look for any possible skin or other problems that might be brewing.

In order to properly groom your Labrador Retriever, you need the proper tools. See the section on grooming tools and products in Chapter 3 for a list of the items you'll need.

The best time to start acclimating your Lab to grooming is when he's a puppy. Spend a few minutes a couple of times a week getting your pup used to the idea of being brushed and handled. Make it a pleasant experience for him so he'll grow up to be cooperative when grooming time arrives.

Brushing

At least once a week, you should brush your Lab's coat with a wire-bristle slicker brush, and a rubber curry brush or a rubber grooming glove. You may want to do this outside if the weather is warm so you don't end up with dog hair all over your house!

When it's time to brush your dog, have him stand quietly while you work. (You can train him to behave during brushing time by telling him what a good dog he is when he's standing still, but reprimanding him with a sharp "No!" if he tries to get away or wiggles around.) Brush your Lab's coat with the wire-bristle slicker brush, moving in the direction the hair grows.

If your Lab is shedding a lot—something that occurs to most dogs in the spring and fall of each year—use a shedding blade on his coat. The blade strips the coat of all the loose hairs in a very effective manner, leaving less of it on the dog to later end up on your carpeting.

After using the wire-bristle slicker brush (and the shedding blade if necessary), you can then go over your dog's coat one more time with the rubber curry brush or rubber grooming glove. This will help get rid of any leftover excess hair.

When brushing your Lab, use this time to examine his body closely. Keep an eye out for any lumps, bumps or sores that weren't present the last time you groomed him. Look for fleas and ticks, too. Ticks can be hard to spot on a dark-colored Lab, but you will probably feel them when you run your hands over your dog's

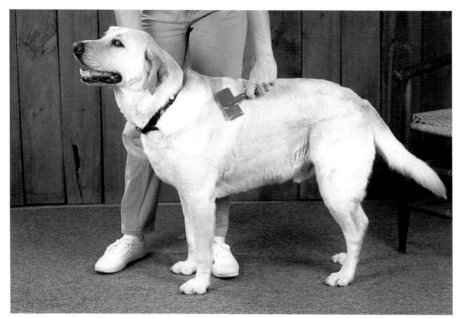

Regular brushing will keep your Lab's coat healthy and your furniture cleaner.

coat. Fleas won't be easy to find at all, especially on a black or chocolate Lab, but if you suspect them because your dog is scratching and biting himself, run a flea comb through his coat to find out if these parasites have latched onto your dog.

Labrador Retrievers shed all year long, but twice a year—typically in spring and fall—their coats get particularly loose. When you notice a lot of hair coming out of your dog's coat, use a wire-bristle slicker brush and a shedding blade to remove it. Doing this a couple of times a week during prime shedding season will prevent your Lab's hair from ending up all over the house.

Bathing

Labs love the outdoors, and consequently, they get dirty. Also, the Lab's oily coat—made to help insulate the dog's skin against water—can get a bit too oily and odorous if not washed on a regular basis.

The amount of bathing your Lab needs will depend on just how dirty he gets, but most Labs require a bath about once a month. Start giving your Lab baths as a young puppy to help him get used to the idea so you won't have to struggle with a wet 60-pound dog once he's grown.

In order to give your Lab a bath, you will need a few items on hand. A mild shampoo and conditioner made especially for use on dogs is a must.

Don't substitute a human shampoo because the pH of a dog's skin is different from that of a human.

You can use your bare hands to wash your dog's coat, or you can opt for a bathing mitt or rubber-nubbed glove to help you work the shampoo into your Lab's fur. These items are available through pet supply stores and catalogs, and while not absolutely necessary, they can help make the job of washing your dog easier.

You will also need access to a tub to wash your dog. Your regular bathtub or a portable tub designed for washing dogs will do. If you prefer, you can take your Lab to a dog wash where, for a nominal fee, you can use the same kind of tub and equipment that professional groomers use to bathe dogs. These tubs allow you to stand up while bathing your dog, eliminating the need to stoop over as you wash. If you have problems with your lower back, you may want to opt for the dog wash because bending over a bathtub while washing your dog is hard on back muscles.

Whatever tub you use to wash your Lab, make sure you use warm water. Resist the temptation to wash your dog in the backyard with the garden hose. The chilly water won't be healthy or pleasant for your dog.

Next, gather together a few old but clean towels that you can use to dry your very wet dog. If you'd like, you can have a hair dryer handy to help facilitate this.

Before you start bathing your Labrador Retriever, brush him first

Most Labrador Retrievers need to be bathed about once a month, depending on how dirty they get.

with a pin brush and slicker. The idea is to remove as much loose hair as you can so the shampoo can do its job getting him clean.

Next, ask your Lab to get into the tub. If he's reluctant, lift him up and put him in there (you may need an assistant for this). Using lukewarm water, wet him over his entire body, doing his head last. Be careful not to get water into his eyes, nose or ears.

Put a dollop of shampoo in your hand and lather up your Lab's coat. Watch out for the eyes, ears and nose when you do this because your dog won't appreciate getting soap in any of those delicate places.

Once you work up a good lather on your Lab's coat and scrub it well, rinse him off with lukewarm water. Again, watch out for the eyes, ears and nose. Make sure you wash all the shampoo out of your dog's coat since shampoo residue can irritate his skin.

If it's warm outside, you can take your Lab out in the backyard to dry. If not, keep him indoors until his coat is no longer damp. Be aware that your dog will probably shake as soon as you are finished bathing him, and if you are too close, you will get wet! Once he's given his coat a good shaking, it's safe to get close and start drying him with the towels to remove the excess water. At this point, you can use the hair dryer to help his coat dry, although you must take care not to burn your dog in the process. Use a dryer with the option of a warm or cool setting only, since these are safest.

The Truth About Flea Shampoo

You can kill fleas with flea shampoo, but the effects won't last. To keep fleas off your dog, you'll need to treat him with an oral or topical flea control product.

Common Illnesses of Labrador Retrievers

While Labrador Retrievers are generally healthy dogs, there are some genetic illnesses with which the breed must contend. As a Lab owner, it's important that you know about these potential problems so you can recognize them quickly should your dog become ill. If you are currently looking for a Lab puppy, talk to breeders about the prevalence of these illnesses in their breeding programs.

Hip dysplasia

A number of larger-sized dog breeds are prone to a condition known as hip dysplasia. Hip dysplasia is the most common genetic disorder in the Labrador Retriever, and can cause mild to severe hind leg lameness. It results when the head of the thigh bone does not fit solidly into the cup of the hip.

Hip dysplasia reveals itself early on with abnormal movement in the hindquarters. Eventually, stiffness and/or lameness will occur. By the time a dog is two years old, hip dysplasia is usually evident, although X-rays are the only way to conclusively diagnose hip dysplasia.

Labs with hip dysplasia are treated with medications that help relieve the pain and increase joint movement. In severe cases, surgery to repair or replace the damaged bone is necessary.

Before buying a Labrador Retriever, make sure the dog's parents were certified by the Orthopedic Foundation for Animals (OFA) as having good hips (see Chapter 9 for contact information). Dogs that have been certified by the OFA with a high rating (excellent, very good or good) are less likely to produce offspring that will develop hip dysplasia.

Bloat

Large dogs with deep chests are prone to a condition called bloat. Bloat is something that all Lab owners should watch for, since the Labrador Retriever fits this general description.

Bloat occurs when a dog's stomach fills with gas or fluid, causing the organ to distend. When the stomach swells, it can twist and cause a dangerous restriction of blood supply to this area of the body.

Bloat is fatal in 50 percent of the cases. If you suspect your dog is suffering from bloat, is it vital that you take your dog to a veterinarian *immediately*.

Bloat can develp by overeating, drinking too much water after exercise, exercising hard after a meal and eating spoiled food. Signs of bloat include excessive drooling, attempts to vomit and defecate, obvious pain when you push gently on the stomach, abdominal distention and extreme distress.

Epilepsy

Also known as seizure disorder, epilepsy is documented in Labrador Retrievers and in several other breeds. Epileptic dogs suffer recurrent and similar seizures during which they may chew rhythmically, foam at the mouth and ultimately collapse. Twitching and paddling are common once the dog goes down. The seizure usually lasts no more than five minutes, after which time the dog slowly recovers. Epilepsy is not life threatening in and of itself unless the seizure lasts more than five minutes.

Epileptic dogs are treated with anticonvulsant drugs that may completely or partially control their seizure activity.

Progressive retinal atrophy

Progressive retinal atrophy, or PRA, is a heritable disease of the eye documented in Labrador Retrievers. PRA is the degeneration of the retina, and it eventually results in blindness.

Signs of PRA include behavioral changes. Dogs that are losing their sight will resist going outdoors in the dark, and walking down stairs and jumping up on furniture if the room is dim.

There is no cure for PRA. However, an organization known as the Canine Eye Registry Foundation (CERF) certifies dogs used for breeding as free from PRA. Make sure the parents of the Lab you purchase receive yearly examinations by a veterinary ophthalmologist (see Chapter 9 for contact information).

Osteochondrosis (OCD)

A disease of the bone and joints, osteochondrosis is a developmental condition that results in the dog's joint cartilage becoming prone to fractures when the dog is exercising. The dog's elbow, shoulder, hock and stifle are the areas usually affected by the disease.

Osteochondrosis is diagnosed with X-rays and an examination of

Labs that exhibit behaviorial changes like refusal to go outside in the dark should be examined by a veterinarian for eye disease.

the fluid that builds up in the joints of affected dogs. Surgery and medication can treat the problem. It's also a good idea to control the kind of exercise a Lab gets when he is young since trauma to growing joints and bones can lead to the condition.

Retinal dysplasia

The eye condition of retinal dysplasia is present when an affected Labrador Retriever is born. It is caused by the retina not forming correctly when the puppy is developing inside the mother's womb.

Retinal dysplasia can be a mild condition that is not even noticeable, or it can be severe enough to cause blindness. Some Labs born with retinal dysplasia show no signs of the condition until they get older.

No known cure or treatment for retinal dysplasia exists. Since the disease is inherited, it's important to make sure that the parents of a puppy you are considering are certified as free of eye disease by the Canine Eye Registry Foundation. However, this is not a foolproof method of avoiding the disease because dogs can carry the gene without having the condition themselves.

Allergies

Labrador Retrievers are prone to developing skin allergies, usually the result of flea bites. Called flea allergy dermatitis, this type of allergy results when a flea bites the dog and the flea's saliva causes a reaction in the dog's skin. Flea allergy dermatitis is characterized by small, reddish bumps that appear in the area where the flea has bitten, usually at the base of the tail. These bumps are extremely itchy and will cause a dog to bite himself and scratch incessantly.

Another type of allergy seen in Labs is called contact dermatitis. It is the result of coming into contact with a substance that irritates the Lab's skin. Red, itchy bumps accompanied by irritated and inflamed skin are characteristic of this condition.

Inhaled allergies are also seen in Labs. Irritants such as pollen, mold and dust are among some of the triggers that can cause your dog to sneeze, cough, and vomit, and develop diarrhea and skin irritation as well.

Canine First Aid

There may come a time when your Lab needs urgent care in an emergency situation. If your dog is sick or injured, you should rush the animal to a veterinarian immediately. In a number of situations, however, you must provide some initial first aid

First Aid Kit for Dogs
- Aspirin
- Antihistamine
- Tweezers
- Antiseptic scrub
- Cotton balls
- Gauze
- Rectal thermometer
- Lubricant jelly or liquid
- Antibiotic ointment (for minor wounds)

treatment even before you put your Lab in the car.

Bleeding

A wounded or injured dog will most likely bleed externally. If the blood is spurting or oozing heavily, the dog needs immediate first aid before being rushed to a veterinarian.

Try to stop or lessen the flow of blood by using a clean cloth and your hand. Put your hand directly on the wound that is bleeding and apply pressure. Keep your hand there until the bleeding stops or slows down.

Burns

Three kinds of burns can affect dogs: thermal, electrical and chemical. Burns are dangerous because they can become infected, and, in cases where 15 percent or more of the dog's body is burned, it can be fatal.

Dogs get thermal burns from open flames, hot water or through contact with a hot surface. Electrical burns are caused by electric shocks, and chemical burns occur when a caustic chemical is spilled on a dog's skin.

Thermal burns cause a reddening of the skin and a loss of hair and possible blistering. Electrical burns are usually red and swollen areas with a light-colored middle that show up on the dog's face. Chemical burns look brown or whitish, and are slick to the touch. If the chemical was acidic, the skin will appear dry and dark.

A dog with a burn needs to see a veterinarian right away. Meanwhile, you can douse minor burns with cold

A Lab that has experienced any kind of physical trauma should be examined by a veterinarian immediately.

ing, may have a blue tongue, may rub its face on the ground, and will probably make choking sounds.

Get a flashlight and open your Lab's jaws as far as you can. Shine the light into the back of the dog's throat and determine if you can see the object. If so, reach into the dog's mouth and pull it out gently.

If you can't see the object, try giving your dog the Heimlich maneuver. Lay the dog on its side and put the heel of both your hands below the dog's rib cage. Press inward and upward using a sharp, quick motion. Do this until the object becomes dislodged.

If you can't dislodge the object, rush your dog to the veterinarian immediately. Even if you are able to remove whatever the dog was choking on, take the dog to the veterinarian anyway since the object may have damaged the airway.

water. Do this by slowly running water over the burn or placing the burned area under cold standing water. Follow up with a cold compress that should stay on the burn while the dog is taken to the veterinarian.

Do not douse severe burns. Instead, cover them with a soft, clean cloth.

Choking

Should you find that your Lab is choking—which means something is blocking its airway—you need to take action right away.

You can tell if your dog is choking because it will have difficulty breath-

Electric Shock

Lab puppies love to chew and will sometimes try to gnaw on electrical cords. This can result in electric shock, which is life threatening.

First aid for electric shock involves first removing the puppy from the source of the electricity. If the electrical current is still live, you must use a wooden stick (like a broom handle) to move the puppy away from whatever gave the dog the shock before you touch the animal.

Cover the dog to keep the animal warm and see a veterinarian immediately. Take your Lab to the veterinarian even if the dog appears to recover from the shock since there could be internal damage.

Fractures

Labs are capable of breaking a leg or tail—especially hunting Labs that work in rough terrain. Being hit by a car is another common cause of broken bones in Labs.

If the break is an open fracture, meaning that the broken bone pierced the skin, the dog will feel a lot of pain. In a closed fracture, the dog will be in pain and the limb will swell or change shape. The dog will also refuse to put weight on the limb.

In either situation, the dog needs veterinary care right away. Stabilize the broken limb before transporting the dog by placing a folded blanket underneath the dog's leg to prevent the bone from further injury. To help prevent shock, cover the dog to keep it warm.

Heat Stroke

Labs left in cars on hot days or left outside in the hot sun with no shade are susceptible to heat stroke, which can be fatal in a very short time. This is especially true of black Labs, who can become overheated very quickly as a result of their dark-colored coats.

Dogs suffering from heat stroke pant excessively and often froth at the mouth, have trouble standing and behave anxiously. If you suspect heat stroke, you should take your dog's temperature rectally using a human rectal thermometer coated with a water-based lubricant (insert the thermometer slowly without forcing it). A temperature of 105 degrees or greater indicates heat stroke.

Provide first aid by placing your dog in a bathtub filled with cold water, or by hosing the dog down with cold water. Keep the dog in the water until the temperature gets down to about 103 degrees (take the dog's temperature rectally every five minutes).

Overweight Labs and those black in color are most prone to heatstroke.

When the dog's temperature is down to 103 degrees, bring the dog to a veterinarian right away for further treatment.

Poisoning

If your Lab ingests a poisonous substance, the dog will exhibit violent vomiting and diarrhea, and he may begin shaking, convulsing, drooling excessively, and show weakness and difficulty breathing.

Call your veterinarian immediately for instructions on what to do for your dog until you can get him to an emergency clinic. The doctor's direction will vary depending on what substance your Lab ingested. If you aren't sure what caused the poisoning, offer your dog some water to drink to help dilute the poison. Get a sample of the vomit or diarrhea and bring the dog and the sample to the veterinarian immediately.

Poisonous Plants

The following plants are among those known to be poisonous to dogs:

American yew
Angel's trumpet
Azalea
Bird of paradise
Black-eyed Susan
Boxwood
Buttercup
Castor bean
China berry
Delphinium
Elderberry
English holly
English ivy
Foxglove
Hemlock
Lily of the valley
Lupine
Mountain laurel
Oleander
Philodendron
Rhododendron
Toadstools
Wandering jew
Bulbs

The decision to breed Labradors is a very serious one that warrants heavy consideration.

Chapter Seven
Breeding Your Lab

It's no accident that Labs remain the most popular dogs in the country. They are a friendly, obedient, happy go-lucky breed, and they make the perfect companions.

It may have occurred to you that you could have some fun—and even make some money—by breeding your Labrador Retriever. After all, Labs are incredibly popular, and plenty of people seem to want them. So how do you embark on the hobby of dog breeding?

Should You Breed?

Having a litter of Lab puppies around the house can be a real blast. Despite this, however, the issue of whether to breed your Labrador Retriever is not a subject that you should take lightly. You need to consider many factors before embarking on this aspect of dog ownership.

Dog breeding is a serious endeavor, and you should approach it with a responsible viewpoint. Go to any city or county animal shelter and you will see why. These facilities are filled with countless dogs, most of whom will be euthanized because there are no homes for them. Purebred dogs are among these unlucky canines, and in fact make up 25 percent of all dogs destroyed each year because they had no one to give them a home.

Given this reality, the decision of whether to bring more dogs into a society where there are already more dogs than there are homes for them is a serious one that requires much thought and soul-searching.

The best way to make your decision is to look at your reasons for wanting to breed and the resources at your disposal, and then weigh them carefully before you bring a litter of puppies into the world. Gauge whether or not you want to breed your dog for the right reasons.

Good reasons to breed your Labrador Retriever—and qualities that would make you a responsible and ethical breeder—include the following:

• Your dog is an excellent example of the Labrador Retriever breed (not just your opinion, but also confirmed by dog show judges) and breeding him or her would help contribute to the quality of the breed.

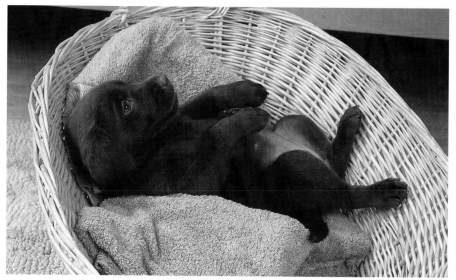

Although it may be tempting to breed your dog simply because Lab puppies are so adorable, it's important to make sure you are breeding for all the right reasons.

• Your dog is free from hip dysplasia and eye disease, and received certification to this effect by OFA and CERF.

• You are actively involved in the purebred dog world, have studied the Labrador Retriever, and feel you are ready to make a contribution to the breed by become a serious breeder.

• You have the money, patience, knowledge and dedication to raise a litter of puppies and find good homes for them. Because you are the person responsible for these puppies' existence, you are willing to take any and all of them back at any stage of their life should their owners no longer want them.

• Your primary motivation for breeding is to contribute to the Labrador Retriever breed, and not to make money or give your children an opportunity to see puppies being born.

Reasons not to breed your Lab include:

• You think it would be fun and educational to have Lab puppies around the house, but you don't know anything about Labrador Retriever genetics, correct conformation and movement, or socializing and raising puppies.

• You don't have the time, patience or inclination to conduct a detailed screening of potential puppy buyers, and are willing to sell a puppy to anyone who writes you a check.

• You aren't willing to give ongoing guidance to your puppy buyers, and take back the puppies at any point in their lives if their owners no longer want them.

• You don't have any intention of getting involved in dog showing or other purebred activities, and don't know much about the Labrador Retriever breed.

• You hope to make money by selling the puppies, when in reality, proper care of a mother Lab and her pups usually results in a loss of money—not a profit.

Breeding Myths

• *Purebred Labs are in big demand.* Even though the Labrador Retriever is the most popular dog in the country, Labs are just as likely as any other dog to end up homeless and ultimately euthanized in an animal shelter. There are more dogs in the world than there are homes for them, and this applies to popular purebreds like the Lab as well. To make matters worse, Labrador Retrievers typically produce large litters of 10 to 12 puppies, and this many homes for each litter are often difficult to find.

• *If I spay or neuter my dog, he will become fat and lazy.* Because most dogs are spayed and neutered at around six months of age or older, owners tend to blame the slowing down that naturally comes with canine maturity on the surgical procedure the dog recently underwent. If a Lab is given a proper diet and sufficient exercise, he will not become overweight or inactive.

• *Breeding purebred dogs is profitable.* The reality is that the costs of prenatal care, possible emergency care and infant puppy care can well exceed any amount you make in selling the puppies. Pregnant females need regular examinations by a veterinarian and treatment if things don't seem right. The actual birthing process may call for an emergency visit to the veterinarian, either to save the life of the mother with a cesarean, or to rescue one or more puppies in distress. Since Labs typically produce large litters, the female dog may not always make enough milk for all the babies, which means the breeder must provide supplemental feeding to the puppies, which can be expensive and time consuming.

• *If I don't breed my dog, he will not be well adjusted.* Studies show that allowing a dog to give birth to one or more litters before spaying or neutering has absolutely no effect on the dog's personality whatsoever. The notion that a dog will feel unfulfilled if not allowed to experience parenthood is a good example of humans projecting their own feelings onto dogs. Labs are not capable of the type of cognitive thinking that humans are, so they don't experience regrets or feelings of longing if they aren't permitted to reproduce. They also don't feel incomplete and start missing their femininity or masculinity after they are spayed or neutered.

• *It's a great way for kids to learn about the miracle of life.* While kids can learn about life from watching a dog give birth, they can also learn first-hand the horror of a tragic death, both of the female dog or one or all of the puppies. Nature doesn't guarantee the safe birth of all the puppies, or that they will live once they are born, nor that your female dog will survive the situation okay.

Getting Started

So you've determined you want to breed Labrador Retrievers for the right reasons, but you aren't completely sure how to start. You are also certain you want to be an ethical and responsible breeder, but how do you go about getting involved and learning all you can?

Your first step to becoming a participant in the culture of dog breeding is to get involved in dog showing. Dog shows are more than just beauty contests for canines; they are opportunities for expert judges to evaluate the quality of dogs and help breeders determine which animals are best used for breeding.

The way to start out in dog showing is to buy a show quality puppy from a breeder and start showing that dog once he reaches six months of age. You can show the dog yourself or with the help of a handler. If you are a beginner to dog shows, you will probably want to hire a professional handler to present your dog in classes. Dog show handling is an art that calls for skill and experience. You can make it your business to learn or simply opt for professional help. In a highly competitive breed like the Labrador Retriever, you will probably have more success in the show ring if you use a professional handler.

In addition to buying and exhibiting a show quality Labrador Retriever, you should also join your local kennel club, as well as one of the national Labrador Retriever associations (see Chapter 9 for contact information).

Go to as many kennel club meetings as you can and start socializing with other Labrador Retriever fanciers. Learn as much as you can about the breed by asking questions; reading books, articles and other materials; and attending dog shows.

If you prefer to focus on the performance aspect of Labrador Retrievers rather than on conformation showing, you will want to get involved with breeders and clubs that concentrate on raising dogs for competitive field trail events. Purchase a Lab bred for field work from a breeder who breeds for performance, and join a local field trial club to learn

Start out your breeding program by buying a show quality female puppy from a reputable breeder.

about this aspect of the Labrador Retriever.

Resources for Learning

The following resources can help you learn about the Labrador Retriever breed:

- Established Lab breeders
- National breed club
- State or local breed club
- Hunting and retrieving clubs
- Books and articles on the breed

Developing a Breeding Program

The objective of every responsible dog breeder is to make a positive contribution to the breed of dog he has chosen. If you plan to breed Labrador Retrievers, your goal should be to create the best dogs you possibly can. This means breeding dogs that adhere closely to the breed standard, both in appearance and in temperament. Ultimately, the dogs you breed should not only look and move like Labrador Retrievers are supposed to, but they should make wonderful companions, too.

If you did your homework, you know a lot about Labrador Retrievers, their genetics and bloodlines within the breed. After you put some time into showing, you hopefully own one or two dogs that received championship titles, either in conformation or field trial events. One or more of these dogs can serve as the foundation of your breeding program, provided they possess the qualities and

One measure of a successful breeding program is the production of Labs that make good pets.

bloodlines you hope to perpetuate in the breed.

Remember that the dogs you choose to mate to create a litter of puppies are likely to reproduce those characteristics that are outwardly visible. If your brood bitch has a strong aptitude for field work but a so-so head, and the stud dog you've chosen has a great head and not much interest in field work, you can hope to get one or more puppies that will feature the best characteristics of each parent: one with a strong aptitude for hunting and a great head. Conversely, you could end up with one or more puppies with the least desirable characteristics of each parent: one with a so-so head and no interest in field work whatsoever. This is why it's important to mate the best dogs together so that even their weakest traits will still be acceptable characteristics in their offspring.

The best test of your breeding program is how well the dogs resulting from your matings do in the show ring or performance venue. You can also consider your breeding program a success if the puppies you produce grow into healthy dogs who make wonderful pets. It's important to realize that the majority of the puppies you breed will not be suitable for showing since dogs good enough to win in competition are the exception rather than the rule. Most of the puppies you produce will end up as pets, so you must also take this into consideration when you develop your breeding goals.

Breeding and Pregnancy

Dogs have successfully reproduced for thousands of years with little help from humankind. However, if you want to make sure your female Labrador Retriever conceives when she should and has a healthy and uneventful pregnancy, you will need to do more than just put her together with a male and then wait for the pups to arrive. Being a conscientious breeder means carefully monitoring both the breeding and pregnancy stages, and providing assistance and prenatal care to your female dog when she needs it.

Before Breeding

It's wise to prepare yourself in a number of different ways before

Labs often have large litters, so it's important to line up a number of homes before you even breed your dog.

you actually breed your Labrador Retriever. You'll need to get your dog ready for breeding and also prepare for placing the puppies long before your dog actually becomes pregnant.

Finding Buyers: Before you present your female Lab to a stud dog for breeding, make sure you secure a number of homes for the puppies you plan to produce. Remember that Labs often produce litters of 10 to 12 pups, so assuming you plan to keep the pick of the litter for yourself, you will need to find anywhere from 9 to 11 homes for your little ones. That's a lot of homes, so you must line up prospective buyers before you breed or you might get stuck keeping the puppies. If you can't find people interested in buying a Lab puppy from you once the pups are born, you should hold off breeding your dog until you have rounded up enough customers.

Once you find prospective buyers, screen them carefully so you are certain they will provide your pups with a good home. Ask each buyer the following questions:

1. *Do you own or rent your home?* If the prospective buyer is a renter, ask for proof that the landlord allows dogs before you sell this person a puppy.

2. *Do you have a fenced yard?* Don't sell a puppy to someone without a fence surrounding their backyard. Otherwise, your dog may spend much of his time outdoors chained up or running around loose in the neighborhood.

When screening your puppy buyers, be aware that families with young children aren't always the best home for a small puppy.

3. *Have you ever owned a dog before? If so, what happened to it?* If your prospective buyer never owned a dog before, make sure this person completely understands the work and responsibilities involved in owning a Labrador Retriever. If the buyer did own a dog before, and it ran away, was hit by a car or suffered some other fate through neglect on the owner's part, do not sell a dog to this person.

4. *Is anyone home during the day to keep the dog company?* If everyone in the family works and goes to school, and the dog will be left alone for long periods of time, don't sell this buyer a puppy unless he is willing to hire a petsitter to care for the dog, or take the dog to a doggy day care center. This is especially important when the puppy is young and needs housetraining and socialization.

5. *Do you have any children? If so, how old are they?* Families with very young children (4 and under) are not always a good choice for a puppy, especially if the children are not closely supervised.

6. *What do you plan to do with your Labrador Retriever?* Find out if the buyer wants a dog to take hiking, camping or jogging, or just intends to keep the dog in the backyard all the time. Labs need plenty of exercise and do best in homes with active owners.

When you find a suitable buyer for one of your puppies, ask the individual for a non-refundable deposit to make sure he is really serious about taking one of your dogs. Once you have the deposits of a handful of buyers, you can prepare to breed your bitch.

Health Concerns: Prior to breeding your female dog, make certain she is healthy. She will need testing for heartworm and other internal parasites, and treatment if she's infected with any of these organisms since they can affect the health and well-being of the puppies. She should also receive an evaluation for hip and elbow dysplasia and a rating from the Orthopedic Foundation for Animals (OFA) to certify that she appears free of these problems. Have her eyes examined so she can receive certification by the Canine Eye Registry Foundation (CERF) as being free of eye disease.

Also, make sure your dog is up to date on all her vaccinations before she is bred, and examined to verify good general health.

Conception

When you first take your Labrador Retriever to a stud dog for breeding, she should be at least two years of age. By the time she is two, her body and mind will have matured, and you will have the opportunity to evaluate her qualities and determine if she is a good candidate for breeding.

On the other hand, you don't want to breed your dog when she is too old, either. Six years of age is the oldest a dog should be when having a litter of puppies, and if it's her first litter, she shouldn't be older than four.

The male Lab is capable of breeding by the time he reaches one year of age. Most Lab breeders wait until a male is older than this, however, because they want to see how the dog matures and fares in the show ring before they breed him. They also need to wait until he is at least two years old to have him certified free of hip dysplasia.

Researchers determined that most female dogs come into estrus, or heat, every seven months on average. Whether you choose to breed your dog during a spring heat or fall heat is a matter of preference. Keep in mind that it usually takes 60–63 days for puppies to gestate, so your pups may be born as long as 2$\frac{1}{2}$ months after you breed the mother.

Two ways exist these days to breed a dog: by natural means or by artificial insemination (AI). If you choose to breed your Lab through natural means, you will need to put the female dog and the male dog together when the female is in heat, and allow nature to take its course. (If you have frequent access to the male, most vets recommend a mating every other day.) If you opt for artificial insemination, all you need is a vile of the male dog's sperm and a veterinarian to inseminate the female at the right moment during her estrus.

The estrus cycle of the female dog lasts around three weeks. However, the bitch is only truly fertile after the ninth day or so of heat. She stays fertile for about four or five days, so this is the time during which you want to breed. It's important to keep close watch on your female dog throughout her estrus period, however, since any male dog with access to her can impregnate her.

You will know the breeding was successful when your female dog starts to show signs of pregnancy about eight weeks after mating. Her teats will swell and some milk may drip from them. She may also start "nesting"—looking for a safe, cozy place to bear her puppies. You may also notice an increase in her girth as the puppies grow inside of her.

Pregnancy

During a bitch's pregnancy, she will require an examination by a veterinarian at least twice. First, have the veterinarian determine for certain that the dog is indeed pregnant by giving her a blood test for the detection of early pregnancy.

The next time the bitch will need an examination by a veterinarian is 35–45 days into her pregnancy. At this examination, the veterinarian will ask you questions about what the bitch is eating, how she's behaving and other health-related factors. The veterinarian can also verify pregnancy at this stage of gestation through the use of X-rays (after 43 days of pregnancy), when the skeletons of the unborn pups appear on radiographs. Ultrasound and palpation can also determine pregnancy at this stage.

If you own a pregnant Labrador Retriever bitch, your veterinarian will give you guidance as to what you should feed her and what kind of general care you should provide. Generally speaking, a pregnant female should receive a normal diet of quality, nutritionally complete dog food for the first month of her pregnancy. After that, you can offer her more food in increasing amounts up until her ninth week of pregnancy. Beyond this point, you should gradually switch her to a special diet created for pregnant and nursing dogs because it contains the higher levels of energy, protein and minerals she'll need to gestate and nurse her puppies.

Before you give your pregnant bitch any vitamin supplements, contact your veterinarian for advice. Most female dogs do not need additional supplements during pregnancy, and in fact can suffer ill health if given certain vitamins and minerals in excess.

Lab Breeding Facts

- Labs typically take 60–63 days to gestate
- Labs often produce 10–12 puppies per litter
- Labs sometimes can't produce enough milk to feed all the pups
- Lab mothers are prone to calcium deficiency

Whelping

At least a couple of weeks before your bitch is scheduled to give birth, provide her with a whelping box where she can comfortably bear her puppies and keep them when she's nursing. It's important to do this so your dog won't go out and find her own place to give birth since she might choose a very inconvenient spot (like the bottom of your closet). You can build a whelping box yourself or purchase one from a pet supply store or mail order catalog.

The whelping box you provide for your Labrador Retriever should be big enough for the dog to stretch out in while still having room for a large litter of 10 or 12 puppies. The sides of the box should be low enough for the bitch to step or hop out of while being high enough to keep the pups inside. The box should also have a ledge overhang to keep the mother dog from accidentally crushing one of her puppies when she leans against the inside of the box.

Place the whelping box in a room where your dog likes to spend a lot of time. Your bedroom might offer the best spot since it will provide familiarity and a modicum of privacy. Line the box with towels for bedding, and make sure the bottom of the box stays at about 80 degrees Fahrenheit.

You will know your Lab is ready to give birth to her puppies when her temperature drops below 100 degrees Fahrenheit (you can take it rectally to determine this). This will happen anywhere from half a day to a full day before your dog goes into labor.

Anywhere from 6–24 hours before labor begins, your dog will become restless and will probably start to pant. She may not want to eat, and might actually vomit and shiver. This is a reaction to the contractions she feels, and there isn't much you can do to help her at this point. Guide her to her whelping box and give her some privacy while also keeping a close eye on her.

The next step will be the actual birth of the puppies, one at a time, while your dog is squatting or laying on her side. The first puppy should be born anywhere from 10 minutes to half an hour after your dog begins straining. Each puppy after that should come out rather quickly, although some female Labs will take a break in between batches of puppies since their litters are rather large. If your bitch strains for more than half an hour with no results, or goes more than two hours in between batches of puppies, call your veterinarian immediately.

When the puppies are born, they will be covered with a clear mem-

Labrador Retriever puppies are born blind, deaf and almost completely helpless.

brane. The bitch will usually lick each puppy after its birth to clear the membrane from its body. Sometimes, the membrane will break on its own when the pup is born. If your dog doesn't lick the membrane off the puppy within a few minutes of the puppy's birth, you can help by gently rubbing the pup with a soft, dry, clean towel.

Your new mother Lab will instinctively know to cut the umbilical cord of each puppy shortly after it is born. She'll do this by chewing the cord until it breaks. If she fails to do this or seems to need help with a particularly large litter, you can sever the cords by using thread, a pair of clean scissors and Betadine solution. Use the thread to tie one knot in the cord about an inch from the puppy, and then another knot about $1/4$ of an inch

higher, away from the pup's body. Cut the cord in between the two knots and dip the puppy's end in the Betadine solution.

After each puppy is born, the bitch will pass some placenta. Remove it quickly since your dog may try to eat it and then will vomit later. Keep track of how many placentas your bitch passes; there should be one for each puppy. If a placenta is missing after all the puppies are born, contact your veterinarian.

Shortly after the puppies appear, they will instinctively begin to nurse. Once your bitch has finished giving birth to her entire litter, make sure all the puppies are attempting to nurse. If one or two seem confused or disoriented, help them by directing them to one of your dog's teats. If a puppy refuses to nurse or seems listless, take it to a veterinarian immediately, taking care to keep it warm in transit.

Caring for Newborn Puppies

You now have a litter (probably a large one) of newborn Labrador Retriever puppies. Your bitch is tending to them carefully, licking them to stimulate their appetites and to keep them clean. Even though their eyes are not yet open and their ear flaps are still shut, they are struggling over the bitch's teats, each trying to get the most milk possible. In a relatively short time, these same puppies will be weaned and ready to go to new homes. In the meantime, you have a lot of work to do!

The First Few Weeks

Although your mother dog will do most of the work when the puppies are newly born, it's vital that you provide the right environment for the pups to thrive. Heat is very important to newborn puppies, and the room where they are living should be kept at a minimum of 80 degrees. Some breeders use heating pads in the whelping box to keep it warm, but others advise against this because it can make the mother dog and pups too warm or cause other problems. If your puppies are comfortable, they will feel warm to the touch and lay about in the whelping box. Puppies that are too cold will huddle together and cry; pups that are too warm will pant and sleep far away from each other.

Because Lab litters are often large, breeders sometimes have to supplement the puppies' diet with bottle-fed formula.

Keep the mother dog comfortable by providing her with her food and water close by so she won't have to go far from her new puppies when she needs to eat. Be prepared to give her plenty of bathroom breaks if she needs them, and let her back in to her pups as soon as she asks to come in. Meanwhile, start handling the pups as much as you can, rubbing their little feet, holding them and talking to them all the time.

You won't need to worry too much about cleaning up after the puppies when they go to the bathroom during the first few weeks after their birth; your bitch will do most of the work for you. It's important that the whelping box stay clean, so you may have to change a towel or two when your bitch releases some residual discharge left over from the birthing process, but the box will stay surprisingly fresh without too much effort on your part considering how many dogs are in it!

During the first few weeks of your puppies' lives, keep an eye on them to make sure they are all thriving. A puppy who is not doing well will feel cold to the touch, will not be nursing, will be pushed away by the mother and may not have the instinct to turn over on its stomach if you place it on its back. A puppy in this condition should be kept warm and taken to a veterinarian immediately.

In the event that your bitch cannot produce enough milk to feed all of her pups, you will need to start supplemental feeding. This means giving the pups bottle feedings of specially-made commercial puppy formula. Your veterinarian can give you information on what kind of supplement and bottles to buy, and how often to feed your babies.

Keep a close eye on your bitch during this period. Since the large size of her litter will cause her to produce a lot of milk, she will be prone to calcium deficiency. If she stops eating, vomits or has tremors, take her to the veterinarian to check her calcium levels.

If you want to have your puppies' dewclaws (the extra claw on the inside of each leg) removed, you should have it done by a veterinarian when the pups are one to three days old. While dewclaw removal is not required by the Labrador Retriever breed standard, it is often recommended in performance dogs since dewclaws can cause problems for dogs working out in the field.

When your pups are around two weeks of age, their eyes will start to open. A few days later, their ear flaps will start to unseal. At this age, puppies will begin to go to bathroom more and your mother dog will have trouble keeping up with cleaning them. You'll have to regularly change the bedding in your box, and may want to add shredded newspaper to help absorb the urine.

When the puppies are three weeks old, you can start offering them solid food a couple of times a day. Choose a product made specifically for young puppies and feed them according to

Start exposing your young puppies to new experiences as early as six weeks.

the instructions on the food label. Serve it in a flat dish or pie pan, and expect the puppies to get it all over themselves as they discover the joys of eating dog food. Your mother dog will clean them up when they finish.

Four to Nine Weeks

When your Lab puppies reach four weeks of age, you will notice they are considerably more active than before. You'll probably want to move them to a larger area than the whelping box in which they have been living up until now. An exercise pen large enough to accommodate all the pups and their mom is the best solution since it gives the puppies enough room to play and exercise.

At around four weeks, your mother Lab will start to gradually wean her puppies. Their sharp teeth and claws will discourage her from wanting to spend too much time in the exercise pen with them. Give her access to her pups a few times a day so they can nurse and she can check on them. The rest of the time, let her stay nearby but don't force her to stay in the pen with the pups all the time.

When the puppies reach six weeks of age, take them to a veterinarian for a check up and their first set of inoculations. You can also start serious work on socializing them at this age. Have friends and neighbors come over to visit so they can handle and play with the puppies. Make sure to include young children in this group as you want your puppies to be familiar with kids.

Ask your puppy visitors to remove their shoes before coming in the house. Also, have them wash their hands with antibacterial soap before handling the puppies. These steps will help decrease the chance of your visitors inadvertently bringing an infectious canine disease into your home.

Other ways you should socialize your six-week old pups include taking them outside in the backyard and

Before you sell your puppies, determine which one is the "pick of the litter"—that is, the show puppy you would most like to keep.

providing them with obstacles to climb on; allowing them to meet a benevolent cat, rabbit or other small pet; and giving them different surfaces to walk on such as sand, plastic and metal.

By the time the pups are eight weeks old, they should be completely weaned from their mother. You should also take care during their eighth week to make sure that their environment is quiet and safe so they are not frightened by anything. Things that scare them at this stage of their emotional development can remain frightening to them for the rest of their lives.

Continue socializing your puppies until they are nine weeks of age and ready to go to their new homes.

Selling Your Pups

Since you were careful to round up a number of puppy buyers before you bred your dog, you should already have homes lined up for most of the puppies. Because your Lab probably had a big litter, you may need to locate a few more homes after the pups are born.

The best way to find responsible owners for your puppies is through word of mouth. Contact other breeders in the area and let them know you have a litter of puppies available. Tell your veterinarian to put the word out, and notify your dog show friends. Avoid the temptation to run an ad in the classified section of the paper or put a sign up at the local pet supply store. If you take this route, you are less likely to get good, quality buyers for your pups.

Several weeks before you send your puppies home with their new owners, you need to register the litter with the American Kennel Club

(and/or the United Kennel Club, if you prefer). The registry will send you paperwork for the individual registration of each puppy, which you will give to the new owners. Unless you are selling any of your puppies as show dogs, each should be sold with the American Kennel Club limited registration, meaning offspring from the dog cannot be registered with the AKC. This will discourage buyers of your puppies from irresponsibly breeding the dogs when they grow up.

To ensure that your puppies are well cared for and that the new owners completely understand the terms of the sale, prepare a contract and ask each pet buyer to sign it. The contract should contain the following points:

1. The name, address and phone number of both you and the buyer.

2. A description of the puppy, its litter registration number and the name of its sire and dam.

3. A stipulation that you have first rights to buy back the dog if the owner no longer wants it. Some breeders stipulate that the dog must be returned to them if the owner doesn't want the dog anymore, but that the owner will receive no money in exchange. If you want certainty that you will get the dog back—and that it won't be sold to someone else who may not take proper care of it— you will agree to buy the dog back rather than just take it back without giving a refund.

4. A requirement that the puppy will be spayed or neutered by six months of age. (This should not apply to puppies sold as show dogs.)

5. A guarantee of the puppy's health at the time of the sale. If you choose to add further genetic health guarantees to your arrangement, such as freedom from hip dysplasia or PRA, stipulate this in the contract and spell out exactly what kind of compensation you will provide should the dog be diagnosed with a genetic illness.

Along with the contract, provide each buyer with a puppy packet containing a few days' supply of the same dog food the puppy has been eating; a three- to five-generation pedigree of the puppy; copies of the parents' OFA and CERF clearances; copies of the puppy's health records showing all the inoculations and other treatments received; and material on how to feed, housetrain and obedience train the puppy.

Give your new buyers verbal assurance that they can come to you with any problems they may encounter with the dog. Also, be prepared to give them a referral to a veterinarian and a school for obedience instruction if the buyer doesn't already have resources in this area.

Questions to Ask Buyers
- Do you own or rent?
- Have you ever owned a dog before?
- Is your yard fenced and secure?
- Why do you want a Lab?
- What do you do in your spare time?
- What do you intend to do with your Lab?

Labrador Retrievers tend to love the outdoors.

Chapter Eight
Activities for Labs

While training and caring for a Labrador Retriever is a reward unto itself, the real perks of owning such an incredible dog comes when it's time to partake in fun activities. Labs live to have fun, and are game for just about anything action you can conjure up. Whether it's just for amusement or with serious competition in mind, you'll find that your Lab is always up for adventure.

Just for Fun

Whether you plan to compete with your dog in a canine competitive activity or just want a companion you can hang out with, a whole slew of activities awaits you and your Labrador Retriever. In fact, Labs seem designed with these kinds of activities in mind.

Swimming

Bred for hundreds of years to swim and swim well, there isn't a Lab alive who doesn't like the water. Labs are born with the instinct to swim and will show a penchant for splashing around in the water at a young age.

You can enjoy your Lab's aptitude for swimming in two different ways. First, you can go swimming with your dog and join him in the water. Or, you can sit on the sidelines, watching your dog do all the splashing around.

The best places to take your Lab swimming are the beach, a lake or a private swimming pool. Get your Lab puppy used to these bodies of water as a youngster. Take him there and bring him into shallow water with you to show him that it's safe and fun. Make sure all of your Lab puppy's interactions with water are pleasant and non-threatening. If you do, he'll grow up wanting to jump right in and swim to his heart's content.

Because Labs are retrievers, they enjoy a good game of fetch, H_2O-style. Try throwing a tennis ball, flying disk or stick into a lake or swimming pool and watch as your Lab goes in after it and brings it back.

For those days when you can't take your Lab swimming, provide him with a small wading pool in the backyard so he can splash around in good weather. This will help satisfy his need to be submersed in water until you are ready to go out swimming again.

Hiking is among the Labrador Retriever's favorite outdoor activities.

Hiking

Because of their great stamina and love for the outdoors, Labs make great hiking companions. Plus, hiking with a Lab means you will see all kinds of wildlife you never would have spotted on your own—our Lab's keen hearing and eyesight make this possible.

Where to Hike: Your Lab will most likely be up to hiking just about anywhere you want to go. Before you venture out for a wilderness hike,

however, you need to make sure dogs are allowed in the area where you want to hike. Check the rules regarding dogs at any local, regional or state parks you are considering, and if dogs aren't allowed, don't break the rules and bring your Lab anyway. If a ranger catches you, you'll be cited and asked to leave.

Most national forests allow dogs on hiking trails, but national parks often do not. While some national parks like the Grand Canyon allow dogs inside the park, they are not permitted on backcountry hiking trails.

When you do find a wilderness area that allows dogs, make sure you follow the rules. Clean up after your dog even though you are out in the middle of nowhere. Other hikers, bikers and equestrians also use the same trails you do, and they won't appreciate having to negotiate dog excrement during their trip. Leaving your dog's poop behind not only creates a health hazard, it also gives a bad impression of dog owners and contributes to anti-dog sentiments that result in dogs being banned from wilderness trails.

Conditioning: Labs seem to have built-in endurance, one of the characteristics that makes them great hikers. You must develop this endurance, however. If your Lab spends much of his time in the backyard and never goes out hiking or on long walks, don't begin your new activity with an all-day trek that is way beyond his capabilities—and yours. Your Lab will be sore and tired the next day, and you'll feel pretty miserable too! Both you and your Lab need to get into condition before you start hiking on a serious basis.

Start out conditioning by going on several short, easy hikes in a local park, and gradually working your way up to all-day treks. Your Lab will build up his stamina this way, and he'll have the opportunity to toughen up his paw pads. You'll also find that *your*

wind is stronger and your muscles less sore the next day if you start out with short hikes and work your way up to long ones.

Wildlife Precautions: Most likely, your Lab will spot wildlife along the trail long before you do. If your dog is on a leash, you can control his behavior and keep him from chasing deer, rabbit and other creatures. Not only is it detrimental to the wildlife (it

Hiking Checklist

Before you head out on an all-day hike, make sure your pack includes:

• A map of the trail, a compass and a flashlight.

• Water for both you and your dog so you don't become dehydrated. Drinking from creeks, rivers or lakes is dangerous and can result in both you and your dog being infected with an intestinal parasite called giardia. Bring your own water from home and carry it in plastic bottles, or bring water purification tablets for use on natural water sources you encounter along the trail.

• A bowl for your dog so you can offer him water on a frequent basis. On warm days, too little water can cause your Lab to overheat—especially if he is black in color. You should offer him water on a regular basis. You can purchase a special lightweight collapsible bowl at a pet supply store or through a pet mail order catalog. This type of bowl will fit neatly into your backpack.

• Dog food if you plan on staying out for a long time, or at least a few treats for your Lab to help keep his energy up.

• A first-aid kit containing medical tape, adhesive pads, gauze, antibiotic ointment and tweezers. If an emergency occurs, these items will prove useful for

both you and your dog.

• A collar, leash and identification tags with your name, address and phone number. Keeping your dog on leash at all times will prevent him from harassing wildlife and getting into trouble. It will also stop him from running into problems with poisonous plants, speeding mountain bikes, horseback riders and unfriendly dogs.

• A pair of rubber dog boots in case your Lab cuts or tears his paw pads when hiking. These are available at pet supply stores and through mail order catalogs.

• Small plastic bags or something to use to clean up after your dog. Bring a larger plastic bag and stash your dog's waste in this sack inside your backpack until you return to civilization where you can dispose of it. (If you are dead set against carrying your dog's waste around, the other alternative is to bring a small trowel to bury it. Make sure the hole you dig is at least 10 inches deep and is located at least 100 feet away from a natural water source.)

• Flea and tick repellent. Apply the powder or spray to your Lab before you begin your hike, and reapply it later on if the product label indicates it's okay to do this.

forces them to use up their valuable energy reserves), but it is also dangerous to your dog. If your dog comes face to face with a wild animal, he could end up bitten, kicked or trampled. He may even face exposure to rabies or another infectious illness. It's also possible that your Lab could become separated from you and ultimately lost in the wilderness while chasing a wild animal.

You may find yourself crossing paths with a snake or other predator while you hike with your Lab. Keep your dog close to you and give the animal plenty of space so he doesn't feel threatened. Wild animals will first try to escape if they are frightened, and will usually only attack if they feel cornered with no opportunity to get away.

If you are hiking in country known for having bears and mountain lions, keep tight control over your dog. Most bear species are not inclined to attack and simply avoid them if you see one along the trail. If you are hiking in grizzly bear country, you should probably leave your dog at home since grizzlies are sometimes unpredictable.

Should you encounter a mountain lion when you are hiking, try yelling and throwing objects at the animal to frighten it away. Keep your dog near you and make sure he doesn't get near the big cat.

Camping

Spending a weekend or even a week out in the wilderness with your Labrador Retriever can be a wonderful experience. Being out in the country living close to the land even for a short while can do wonders to relieve stress for you and provide loads of fun opportunities for your dog.

If you are camping at a designated campsite with your dog, show courtesy to your fellow campers. Keep your dog leashed or staked out at all times, and don't allow him to roam. Not only are loose dogs not allowed at most campsites, but they can also pose a nuisance to wildlife and other campers. Be sure to pick up your dog's waste, too, and don't let him bark at other dogs or people at the site.

When nighttime rolls around, keep your dog inside your tent or camper instead of tied outside. Many campsites don't allow dogs to be kept outside at night, but even if it is allowed where you are camping, it's a bad idea to do it. Your dog's safety is jeopardized if he's outside all alone where a predator or poisonous reptile or insect could harm him. Besides, your Lab will be happier if he can sprawl out near you inside where it's nice and warm.

When you pack for your camping trip, don't forget to bring everything your dog will need, including his regular food and safe water to prevent stomach upset and diarrhea; his collar, leash and identification tags; a water and food bowl; flea and tick repellent; a first-aid kit; and plastic bags or something else to clean up after your dog.

When traveling with your dog by car, don't let him hang his head or body out the window. Instead, confine him to his crate or use a seat belt harness for dogs.

Reasons to Keep Your Dog on Leash

• Protects him from cars, predators and getting lost
• Protects humans and animals from your dog
• Is required by law
• Allows you complete control

Jogging

If you're a jogger and you own a Labrador Retriever, you definitely picked the right breed. Labs make great jogging companions because of their love of exercise, their propensity for endurance, their trainability and their desire to accompany humans in everything they do.

If you jog, you already know the benefits of this activity for you. Jogging is good for your body, and it's a terrific stress reliever for the mind as well. Jogging is also great for Labs because it gives them a chance to burn up some of their energy and be outside and close to the humans that they love.

What You Need: In order to run safely with your dog, you will need to bring a few items with you on your jaunts. Your dog should have a secure buckle collar equipped with identification tags and a leash about six feet long. Don't let your dog run with you off leash. While this might be tempting because it's easier than dealing with having to hold the dog when you run, but you won't have sufficient control over your dog if he's running loose. If your dog is out of your control, he could dart out into traffic, get into a fight with another dog, or trip you when you are running.

Make sure to also bring along plastic bags or something you can use to clean up if your Lab decides to relieve himself along the way. Just because you are in the middle of a run doesn't mean you should leave your dog's waste behind. Stop and pick it up so other joggers don't have to dodge it when running down the trail.

Proper Training: Jogging with your dog sounds easy enough. You just grab the leash and run, right? Wrong! Your Lab needs to follow your lead as you jog. An out-of-control canine jogging partner can literally drive you crazy.

Before you even attempt to jog with your dog, make sure he is reliably obedience trained. With formal training, he will have more inclination to pay attention to you out on the jogging trail and obey commands when you give them. He must also know how to walk on a leash calmly and at your side before you start running with him. A dog that won't walk quietly on a leash may prove uncontrollable when you are running.

When you begin running with your dog, hold the leash in your left hand. Keep your dog at your left side just as you would when walking him on leash. Don't allow your dog to pull you or drag behind you when you are running. Give him a collar correction if he does this, and praise him when he runs at your side.

Conditioning: If you are already jogging on a regular basis, but your dog hasn't performed this activity with you, you will need to condition your dog to build him up to your level before you start taking him out on regular runs. If you haven't been jogging yourself but want to start, you will both need to start conditioning together.

Before you begin conditioning your Lab, make sure he is at least a year old. A dog's bones and muscles are not ready to take on the stress of a regular, high impact activity like jogging until adulthood. When he reaches six months of age, you can take him on short runs just to get him used to the idea, but don't do any serious jogging until he's fully grown.

Conversely, don't start a jogging program with a geriatric Lab either. If your dog is older than six years of age, talk to your veterinarian to determine if your dog is healthy enough for this level of regular exercise.

To begin conditioning your Lab for jogging, do the same thing you did or would do to condition yourself. Start out with short, slow runs of a mile or less and gradually over a period of a few months build up to several miles or more at a faster speed. Try to run on dirt if you can, both during your conditioning and whenever you jog at your ultimate pace. The constant pounding on concrete is hard on both your joints and your dog's, so running on softer ground is preferable.

As you increase the amount of distance you run with your dog, keep an eye on him to make sure he seems comfortable and isn't limping or showing signs of exhaustion. Watch him that same night and the next day to determine if he is sore and overly tired. If he is, you need to back off on the amount of running you are doing and build up more slowly.

Hunting

Labs were bred to retrieve game, and if hunting is an activity you enjoy, consider training your Lab to work alongside you in the field.

When hunting fowl, your Lab's job includes marking the fall of shot birds, and ultimately retrieving these birds. This will involve swimming in lakes and streams, and moving through difficult cover. Your Lab must also know how to follow your commands out in the field when he is not controlled by a collar and leash.

If you are serious about hunting with your Labrador Retriever, find a good dog trainer who specializes in teaching retrieving dogs. Then, train with him to get your dog to the point where he will work reliably with you using voice commands and hand signals.

If your Labrador Retriever is still a puppy, start encouraging his hunting skills at a young age by praising him when he retrieves objects and exposing him to birds to develop his interest in the activity. Give him a bird wing to carry around in his mouth, or get a frozen bird from a local hunt club to break him to birds. When he's old enough, take him camping and hiking with you, and encourage him to swim as much as you can. Make retrieving as fun as possible to help build his enthusiasm for becoming a hunting dog when he grows up.

Canine Competition

You could spend all of your spare time doing purely fun activities with

Labs were bred to retrieve game and make excellent hunting companions.

your Labrador Retriever, and that's fine. But you and your dog might enjoy the challenge of a competitive canine activity, and you'll find plenty to choose from.

When it comes to competitive canine activities, any level of involvement will prove fun for you and your dog. If you prefer to compete with your dog on an occasional basis, you'll find local dog clubs that sponsor small events that you can take your dog to whenever the mood strikes you. If you are serious about becoming number one in the sport you have chosen, you and your Lab can strive for success on a national level.

If competition sounds like something you want to pursue, examine the following list of activities and see which ones most appeal to you—and feel right for your dog. Remember, your Lab must have an aptitude for the sport if you stand a chance of doing well in it. Contact a local kennel club or a specific national organization for information on how to get involved.

Canine Good Citizen

Unlike such informal activities as hiking, camping and jogging with your dog, the activity of training for and earning an American Kennel Club Canine Good Citizen (CGC) title requires discipline and work. However, moving toward this goal can offer plenty of fun for both you and your dog. The end result is a closer bond between you and your Lab, a dog who is an excellent companion,

and a neat title to add after your dog's name.

The Canine Good Citizen Program was developed by the American Kennel Club to help reward dogs for being well-behaved and properly trained. Your Labrador Retriever doesn't need to be registered with the American Kennel Club or any registry in order to earn a CGC title but he does need to be a good dog with some obedience training.

To earn a CGC title, you and your Lab must attend a Canine Good Citizen test, usually held by a local dog club at a park or school play field. In order to pass the test, your Lab must do the following:

• While holding the sit position, your dog must allow a stranger to approach both of you without acting shy or aggressive. The stranger will shake your hand and say hello to your dog. Your dog must stay in the sit position and not jump up or do anything inappropriate.

• While sitting at your side, your Lab must allow a stranger to pet him without acting aggressive or shy, or breaking the sit.

• Your dog must walk alongside you quietly on a leash through a crowd of other people and dogs. No pulling is allowed.

• Your Lab must perform a sit, down and stay, all on command.

• Despite several distractions such as a loud noise, another dog, or the opening and closing of an umbrella, your dog must stay calm and composed.

Conformation showing will determine your Lab's suitability as a breeding animal.

• Your Lab must be tied and left alone for five minutes without getting visibly upset.

Depending on the judges, you may find a few more activities added to the test to help determine if your dog is well-trained and well-behaved. If the judges decide your dog fits the description of a Canine Good Citizen, they will award your dog a certificate identifying him as such and giving you permission to use the title CGC after your dog's name.

Conformation Showing

If you have ever watched the Westminster Kennel Club Dog Show on television, you have seen conformation showing at its finest. At the Westminster dog show, top purebreds from all over the country compete for the grand title of Best In Show.

In conformation dog shows like the Westminster Kennel Club Dog Show, purebred dogs are judged both on the way they are built (their conformation) and the way they move. The purpose of the conformation dog

show is to identify the best dogs within each breed. Dogs nearest to the ideal—that is, they adhere closely to the breed standard—are rewarded and considered the best dogs to use for breeding. This is why only male and female dogs who are intact (not spayed or neutered) can participate in conformation showing.

How It Works: Most conformation dog shows around the country are sanctioned by the American Kennel Club and follow the rules determined by this governing body.

AKC dog shows consist of different classes for each breed of AKC-registered dog. The classes within each breed consist of different categories, judged in sequence: Puppies 6–9 Months, Puppies 9–12 Months, Puppies 12–18 Months, Novice, Bred by Exhibitor, and American Bred or Open.

In order to become a champion and have the letters "Ch" added to the beginning of its name, the dog must receive a total of 15 points within one or more of these classes. Points can only be earned if the dog wins one of these classes and then continues on to beat the winners of other classes in the Winners Dog or Winners Bitch competition. The points awarded toward a championship at each show varies from one to five points, depending on how many dogs were entered in the classes.

The Labs named Winners Dog and Winners Bitch then go on to compete with dogs who are already champions in the Best of Breed class. The winner of the Best of Breed class goes on to compete against dogs of other breeds in the Group competition. Since the Labrador Retriever is in the American Kennel Club Sporting Group, the Best of Breed Lab competes against other Sporting Group dogs like the Golden Retriever, Weimaraner and English Springer Spaniel.

The dog who wins the Sporting Group then goes on to compete with the winners of the other six AKC groups in Best In Show competition. The dog deemed the best of all Group winners is awarded Best In Show and receives a trophy along with considerable accolades.

Getting Started: If conformation showing sounds like the perfect activity for you, you will need to do several things in order to get started.

First, study the Labrador Retriever breed by reading as many books on the subject as you can find, visiting Labrador Retriever sites on the Internet, and attending dog shows and watching the breed being judged.

Next, join a national Labrador Retriever club and a local kennel club and start networking with people in the breed.

If you already own a Lab, chances are your dog won't be suitable for conformation showing unless he was sold to you as a show dog by a reputable breeder. In order to participate in conformation showing on a serious level, you need to own a show-quality Lab. Using your contacts, start searching for a show-quality puppy.

You may also want to consider the possibility of co-ownership. In a co-ownership situation, you are part owner of a dog, and another person— usually the dog's breeder—is the other owner. You can opt to have the dog live with you as a family pet and then allow your co-owner or a professional handler to take the dog to shows on the weekend for a week or two at a time. This kind of arrangement is often very attractive to breeders who would like to keep and show a good puppy but don't have room in their own homes to house another dog. By becoming a co-owner and keeping the dog with you, you allow the breeder the chance to have an interest in a dog that he might otherwise have to sell.

The downside of co-ownership for you is you won't have your dog around for many weekends when he is off at dog shows. You'll also have to put up with your dog's hormonal behavior because only unaltered dogs can be shown in conformation shows.

If you purchase a show-quality Lab puppy from a breeder, you will need to start training the dog for the show ring at an early age. The breeder you purchased the puppy from can help guide you in this area, and assist you in determining which shows to enter and how to best handle your dog's career.

Titled Activities

The following activities allow you to earn a title for your dog that will go at the end or beginning of his name:

- Canine Good Citizen Test
- Conformation showing
- Obedience trials
- Hunting tests
- Field trials
- Tracking tests
- Agility trials

Obedience Competition

Go to any dog show and take a look at the obedience competition. You are bound to see plenty of Labrador Retrievers competing and taking home titles. Since obedience training is second nature to Labs, they make great competitive obedience dogs.

How It Works: While dogs in conformation classes are judged on their appearance, dogs in obedience competition are judged strictly on their performance and how well they execute obedience commands. Any purebred dog registered with the American Kennel Club can participate in obedience competitions sanctioned by the AKC. Most obedience competitions are held in conjunction with local conformation shows.

A dog can earn five different obedience titles in American Kennel Club obedience competition. The first title a dog earns is the Companion Dog (C.D.) title. Next comes Companion Dog Excellent (C.D.X.), then Utility Dog (U.D.), Utility Dog Excellent (U.D.X.), and finally Obedience Trial Champion (O.T.Ch.), When a dog earns an obedience title, the corresponding letters are adding to the end of the dog's name.

When a dog earns a new title in obedience competition, the lower title is replaced with the higher one. This means that a dog with a Companion Dog title (C.D.) after its name who then earns a Companion Dog Excellent title (C.D.X.) will have the C.D. title replaced with the C.D.X.

In order to earn an obedience title, your Lab must successfully obtain a *leg* in each title divisions. To receive a leg, your dog must compete in individual obedience classes based on his level and the specific title for which he is vying.

Obedience trials feature six different classes. Dogs who have not yet earned a C.D. title are eligible for Novice A and Novice B classes. Dogs working toward their C.D.X. are eligible for Open A class. Open B is for dogs who already won a C.D. or a C.D.X title. Utility A is for dogs that have won the C.D. title, but not the U.D. title, and Utility B is for dogs with a C.D. or U.D. title.

In obedience competition, dogs are not judged against each other. Instead, they are judged against a perfect standard of 200 points. A dog must earn at least 170 of the 200 possible points in the judge's opinion in order to obtain a leg toward an obedience degree.

The award of High in Trial is given to the dog with the highest number of points.

Getting Started: Any Labrador Retriever is eligible to earn obedience titles in American Kennel Club-sanctioned events as long as the dog is registered with the AKC. You don't need a special show dog or even a dog that looks remotely like a show dog, and your dog can be spayed or neutered. All you need is a purebred Lab that's been obedience trained and shows an aptitude for this type of competition.

It's easy to get started in obedience competition. Begin training your Lab puppy early on, and take him to puppy kindergarten class as soon as he is old enough. Talk to your obedience instructor and tell him you would like to pursue an obedience title for your Lab. The instructor will help you enroll your dog in classes that will prepare both of you for obedience competition, and will give you guidance on how to work with your dog at home. You may also want to consider joining a local obedience club where you can network with others who are working toward obedience titles on their dogs.

Remember that even though your Lab might be great at performing obedience exercises at home in his

Agility is a fun sport for both Labs and humans.

backyard, he may find the environment of an obedience trial very distracting. Be sure to work with him at the park and other public places so he gets used to paying attention to you no matter what is going on around him.

Agility

One canine activity that is growing in leaps and bounds is the sport of agility. In this activity, dogs are asked to negotiate a number of different obstacles at their owners' request. The dog at an agility trial who performs these tasks in the shortest amount of time with the most precision is deemed the winner.

How It Works: The obstacles dogs are asked to tackle include such objects as dog walks (the canine version of a cat walk), A-frames, collapsible tunnels and jumps.

American Kennel Club agility trials consist of three different classes: Novice Agility, Open Agility and Agility Excellent. By entering these classes, dogs earn the agility titles of Novice Agility Dog (N.A.D.), Open Agility Dog (O.A.D.), Agility Dog Excellent (A.D.X.), and Master Agility Excellent (M.A.X.).

Division A classes in Novice Agility are for dogs and handlers who never earned an agility title. Division B in Novice Agility is for dogs who haven't earned a title but have handlers that successfully earned an agility title on another dog. Open Agility is for dogs who obtained the Novice Agility or Open Agility titles, but do not yet have the Agility Excellent title. Agility Excellent classes are for dogs who already have either an Open Agility title or Agility Excellent title.

Getting Started: In order to earn AKC agility titles, your Lab must be registered with the American Kennel Club. If you have a Lab puppy and would like to try agility with him when he grows up, introduce him to agility-like obstacles at a young age. Provide him with little tunnels he can run through and boards he can walk over. Meanwhile, start practicing obedience exercises with him, since focusing on you and executing commands are part of the job of a well-trained agility dog.

When your dog is around six months old, you can enroll him in an introductory agility class for puppies offered by many obedience dog clubs and schools. Here he will have a chance to negotiate some serious agility obstacles and learn the basics of this exciting sport. As your puppy builds his skills over obstacles, you can move him up to a higher level class and hone his abilities until he is ready for competition.

Flyball

When it comes to excitement, no canine activity can top the sport of flyball. Flyball is a high-speed game that calls for the kind of energy for which Labrador Retrievers are famous.

How It Works: The concept of flyball is a simple one. The sport is basically a race made up of teams of dogs who work in a relay at catching a ball and bringing it back to the starting line. The team that is the fastest wins the race.

In flyball, each team is made up of four dogs who take turns running down a short track toward a mechanical flyball box. When the dog touches the box with his foot, a tennis ball shoots into the air. The dog catches the ball in its mouth and runs back to the other end of the track. The dog's handler and the next dog on the team are waiting there, and as soon as the dog arrives with the ball, the next dog is sent down the track, and the relay continues.

Flyball teams compete two at a time, so while one team of dogs is running back and forth for the balls, the other team is doing the same thing at the same time on an adjacent track.

Although the sport of flyball is pretty much dominated by the speedy Border Collie, that doesn't mean Labs can't enjoy the sport and even win. But whether you win or lose, you and your dog will have fun playing this exciting game.

Getting Started: Flyball is a high-energy sport that calls for the right personality in both dog and handler if a team is to find success. Are you a high-energy person who likes the thrill of competition? Does your Lab like to retrieve balls and seems to hardly ever get tired of playing? Is he a fast sprinter and easy to control when lots of other dogs are around? If so, this may indeed be the sport for you.

Flyball is not sanctioned by the American Kennel Club; it is governed by the North American Flyball Association. Any dog can participate in this event, purebred or not. Your Lab does not need to be registered with any organization to become a flyball participant.

Before you get started in flyball, your Labrador Retriever must be well trained in obedience. He must learn to focus on you and follow your commands before you can even begin training in the sport. If your Lab is still a puppy, start him out with basic obedience training classes so he learns to pay close attention to you while there are lots of other dogs and distractions around.

You should also encourage your Lab puppy to play with tennis balls, and fetch and retrieve them on command. A penchant for retrieving tennis balls is at the heart of all good flyball dogs.

Meanwhile, attend a few flyball competitions to get an idea of what the sport is about. Contact the North American Flyball Association and request regulations, along with dates and places where you can see some flyball events in person. Start looking for a flyball group in your area and contact them for information on where you can start formally training your dog for this exciting sport.

Tracking

Ever see pictures or newsreels of Labrador Retrievers seeking out victims of earthquakes, bombings or avalanches, searching through rubble or digging beneath the snow? Have you seen Labs leading their handlers through the wilderness, looking for a lost child or hiker that a family is

The sport of tracking takes advantage of the Lab's natural ability to locate objects using its keen sense of smell.

frantically worried about? These Labs—officially known as Search and Rescue dogs—can perform their very important jobs because they developed the skill of tracking.

The American Kennel Club provides owners of purebred dogs the opportunity to earn tracking degrees for their pets. Dogs with these degrees sometimes go on to become Search and Rescue dogs, or simply work with their owners to hone their tracking skills and earn higher degrees.

How It Works: Dogs have an incredible olfactory system that is 100 to 1 million times more sensitive than that of humans. The activity of tracking puts the Lab's amazing sense of smell to the test.

To earn an American Kennel Club tracking title, a Lab must locate a specific object over a distance of about 500 yards by using his sense of smell. The dog works closely with his human handler as the two search for the "missing" object using the dog's nose as a guide.

Unlike some other canine activities, dogs do not compete against one another in AKC tracking events. Instead, dogs are measured against a tracking standard, and either pass or fail the test.

Tracks for tests are set up the day before the main event by track layers and judges, while the contest track is actually laid the following day. On the day of the test, a track layer walks the track. At the end of the track, this person drops an article he has carried. This is the object the dogs must find.

During the test, the dog and handler must follow the track laid all the way to the end—and to the article—without becoming distracted and venturing off the mark. Instead of wearing a collar, the dog wears a tracking harness. The handler walks behind the dog at the end of a 20–40 foot leash in most tracking tests, and is not allowed to influence the dog's movement.

Three levels of competition exist in AKC tracking. Dogs can earn titles of Tracking Dog (T.D.), Tracking Dog Excellent (T.D.X.) and Variable Surface Tracking (V.S.T.), depending on their skill level.

The Tracking Dog (T.D.) test is the first examination a tracking dog must take toward earning a tracking degree. At this level, the track is the shortest of the three tests, and requires the dog to follow a track on moderate terrain that was laid 30 minutes to two hours prior to the test. The dog must find a glove or wallet at the end the track.

For the Tracking Dog Excellent (T.D.X.) test, the dog must follow a scent laid three to five hours earlier over extensive terrain and a number of obstacles. Four different articles are dropped along the trail, and the dog must locate each of them.

The Variable Surface Tracking (V.S.T.) test is designed for dogs and handlers interested in becoming involved in Search and Rescue activities and involves following a track laid three to five hours earlier over surfaces commonly found in urban environments, such as asphalt, bricks and concrete. The dog must locate several articles along the track.

Tracking dogs that acquire all three titles of T.D., T.D.X. and V.S.T. earn the Champion Tracker title.

Getting Started: Before you can enroll your Lab in tracking tests to earn an American Kennel Club tracking title, your dog must be registered with the AKC and pass a tracking certification test given by a local tracking or obedience club. This test will determine if your Lab possesses basic tracking abilities before he tries out for a tracking title.

Start training your Lab to track at a young age so he'll be ready to pass the tracking certification test when he is six months of age. Begin in your backyard by showing your puppy a treat or his favorite toy, then dragging it across the lawn and hiding it from him. Encourage him to find it by using his nose.

Meanwhile, start obedience training your puppy so he learns to listen to your commands and pays close attention to you. Do this when he is a young pup and continue it with formal obedience classes once he is older.

To seriously train your Lab to track, it's a good idea to join a local tracking club or sign up for tracking classes at a dog obedience school.

Part of your training will include practice sessions with your dog. For this, you will need access to an open, grassy field where you can rehearse what you've learned. Ball fields and parks make great places to track. You will also need to purchase a tracking harness and a lead at least 20 feet long. Bring along treats and a personal object for the dog to find. Prepare to do a lot of walking as you train.

Hunting Tests

The Labrador Retriever was originally developed as a hunting dog, and no canine activity does more to evaluate the breed's innate skills than the AKC hunting retriever test.

How It Works: AKC hunting tests designed for retrievers are not competitive activities. Instead, these events measure the amount of hunting instinct and ability held by individual dogs.

At retriever hunting tests, two judges evaluate each dog for its attributes in marking, style, nose, perseverance and trainability, and give it a score of 1–10 in each area. To earn a qualifying score and obtain a hunting test title, the dog must pass all sections of the test with certain minimum scores.

Dogs can enter one of three types of tests: Junior Hunter, Senior Hunter and Master Hunter. Junior Hunter tests are the easiest and require the dog to retrieve a minimum of four birds, two on land and two on water. Dogs that pass this test receive the title of Junior Hunter (J.H.) after their names. Senior Hunter tests call for the dog to retrieve a minimum of four birds under more difficult conditions.

In retriever hunting tests, Labs are evaluated on their aptitude for working in the field.

Dogs passing this test receive the Senior Hunter (S.H.) title. The Master Hunter test demands that a dog perform in five different and even more difficult hunting situations to earn the Master Hunter (M.H.) title.

Getting Started: If you are already hunting game birds with your Lab, your dog may already possess the skills needed to earn a Junior Hunter or even higher title. Obtain a copy of the American Kennel Club hunting retriever test regulations to determine if this is true for your dog. Consider joining a local retriever hunt club where you can learn even more about earning hunting retriever titles for your dog.

If you never hunted with your Lab before, but would like to pursue a hunting retriever title for your dog, start by obedience training your Lab so he is extremely reliable off leash. Encourage him to retrieve balls, toys and even dummy birds from a young age. Join a local hunting retriever organization and get started with a hunting training group or class once your dog is at least six months old so he can learn the necessary skills.

Field Trials

Since Labs are such masterful hunters, it's only natural that they participate in a competitive hunting activity such as field trials. At field trials, Labs demonstrate their hunting-retrieving skills as they work alongside their handlers to earn championship points and coveted titles. Dogs at least six months of age can participate in AKC field trials provided they are registered with the AKC. Dogs that are spayed and neutered are eligible for field trials, as are dogs that are intact.

American Kennel Club field trials resemble actual hunting conditions that test the skills and instincts of hunting breeds. Different types of field trials exist for different types of hunting dogs. Labrador Retrievers are eligible to participate in AKC Retriever Field Trials.

How It Works: AKC Retriever Field Trials are held over two-or three-day periods in wilderness areas easily accessed by car. Dogs are evaluated by judges on obey their handlers and retrieve game birds in the field.

Typically, dogs are asked to sit quietly until a bird is shot by an official gunner and the handler asks the dog to retrieve it. The dog must then bring back the bird and deliver it to the handler.

The field trial titles given to dogs who successfully compete at these events are Field Champion (F.C.) and Amateur Field Champion (A.F.C.). These titles appear before the dog's name.

AKC field trials offer number of different regular stakes for dogs of varying ages and abilities. They include the following:
• *Derby*—Dogs under 24 months
• *Qualifying*—Dogs who never placed in Open All-Age, Limited All-Age, Special All-Age, Amateur All-Age or Owner-Handler Amateur All-Age Stakes, or won two first places in Qualifying Stakes
• *Open All-Age*—Dogs over six months of age
• *Limited All-Age*—Dogs who previously placed in Open All-Age, Amateur All-Age, or Owner-Handler Amateur All-Age carrying championship points in each, or who placed first or second in a Qualifying Stake
• *Special All-Age*—Dogs who recently placed in an Open All-Age, Limited All-Age, Special All-Age, Amateur All-Age, or Owner-Handler Amateur All-Age Stake, carrying championship points, or who placed first or second in a Qualifying Stake
• *Restricted All-Age*—Dogs who previously placed in Open All-Age, Limited All-Age, Special All-Age,

Amateur All-Age, or Owner-Handler Amateur All-Age Stakes, carrying championship points in each class
• *Amateur All-Age Stake*—Dogs handled by amateurs (not professional dog trainers or handlers)
• *Owner-Handled Amateur All-Age*—Dogs handled by amateur owner handlers

In order for a Lab to win an Amateur Field Champion (A.F.C.) title, his handler must be an amateur and must have handled the dog to a National Championship Stake win or a National Amateur Championship Stake win. Or, the dog may have been awarded a certain number of points in Open All-Age, Limited All-Age, Special All-Age, or Restricted All-Age Stakes when handled by an Amateur, and in Amateur All-Age Stakes or Owner-Handler Amateur All-Age Stakes.

A Lab must win a National Championship Stake or a certain number of points in Open All-Age, Limited All-Age, Special All-Age, or Restricted All-Age Stakes to receive the Field Champion (F.C.) title.

Getting Started: Many Lab owners who enter their dogs in AKC field trial events are recreational hunters who already trained their dogs to retrieve game birds out in the field. If you fit this description, chances are your dog possesses many of the skills required to participate in an AKC field trial. Obtain a copy of the AKC rules and regulations on Retriever Field Trials and study them to determine which areas you may

Labrador Retrievers who successfully compete at American Kennel Club Field Trials are awarded Field Champion and Amateur Field Champion titles.

need to work on, if any. Meanwhile, join a local retriever hunt club to network with other field trialers and find out more about what your dog must learn to win a field trial championship.

If you never hunted with your Lab but would like to get involved in field trailing, start by obedience training your dog so he is extremely reliable with voice commands, and also encourage him to retrieve. Join a local retriever hunt club and locate a training group or instructor who can help you start your dog on birds. In order to obtain a field trial championship, your Lab must be highly trained in the activity of retrieving.

Jobs for Labs

There's nothing a Labrador Retriever likes more than helping people. The instinct to work in the service of humankind has been bred into the Lab for generations. A Lab that's employed helping people is a happy Lab.

Even though your Labrador Retriever's primary purpose in life is to serve as your buddy and keep you company while you are jogging, hiking or just watching TV, your dog can still work at another job, one that helps those in dire need.

You and your Lab will find volunteer work in the areas of animal-assisted therapy and search and rescue extremely rewarding. If you have the time and inclination, consider getting involved in either one of these activities with your dog.

Animal-Assisted Therapy

Over the last several years, the art of animal-assisted therapy became widely known and accepted throughout the medical and hospice-care communities. Animal-assisted therapy uses dogs, cats, horses and other animals to help humans who have physical and/or emotional difficulties.

Research proves animals can do wonders to help people relax, learn to communicate better and live longer, happier lives. In animal-assisted therapy situations, people with special problems show remarkable improvement and recovery with the help of animals.

Dogs are the most popular creature used in animal-assisted therapy because of their interactive natures and talent for sensing human moods. Many dogs—Labs included—take on the role of animal therapist by visiting nursing homes, orphanages, hospitals and other facilities. Most dogs who provide help to people in these special-need situations are the pets of volunteers. Simple acts performed by these dogs—such as laying a head in the lap of an Alzheimer's patient or standing for petting by a handicapped child—can help with the healing process and improve the quality of life of those in need.

If you like the idea of helping people, and have time to take your dog to a nursing home, hospital or other care facility at least once a month or more, consider getting involved with an animal-assisted therapy group in your area. Many local kennel clubs and obedience clubs regularly organize visits to local nursing homes and hospitals, and are always looking for volunteers and dogs to help out.

Before your Lab can start his volunteer job in animal-assisted therapy, he will need to possess certain skills to ensure that he's ready for the work involved. First, he must be reliably obedience trained. Only calm dogs that are easily controlled can visit with residents of nursing homes and other care-giving facilities. Second, your dog must be friendly and like people.

Many dogs that participate in animal-assisted therapy are certified by an organization called Therapy Dogs International, Inc. (TDI). If your dog is TDI certified, hospitals and other places are assured he is properly trained for the job of animal-assistance and will welcome him into their facilities.

In order for your Lab to become a certified Therapy Dog, you both must pass the American Kennel Club's Canine Good Citizen test. The dog must also pass a temperament evaluation test conducted by a TDI-certified evaluator to make sure he can handle being around special equipment like crutches, wheelchairs and other items one encounters in a hospital setting.

Before your dog gets temperament tested, he must be at least one year old, pass a physical exam conducted by your veterinarian, and have received inoculations for rabies, distemper, hepatitis, para-Influenza, parvovirus and possibly leptospirosis.

For the name and phone numbers of TDI evaluators in your area, contact Therapy Dogs International, or call a local kennel club or obedience club to find out if they offer an animal-assisted therapy dog program.

Search and Rescue

You have probably seen television footage of dogs hard at work after a tornado, bombing or other disaster, desperately trying to locate survivors trapped in the rubble. You may also have heard about dogs who perform searches for lost people, spending hours combing through wilderness areas until the missing person is found. Such specially-trained dogs, known as search-and-rescue (SAR) dogs, are often called upon whenever disaster strikes.

While the dogs who do this work are considered heroes by the families of the victims they help, any dog with a strong love of humans and a penchant for tracking can become a search-and-rescue dog with the appropriate training.

Labrador Retrievers are particularly good at search-and-rescue

The Lab's innate attraction to people makes it an excellent choice for animal-assisted therapy programs.

work, probably because they are so trainable, people-oriented, and bred to retrieve. In fact, most of the search-and-rescue dogs working today are Labrador Retrievers.

The dogs and handlers who do search-and-rescue work are mostly volunteers. They are always on call, ready to leap into action should local authorities contact them looking for help. Some search-and-rescue teams even work outside their communities, flying to far away places when their help is needed.

If you are interested in volunteering as a search-and-rescue team for your community, state or on a national or international level, you must make a serious commitment to train both yourself and your dog. The rewards from this work are tremendous, but a lot of preparation is required before you and your Lab will qualify to participate. Also, once you and your dog are trained and committed to doing search-and-rescue work, you'll find it very demanding, both on your time and emotions.

Before you can start training for SAR work, you need to determine if your Lab possesses the right personality for the job. Does your dog love to play? Is he especially fond of retrieving? Does he get along with other dogs? Does he like people? If you answered yes to these questions, your dog is a good candidate for search-and-rescue training.

Next, your Lab needs to be reliably obedience trained. You cannot teach him the nuances of search-and-rescue work if he's not completely controllable and focused on you. Obedience training serves as a great foundation for SAR training.

To get more information on SAR training and how to get involved in your community, contact the National Association for Search and Rescue or the American Rescue Dog Association (see Chapter 9 for contact information).

Useful Addresses and Literature

Purebred Dog Clubs

American Kennel Club
5580 Centerview Dr.
Raleigh, NC 27606-3390
(212) 696-8200

United Kennel Club
100 East Kilgore Rd.
Kalamazoo, MI 49001-5598
(616) 343-9020

Canadian Kennel Club
Commerce Park
89 Skyway Ave., Suite 100
Etobicoke, Ontario, Canada M9W 6R4
(416) 675-5511

Labrador Retriever Clubs

National

Labrador Retriever Club, Inc.
Corresponding Secretary, Mr.
Christopher G. Wincek,
12471 Pond Road
Burton, OH 44021

National Labrador Retriever
Club, Inc.
Membership Chair, Patty
Streufert
e-mail: *patty@gatewaylabs.com*
http://labradorretrievers.org

By State (note: not all states have Labrador Retriever clubs)

Arizona
Papago Labrador Retriever Club of Greater Phoenix
Debbie Sheppard
6632 E. Holiday Dr.
Mesa, AZ 85215-2930

California
Golden Gate Labrador Retriever Club
Georgia Burg
16306 Redwood Lodge Rd.
Los Gatos, CA 95033-9265

Labrador Retriever Club of Southern California
Chris Bunch
3844 Mound View Ave.
Studio City, CA 91604-3630

San Joaquin Valley Labrador Retriever Club
Laura Fletcher
144 Loma Vista Way
Modesto, CA 95354-2626

Colorado
Labrador Retriever Club of Greater Denver
Denise Hamel
6259 S. Monaco Way
Englewood, CO 80111-4464

Connecticut
Labrador Retriever Club of Central Connecticut
Bobbie-Lynne Dehart
25 Tower Rd.
Middletown, CT 06457-1565

Labrador Retriever Club of Southern Connecticut
Linda Ronchi
29 Red Barn Rd.
Trumbull, CT 06611-1060

Labrador Retriever Club of the Pioneer Valley
Maureen Brennan
11 Sandpiper Rd.
Enfield, CT 06082

Florida
South Florida Labrador Retriever Club
Lee Wullschleger
1301 Mango Is.
Ft Lauderdale, FL 33315-1333

Georgia
Greater Atlanta Labrador Retriever
Club
Carol A. Quaif
2263 Ashton Pl.
Marietta, GA 30068-3401

Hawaii
Labrador Retriever Club of Hawaii
Marie Tanner
95-138 Kuahelani Ave., Apt 120
Mililani, HI 96789-1563

Indiana
Winnebago Labrador Retriever Club
Barbara J. Holl
1291 Joliet St.
Dyer, IN 46311-2022

Hoosier Labrador Retriever Club
Clint Furgason
631 Lakeview Dr.
Noblesville, IN 46060

Kansas
Shawnee Mission Labrador Retriever
Club
Michelle Lewis
4622 W 69th Terrace
Prairie Village, KS 66208-2546

Kentucky
Miami Valley Labrador Retriever Club
Connie Stutler
13394 Green Rd.
Walton, KY 41094-8738

Massachusetts
Labrador Retriever Club of Greater
Boston
Karen Kennedy
343 Locust St.
Danvers, MA 01923-1201

Michigan
Huron River Labrador Retriever Club
Albert Reich
5558 Sunkist Dr.
Oxford, MI 48371-3040

Minnesota
Labrador Retriever Club of the Twin
Cities
Linda L. Weikert
51767 Highway 57 Blvd.
Wanamingo, MN 55983-6600

New Jersey
Mid Jersey Labrador Retriever Club

Mary Ann Debalko
46 Long Hill Rd.
Long Valley, NJ 07853-3075

New Mexico
Labrador Retriever Club of
Albuquerque
Juxi Burr
4401 Yale Blvd. NE
Albuquerque, NM 87107-4114

New York
Iroquois Labrador Retriever Club
Phyllis L. Beemer
84 Crescent Hill Rd.
Pittsford, NY 14534-2429

North Carolina
Labrador Retriever Club of the
Piedmont
Elizabeth Mayo
3653 US Highway 601 N.
Mocksville, NC 27028-6270

Raleigh-Durham Labrador Retriever
Club
Tara Glodic-Powell
2700 Mcneill St.
Raleigh, NC 27608-1759

Pennsylvania
Greater Pittsburgh Labrador
Retriever Club
Teresa Wild
1277 Brooklawn Dr.
Pittsburgh, PA 15227-4313

Texas
Dallas-Ft. Worth Labrador Retriever
Club
Cathy Brown
2617 Fairbrook St.
Irving, TX 75062-6616

Virginia
Labrador Retriever Club of the
Potomac
Rachael Shatz
909 W Maple Ave.
Sterling, VA 20164-5022

Washington
Rose City Labrador Retriever Club
Lisa Cruanas
14410 NE 76 Ave.
Vancouver, WA 98662

Puget Sound Labrador Retriever
Association
Shelah Frey
14701 SE Allen Rd.
Bellevue, WA 98006-1671

Canine Activity Clubs

North American Flyball Association
1400 W. Devon Ave, #512
Chicago, IL 60660

United States Dog Agility
Association, Inc.
P.O. Box 850955
Richardson, Texas 75085-0955
(972) 231-9700

North American Dog Agility Council
HCR 2, Box 277
St. Maries, ID 83861

American Kennel Club (tracking,
agility, obedience, field trials,
hunt tests)
Performance Events Dept.
5580 Centerview Drive
Raleigh, NC 27606
(919) 854-0199

National Hunting Retriever
Association
P.O. Box 5159
Fredericksburg, VA 22403
(540) 286-0625

North American Working Dog
Association
Souteast Kreisgruppe
P.O .Box 833
Brunswick, GA 31521

National Association for Search &
Rescue
P.O. Box 3709
Fairfax, VA 22038
(703) 222-6277

American Rescue Dog Association
P.O. Box 151
Chester, NY 10918
(914) 774-1054

Search & Rescue Dog Alert
P.O. Box 39
Somerset, CA 95684

Dog Training Associations

American Dog Trainers Network
New York, NY
(212) 727-7257

National Association of Obedience
Instructors
Attn: Corresponding Secretary
PMB # 369
729 Grapevine Hwy. Suite 369
Hurst, TX 76054-2085

Association of Pet Dog Trainers
P.O. Box 385
Davis, CA 95617
(800) PET-DOGS

Tattoo Registries

National Dog Registry
Box 116
Woodstock, NY 12498
(800) 637-3647

InfoPet
P.O. Box 716
Agoura Hills, CA 91376
(800) 858-0248

Tattoo-A-Pet
6571 S.W. 20th Court
Ft. Lauderdale, FL 33317
(800) 828-8667

Health Organizations

Orthopedic Foundation for Animals
(OFA)
2300 E. Nifong Blvd.
Columbia, MO 65201-3856.
(573) 442-0418

Canine Eye Registration Foundation
(CERF)
Veterinary Medical Data Program
South Campus Courts, Building C
Purdue University
West Lafayette, IN 47907
(765) 494-8179

Veterinary Pet Insurance (VPI)
4175 E. La Palma Ave., #100
Anaheim, CA 92807-1846
(714) 996-2311

National Animal Poison Control
Center
1717 S. Philo, Suite 36
Urbana, IL 61802
(800) 548-2423

Index